CW00469581

# HEART
# ATTACK

# HEART ATTACK

## BRITT VAN DEN ELZEN

NEW DAM PUBLISHING

Copyright © 2023 Britt van den Elzen

First edition

Cover Design by Maria Spada

ISBN 978-9-0832-0969-2 (hardback)
ISBN 978-9-0832-0968-5 (paperback)
ISBN 978-9-0832-0967-8 (ebook)

Published by New Dam Publishing
www.brittvandenelzen.com

*To the people who don't give up
when things get hard*

BORZIA
OSTRA
N
W
E
S
DAMRUIN
SHADOW PLAINS
BARAK
ELM
ARDENZA
SSU BASE

# ARMY RANKS

| | |
|---|---|
|  SOLDIER | — FIRST LIEUTENANT |
| ||| CORPORAL |  MAJOR |
| || SERGEANT |  LIEUTENANT COLONEL |
| \| SECOND LIEUTENANT |  COLONEL |

 BRIGADIER GENERAL

 MAJOR GENERAL

 LIEUTENANT GENERAL

 GENERAL

# PROLOGUE

## THE YEAR 2163
## OSTRA, BORZIA

General Zander walked through the royal palace with purpose, an even deeper scowl than usual marring her fine-featured face. She clasped her fingers around a newspaper in her hand as if it was the neck of an enemy. Going by the frightened expressions of the staff, it was likely war would soon rain upon them.

That guess wasn't far off, as the paper in her hand was *Ardenian*.

"*Move*," she barked at the soldiers in her way, who fell in line quickly. Not even a brush of clothing touched her as she stormed past.

The guards opened the large wooden doors and let her through without hesitation.

King Sergei looked up from his morning tea, his eyes narrowing as he tried to decipher her expression. "What is it?" he asked stiffly.

"*This*," General Zander hissed as she threw the newspaper on the table, looking like an animal narrowing in on its prey after being left to chew on only bones for too long.

The king turned the newspaper to face him and unfolded it carefully, as if it had a bomb planted inside. He skimmed the page. With each passing sentence, the frown between his eyes deepened. Finally, he lay down the paper and turned his gaze to her. "Is it true? Ardenza found a solution against the mutation?"

She scowled. "Unfortunately, it is."

"*Unfortunately*," the king repeated calmly. "Ardenza finding the serum before we did is… *unfortunate*?" he asked, voice steady but eyes blazing.

General Zander sat down in the chair opposite him. "They're already working on a vaccine." Her eye twitched as she tried to remain composed. She flicked her knife free from its sheath and twirled it around in her hand. "But that's not what pisses me off. We're rich; we'll pry the vaccine from their hands with gold. Ardenza has a price, just like everybody else."

The king only watched, unfazed by her display of anger. "What, then?"

"Just continue reading," she spat, turning a couple of pages and shoving the paper back to him, showing another article. The General turned away as if she couldn't even stomach looking at it.

He turned the paper, his hand splaying over the black-and-white print. Slowly, his fingertips turned white as he seemed to increase pressure.

"Is it her?" he asked through clenched teeth.

"Of course it is."

King Sergei's frown was the only sign of his distress. "*How?*"

"She survived. Changed last names," the General answered with effort, making sure she didn't raise her voice.

The king's anger didn't subside, but, slowly, his eyes darted back to the page she held open. "*Impossible*," the king replied, shoving back the newspaper.

General Zander shook her head. "It is possible. I asked my contacts in Barak, and they searched for her birth certificate—it wasn't there. They did, however, list some of her information in the military system."

"She was presumed dead."

Clenching her teeth, General Zander stashed away her knife. She calmed her breath through sheer will and determination. "Does she *look* fucking dead to you?" The General pointed to the picture in the Ardenian newspaper.

King Sergei suddenly stood, tearing his eyes away from the picture. "Remember your place, *Tatiana*."

General Zander—Tatiana—breathed a dramatic sigh of relief. "What a marvelous way to deflect, *Papa*. From now on, I shall keep my mouth shut like the obedient little princess you want me to be," she snarled, eyes turning sour.

The king looked her dead in the eye. "Watch your tongue, *girl*, or I will put all of it in Alek's name. You know just as well as I do that the public would much rather see you step down."

Tatiana clenched her jaw and turned red from anger. She exhaled slowly, and her expression changed, her lips curving into a manic smile. "The public would rather *not* see a Zander on the throne at all. That's why we need to rip this problem from the world. Have no one questioning our claim."

"She might not know," the king murmured. Thinking. Contemplating.

Tatiana stood, grinning darkly, and walked over to the windows of her father's sitting room, looking out onto Ostra. "Of course she doesn't. All the more reason to act fast—*before* anyone finds out."

The king grunted. "Don't we have anyone in Ardenza to do the job?"

"And let an Ardenian do it?" she snorted.

The king tutted as he agreed. He was tapping his finger on the paper before him, mulling it over, thinking of different scenarios. "There must be an easier way."

"Easier than killing her?"

The king raised a brow. "You think your team can do it?"

"*Think?*" she exclaimed. "I *know*."

"That arrogance of yours won't ever do you any good but make you blind to your weak spots," he snarled, pointing a finger in her face.

His daughter raised her chin defiantly. "I'm not arrogant. I'm confident."

"That's a very thin line to cross, Tatiana, and I will make you pay for it if you do."

"*I won't,*" she countered.

"Do it, then. But I swear to you—if you fail, you will account for it personally. Your inheritance hangs in the balance."

"Don't I know it," Tatiana replied, a wolfish grin marring her pretty features. "As I said, dear Papa, everyone has a price—and I know just the person who will help me do almost anything."

# CHAPTER 1

## THE YEAR 2146

# BORZIA IGNORES CRY FOR HELP

There has been an ear deafening silence from Borzia ever since Ardenza declared the mutation-crisis an emergency. Now that the shadow plains are expending rapidly, we are running out of time-and solutions. Many citizens have been forced to leave their homes. The world is changing fast, and the scarce transportation to the west proves expensive.

The petition for help has been so far left unanswered; King Sergei refuses to send aid to Ardenza's exposed borders. Only General Zander has made a comment on the situation: "We have our own problems to deal with." Which has left a foul taste in many mouths, since Borzia already dealt with the crisis by reinforcing their own borders-pointing the expansion towards the connecting mainland of Ardenza.

Raven was eight years old when her mother got sick.

It started with hunger.

This didn't ring any bells because it was a regular occurrence with the food shortages.

But then her mother began sweating profoundly and started saying weird things in her sleep—which frightened Raven, especially at night.

Her mother often had seizures, during which Raven was told to go to her room. She always did, but she would lean against her door and watch the living room through the keyhole. When her mother's body finally slackened, she would listen to the conversation between her parents.

"You must bring me to the hospital, Leon, and take Raven to West-Ardenza. You'll both be safe there."

"What about Borzia?" she heard her father ask softly.

"No." Her mother was shaking her head.

"But many—"

"I said *no*, Leon," she said sternly.

Raven didn't know what Borzia was.

Her father stared at their entwined hands. "If it's the mutation… I can't lose you, Natasha."

"It is the mutation," her mother said. She clasped a hand on his arm. "And I don't want to endanger either you or Raven. I won't. Call them."

*Them.*

This, Raven understood. *The people in the white suits.*

She barged into the room. "No!" she exclaimed loudly and fell to her knees beside her mother. "Mama, they picked up Dany's brother, and they never saw him again."

Her mother took her hand. "You're going to see me again, dear. I promise." But her mother's hand was shaking, and her voice broke on the last word.

Raven put her head on her mother's chest and listened to her heart. She nodded. The possibility of her mother being taken away wasn't one she wanted to think about. So, if her mother said she would see her again, Raven believed her. She *willed* herself to believe her.

One day later, the people in the white suits picked up her mother.

☆ ☆ ☆

A week had gone by when Raven woke up in the middle of the night to the groaning of the wooden floor. She clicked on her bedside lamp, which she rarely used. The light flickered weakly, as it usually did nowadays. Bracing herself against the cold with her robe, she opened the door to the living room where a burning light showed her father packing a suitcase.

"Papa?" Raven asked as she rubbed the sleep from her eyes. "What are you doing?"

Her father paused for a moment, but then continued packing. "We're going on a trip, dear."

Her jaw dropped. "What?" Tears rushed to her eyes. "To where? And what about Mama?" Raven had never been anywhere outside her hometown, Damruin.

She didn't know it then, but hell had broken loose in a city nearby, and people had been banging on the doors. Not to seek shelter, but to tell everyone to get out of there as soon as possible.

"Mama knows we're going."

Raven's bottom lip trembled. "I'm scared, Papa. I don't want to leave." Something wasn't right. A fun trip meant they would be happy—and her father was far from it.

He straightened and knelt in front of her, planting a kiss on her forehead. "I know you're scared, Raven. But I have to ask you to be strong right now. Just for a little while."

She blinked through her tears.

"For Mama?" he asked, swallowing.

BRITT VAN DEN ELZEN

She nodded.

✯ ✯ ✯

After what felt like an eternity, they arrived at a refugee camp near the border of Borzia, which Raven had learned in the little makeshift school she went to with the other children, was a neighboring continent.

Raven celebrated her ninth birthday at the camp.

This year, there were no presents, not her parents singing to her or her mother baking her favorite cookies. But her father *was* there, and he had gifted her a tiny cupcake with an unlit candle. She didn't know where he had gotten it from, but it tasted divine. It made her forget they couldn't even light the candle for her to blow out.

The days blurred together, and the food grew scarce. Panic rose among the people in the camp. Raven felt like everything around her was crumbling, and she couldn't do anything about it.

She didn't know it then, but the mutation left no survivors. Once the genetic changes kicked in, you either died or turned into a mutant. Years later, she would discover that there had been many sick people *everywhere*—that they had all been taken to hospitals, like her mother. Too many of them had been packed together in one room because the doctors didn't know what to do with them. The nurses and doctors took care of them to the best of their abilities. That was the first problem: the hospitals were the first to fall when the mutation finally expressed itself.

One day, at camp, a family came in. With them was a sick person—sick like her mother had been. They were sweating, seeing things that weren't there, jolting in their unconscious state. The family refused to bring the person to a hospital.

Raven went to her father and asked, "Papa, why did Mama have to go when she was sick?"

Her father gave her a quizzical look. "People with Mama's illness have to go to the hospital."

She shook her head. "Someone downstairs is sick, too."

His eyes widened. "Sick like Mama?"

Raven nodded.

Her father cursed, stood abruptly, and walked down the stairs. An hour later, her father had repacked the worn-out suitcase and stroked Raven's hair. "Let's go. We're continuing our journey."

Raven's body shook, but she nodded—tried to put on a brave face for her father. She understood they hadn't arrived yet where they needed to go. But every step they took onward was another step away from her mother.

✫ ✫ ✫

A couple days later, they stood on a crowded square before tall golden fences.

Raven could only see the top of the fence, and grabbed her father's hand more tightly as she got swallowed up in the masses.

"Let us in!" someone shouted.

Her heart started pounding in panic.

Another person cried, "They're already so close, you can't let us walk all the way to the wall! We won't make it."

Yet another person used words her mother wouldn't allow to be repeated and ended with, "Borzian scum!"

Shocked and wide-eyed, Raven had looked up to her father, who didn't seem to be the least bit shaken by the comments. She was sure her mother would have put the man in his place for using such vulgar words. She always scolded Raven for them, too.

Raven missed her mother. She hoped she was doing well.

The crowd went wild when the fence opened and some people were allowed to enter.

Her father dragged her through the crowd, all the way to the front, until people in grey uniforms appeared before her. *Soldiers*, Raven realized. They were at the Borzian borders. *Why* were they at the Borzian borders? Didn't her mother tell them not to go there?

Tugging her father's hand, she tried to get his attention, but he kept walking.

Her father said something to the soldier she couldn't understand.

The soldier looked down at Raven, which made her feel uneasy—saying something that didn't sound very nice. After that, the man looked back at her father and held out his hand like he had all the time in the world.

Her father retrieved some papers from his inner pockets and handed them to the soldier, who skimmed them and looked back at Raven with pinched brows. He walked over to another soldier and let him read through the paperwork— who looked to her, too. He retrieved a device from his jacket and made a call. Then, he nodded to the soldier, who came back and spoke to her father again in harsh tones.

Raven's eyes were glued to the soldier in the back, who was still looking at her as he held a large device to his ear and talked, reading something from the document still in his gloved hand, misty clouds escaping from his mouth in the chill air.

Suddenly, a large hand gripped her shoulder, and she looked back up at her father, who was urging her forward.

"Come on, sweetheart." He held the suitcase in his other hand and gave her shoulder a reassuring squeeze—but the soldier put a hand on her father's chest.

He barked a command.

Her father's face turned outraged. "What? I'm her father." These words she understood.

"And an Ardenian one at that," the solider replied coolly, with an accent.

"No way," her father countered as his voice turned desperate. "I'm all she has."

Raven frowned. *That wasn't true. She also had her mother.*

The soldier ignored him and grabbed her by her shoulders as he urged her forward. Raven quickly took her father's hand and held on to it for dear life. "What's going on?" She asked, and her father cursed as the soldier put more pressure on her body, forcing their hands to part. "Papa!" she said again, louder this time—more afraid.

The frown on her father's forehead drew deeper.

Another soldier walked over to her father and pushed him back into the crowd.

"No! *Raven!*" he shouted.

The sound of his voice got swallowed by the loud yelling of the people, and he, too, disappeared.

She kept shaking her head, resisting the soldier's insisting hand on her back. "I don't want to go without my papa!" she yelled to the soldier. Panic fought its way through her small body.

The soldier didn't even look down as he said, "You'll be safe inside." As if the words were reassuring.

"No!" she shrieked as her father's voice reached her again, and by some miracle, she pulled herself free from the soldier's grasp. She tried to walk back into the crowd but was too slow, and he grabbed her again, pushing her in front of him. "You *will* walk inside, *little girl*, or I'll carry you—*oh*."

Raven punched him hard in the crotch, the place her mother had pressed her to avoid as she fought with the boys in her class. She must have hit him well because the soldier heaved over, letting go of her, and used curses she didn't know. Before he had time to recover, Raven sprinted away.

Her father watched it happen and immediately disappeared into the crowd, towards where she was sprinting. Suddenly, she felt her father's firm hand grab hers, and he pulled her closer. Raven was glad there were so many people in the square, because whistles sounded, and harsh orders were shouted, but the Borzian soldiers couldn't get past the dense crowd.

Her father's eyes were red, but he held on tightly to her hand while they escaped—almost to the point of pain. "I'm so sorry, Raven. *So, so sorry*."

She clung to his grip—the only thing left in her life that she could hang on to—as she could hear the soldiers yell, "*Stop the girl!*" A sharp whistle. "*Stop the girl!*" But either no one knew who they meant, or no one cared.

Most likely, the latter.

They walked and walked and walked. Raven had never walked so much in her entire life, maybe not even all of her life combined. Their shoes were threadbare, but even as her feet started hurting and she had gotten tired, her father had carried her on his back. Day and night blended together until they couldn't separate the two anymore.

After a while, her father stumbled, which dragged Raven from her sleep as they fell onto the cold, hard ground. The frozen skin of her hands tore open as she broke her fall, and her father clasped one of his knees, dazed.

She told him she could walk on her own, but her father instead insisted that they needed a quick break. He said he needed to close his eyes for just a moment.

But the break turned into a very long one. So long that Raven ended up sitting in the dark, way past the point of shivering, just looking up at the stars. She did that often these days. It was the only light they could see. She wondered if the stars could see them, too. Every time she blinked, she wished on them for help.

In the distance, she could see two enormous lights coming their way after what seemed like forever. *A car*. She tried to wake up her father, shaking his cold arm. "Papa. Papa! Wake up."

When he didn't respond, she got up slowly. She waved, even though her arms felt heavy and ached with every movement she made. Her frozen, stiff limbs worked just enough to stand.

The car came straight for them, and in a moment of madness, or numbness, Raven stood in the middle of the road to slow it down. To this day, Raven still doesn't know what came over her at that moment. It might have been dehydration or malnourishment—lack of sleep, even—but it had seemed like the only solution.

She knew, however, that if she didn't stop that car, her dad would die—and she would too.

The car came to an abrupt halt, the tires skidding on the sandy road. A soldier quickly got out, pointing a sharp light her way. "Are you out of your damn mind?" he yelled. "I almost ran you over."

Raven didn't flinch. Didn't even cry. She wasn't afraid,

just pointed to her father. "We need your help."

The soldier stepped closer and grabbed her chin to take a better look at her as he shone the light in her face. He inspected her clothes, her shoes. He whistled loudly, and another door in the vehicle opened—two footsteps coming closer.

"Help her," the soldier said, and a sense of relief washed over Raven as he walked over to her dad, who still lay at the side of the road.

The other soldier, a female, came closer and looked toward her father. "How long have you been here, sweetheart?"

Raven shrugged. "I don't know." Her head hurt.

The soldier squatted in front of her and handed her the tube to a water bag. "Not too much at once."

She nodded and took a sip.

The soldier in front of her pointed to where the other soldier was working on her dad. "Is that your father?"

Raven nodded. "Is he okay?"

Then, as if she couldn't stop herself, she continued drinking from the tube. The soldier whisked it from between her cracked lips. "Not so quick; you'll get sick. Tiny sips."

The female soldier guided her toward the car and opened a door. "Get inside. It's warmer there."

Hesitating, Raven looked behind them. "My father…"

"Will be here in a minute," the soldier finished.

Raven looked at her.

"I swear," she said.

And she hadn't lied. A couple minutes later, she and her father sat in the back of the warm car, and they were driving back to wherever the soldiers had come from.

She gripped her father's hand, who gripped hers back

weakly, but it was enough reassurance. Raven drifted off into sleep now and then, but in the dim light of the car, her eyes focused on the soldier's shoulders—on the stars embroidered there.

And from that moment on, Raven swore to do everything in her power never to feel helpless again.

# CHAPTER 2

I focused on the four embroidered stars on Nikolai's shoulder that were pierced by the two crossed swords, like the ones he always had strapped to his back.

Tears were streaming down my face while I tried to think about what else I could do for the General. I tried to calm my breathing.

"Raven?" resounded from the hallway, and relief forced its way through my body.

"Hunter, here," I answered, completely worn-out.

Hasty footsteps echoed through the bunker, and Hunter ran into the room a moment later. Her eyes flew to the General, who lay on the table before me, and I followed her gaze.

"Nigel?" she asked, transfixed by the man in front of her.

I shook my head and swallowed audibly. My heart pounded an unsteady rhythm, and I felt new tears pricking behind my eyes—the pressure in my head increasing.

Hunter ran her hands over Nikolai's chest and asked, "How much anesthetic have you given him?"

"Everything that was left," I answered, voice trembling, and I shook my head. "I used the last syringe before cleaning his wounds and drilling a hole in his skull to relieve pressure on his brain."

"You did well," she said, and grabbed my arm. She tried to catch my eyes. "You made the difference between life and death for many people today, Raven."

I averted my gaze and tried to hide the emotions that fought their way to the surface. I looked back to Nikolai. "The General went back for Kent. He got caught with his leg under a large chunk of concrete that we couldn't lift. We soon learned we had to amputate his leg if we wanted to save his life, and General Zaregova would not leave him— so he performed the procedure despite his own injuries." I swallowed.

"But the collapse of the building attracted even more mutants to the sound, so we took Kent along, and it slowed us down a lot. We had come a long way until the mutants caught up with us. That last fight would have been the end if the General hadn't drawn his gun."

I blinked and focused on Hunter's hand as she tried to keep Nikolai awake by tapping his chest.

"Nigel died half an hour after I spoke to you," I explained. "He had lost too much blood."

"You gave everything, Lieutenant," I heard a voice say from the door, and I looked up. It belonged to Major General Locke, and I did not know why, but more tears gathered in my eyes.

"Everything wasn't enough," I simply said.

Hunter looked straight at me. "Clean yourself and try to get some rest. I'll take over."

I had refocused on the General when I felt a hand on my shoulder. Stunned, I looked straight at the Major General, who stood beside me. I wanted to tell him he didn't need to help me, but I couldn't get the words past my throat. After one more look at Hunter, I nodded and let the Major General walk me out of the room.

Major General Locke led me into a separate space at the end of the hallway, where he closed the door behind us. He sat me down on a chair at a small table I hadn't seen before, but I didn't bother taking in more of the space.

When he turned on the faucet, I felt my eyes sting again. This time I let my tears flow in silence as I stared at a point on the table.

A second later, Major General Locke sat down across from me and shoved a glass of water my way. "Drink up," he ordered.

My hand immediately enclosed the glass and pulled it to me, hands shaking, before I brought it to my lips to take a few mouthfuls of water—which proved to be an exercise because my throat was taut with emotion.

After finishing the glass, I put it back on the table and wiped my face clean, drying it with one of my uniform sleeves. "Thank you."

He looked at me and bowed his head almost imperceptibly. "Major Jameson is an exceptional trauma surgeon. She will get the General back on his feet."

I nodded. "I don't doubt it."

The Major General tilted his head a little to the side.

"I know Hunter is an amazing surgeon. It's not about that. It's—" I took a deep breath and searched for the right words. "When I realized I was the last one standing, it felt like the floor was dragged from underneath me, and I was free-falling into endless depths. I felt so fucking powerless."

"And now you're blaming yourself for Kent's death?" he guessed.

I studied my hands. "I *know* I'm to blame. If I'd just been better trained, I could have done more and been the person he needed the most at that moment. I might have had a way to stop the mutants—to treat his wounds."

The Major General frowned at me. "Listen. This is *not* your fault. If you had been better trained, it still wouldn't have mattered against a mutant. Let alone multiple. You still could have felt powerless."

I didn't entirely agree, but… "Is that how you felt?" I asked him. "When Hunter…" I trailed off, unsure if he wanted to talk about it.

"Saved me?" He nodded. "Yeah." Carefully, he loosened one clasp of his uniform and pulled down the top of his undershirt, revealing a large, reddened scar that spanned from his throat to his shoulder.

I bent forward a little and inspected the fresh scar tissue. "I heard about it."

Jordan let his fingers trail over his scar as a strained smile played on his lips. "It was just as gruesome as it looks."

"Gruesome?" I asked and looked back at his scar. "It must have felt terrible, but that scar isn't."

He let go of his shirt and frowned.

I pointed to his neck. "It looks good."

"My *scar*?" A cynical laugh escaped him like he thought I was messing with him.

But I nodded gravely. "A sign of survival—any kind—is powerful. It tells me we are strong enough to overcome any crisis thrown our way."

"Yeah, I bet the women out there will find it *irresistible*," he responded with a dull edge to his tone.

"It is," I said matter-of-factly, and looked at him, which made me realize he wasn't being sarcastic. His eyes betrayed him, and I could see he only used the emotion as a shield to hide his vulnerability.

Don't get me wrong: this man knew he was attractive. But, for whatever reason, he believed he wasn't allowed to be any less than *perfect*.

But perfect is boring.

"You're resisting it just fine," he countered, but his lips twitched slightly.

It did not deter me. "It's universally decided that being a survivor *is* attractive, it's *badass*. No matter what shape it comes," I repeated, granting him a small, earnest smile, which he answered.

The memories of what had happened today rushed back and suddenly caught up with me again. *Who was I to be smiling right now?*

I had allowed myself to forget what was going on. But the feeling of control slipping through my fingers like quicksand returned.

I cursed. "Why do we have to live in a world that's so messed up?"

The Major General stood, refilled my glass with water, and held it out to me. "Fairness is a human construct." He didn't say it as a joke, but grim humor shone through the surface of those blue eyes.

I took the glass from him and inhaled deeply. "Such positivity," I murmured.

Major General Locke's eyes turned lighter as he pulled up his chair and walked over to the door—but not before he pinched the back of my neck in a familiar gesture.

"Thank you, Major General," I said as he turned around.

"It's Jordan," he responded softly, and left the room.

# HEART ATTACK

## 3 YEARS LATER
## THE YEAR 2166
## NOW

I had just sat down on the couch to read when there was a knock on the door.

"Could you open that, Raven?" my father asked from the kitchen.

I had already put my book face-down on the side table. "Are you expecting someone, Papa?" I asked him. I opened the door and immediately took a step back—shook my head.

"Not that I know of," my father called back. "Who is it?"

Wide-eyed and with a hand covering my mouth, I stared at my mother. She looked exactly the way I remembered: her curling, thick brown hair, warm brown eyes, and above all, her easy smile.

"Mama?" I said, and my voice broke. Without noticing, tears had spilled from my eyes, one by one parting from my lashes.

She just stood there, smiling—a distant look in her eyes.

I stepped closer, her eyes tracking my movements. "Mama, is that really you?"

She still said nothing, but this time she nodded.

"What is it, Raven?" my father asked, walking out of the kitchen and wiping his hands clean on his pants. He froze midway, his eyes widening.

"It's Mama," I said, grateful tears already streaming down my cheeks.

"Raven," my father said carefully, "get away from the door."

My smile fell as goosebumps rose all over my skin.

"But—what? Mama—"

"Raven, get away from that door *right now!*" he thundered.

I looked from my father back to my mother, who was now focused on him. She was still smiling. This time, however, I could feel only shivers.

Slowly, I started backing away into the room.

"That isn't your mother," my father said, and I jerked my head to the side. "That's a mutant."

And when I looked back, I really saw her—*it*. Her gaze focused solely on me.

The wiry, skeletal creature standing at the door wasn't my mother. The clothes she was wearing were torn. Her head was sprinkled with bold spots, the curls she once had were now straight. There wasn't anything left of her beautiful brown locks. Even her brown eyes had changed, replaced with the milky white I'd often seen.

Only her smile remained. But it didn't feel the same. Not by a long shot.

I blinked, shaking my head as I clutched my neck. "*No.*"

The mutant took a step into the room, and my father told me to walk further away again, but my back bumped into a solid surface. I turned around and saw I was flush against a wall. My father's voice sounded from afar while the mutant kept getting closer.

I blinked, and the room had changed. I was in a space that had no doors or windows. Even my father was gone.

There was a gun on the floor, and I dived for it.

The mutant walked closer, but when I held up the pistol with trembling hands and aimed it at her face, she changed back into my mother.

I lowered the gun, and she changed back to the mutant. She lashed out at me.

"Stop moving!" I yelled and aimed the gun again, making my mother reappear. My hands started shaking intensely, and my face crumpled. "Mama, please, you're scaring me."

My mother's face softened, but I didn't dare lower the gun again. "Damn it!" I cried, aiming the gun straight into her face. "Stop, *please*! It's me—*Raven*," I tried again, but she continued moving forward.

I could count the hairs on her head by now.

"If you want me to stop, pull the trigger," she said lovingly—as if she understood.

My mother's voice weakened my knees. "No." *This isn't real. This isn't real.*

Her face mutated back. "Then you're dead," she spat, her tongue and missing teeth visible through her wide-open, rotting cheek.

Then she attacked.

I woke up screaming.

My hands went to my sore throat immediately. I was safe. It wasn't real. My breathing came in deep gulps of air. *It wasn't real.* With my hand on my chest, I tried to steady my thrashing heart.

I sat up straighter in bed. My whole body was damp—my legs entangled in the clammy sheets. The pain in my throat started easing, but the pressure built. I tried to push away the tears fighting their way into my eyes.

It was a dream. *Just a dream.*

I pulled my knees closer to my body and let my head rest on top. After a few deep breaths, I let go and stepped out of bed. The cold floor of my room anchored me back into the present moment, and I entered the bathroom to drink some ice-cold water straight from the tap.

Eventually, I met the eyes of my reflection. I stared at

myself for a while before nodding and started wrapping my hands.

✭ ✭ ✭

When I was younger, the nightmares occurred more often until my father sent me to a psychiatrist who taught me to anchor before I went to sleep, and worked through my nightmares with me until they went away. Of course, it had been a risk to go back into the shadow plains with everything it had taken from me—but I had to fight my demons. Real and otherwise.

The first few months at mission 3B were great. I felt better than I had in years.

But my nightmares had flared back up since I lost Nigel Kent in the field and had barely kept Nikolai alive.

I craned my neck as I stepped into the ring—blocking out the roaring crowd surrounding us. My vision zoned in on everything within the metal bars of the fighting ring; me and my opponent. The square was lit up; making the match easier to watch for outsiders, and harder for the fighters to get distracted. It didn't stop people from reaching inside and clanging metal against the bars, though.

The first time I had visited this hole, I had been *so ready*—*so done*. When I'd told Tania, one of my friends from 3B, I was going to this place someone had recommended, she insisted on going with me. Not because she thought it was too dangerous for me to go alone. No—it was *all* excitement. *Of course* Tania knew this place.

*The Sewers.*

She had warned me they fought dirty down here, but I hadn't cared. I relished the pain and the feeling I got when I stepped into this ring. Though the first time it had primarily been pain.

The way I had learned to fight was technically perfect, but technique didn't matter here. It was winning or losing—by whatever means necessary. No fights to the death, but fights to survive.

For some fighters, it's how they made a living. Winning a fight paid for their medical bills—if they cared about themselves enough to seek the help—and the leftover was enough to survive for a few days, weeks even, until they did another fight.

For other fighters like me, it was a way to forget—to feel *alive*.

My first time here was also the first day I had been back from the shadow plains for the second time—this time after a stay of *years*. I had been running away for too long, and I was *done*. At the end of my life, I wanted to look back and be proud of what I did, how I lived, and how far I'd come. Hiding away on some mission, moving around in the shadows, living like a ghost of myself, while ignoring and pushing away the feelings brewing in my chest—no, that wasn't a life.

At least, not the life I had imagined.

Sounds of a cheering crowd invaded my thoughts, and the man in front of me grinned.

The last time I fought Razor, I lost. And going by his smile, he thought we would repeat that fight. But, different from the people who fought in the Sewers for a living, I was educated by the military. Every time I fought, I fought to improve, and *learn* from my mistakes. Not to earn money.

It had made me a brigadier general in under three years. A *general*.

That fight against Razor had been the first and last

time I had lost a fight down here, and everyone knew it. Just like everyone knew I would win this time—now that I had learned his weaknesses like they were my own. Now that I knew how to fight down here. But it seemed he still underestimated me.

Though I should be grateful. He had taught me just how dirty people could fight. He'd quickly shown me why they called him Razor, carrying the little blades on him everywhere. I had been severely cut in multiple places that first night, but I had taken the loss with a smile on my face.

Because while everyone was fighting me, I fought myself too. And I desired nothing more than feeling powerful. To win for the sake of winning.

There were only two rules: no weapons (except for the clothes you wore, apparently), and when the other relented, you stopped. This also applied to a contender being unable to continue. We didn't fight people that couldn't fight back.

Not all of us, anyway.

I cracked my neck and loosened my shoulders as I stepped forward into the ring.

"Come back for another beating, sugar?" Razor spat.

I smirked as we started circling each other. "Something like that."

The crowd would get restless if you took too long to fight.

He pounced.

His fist soared straight to my face, but I blocked the punch with both arms raised, and I felt something sharp cut through my skin. Not a popular move, but I didn't need the crowd's favor to win.

I jumped sideways and dropped my hands to the ground the next second, swinging my leg up in the momentum, kicking him in the face.

Razor stumbled back a few steps, and he looked enraged. I crouched close to the ground, hands still touching the filthy, sticky floor.

I smiled. Because I knew how much that infuriated him.

He barged forward again, kicking, but I rolled away and straightened, his leg only skimming my body.

We jumped at the same time, both our arms in front of our faces. He kicked, and I braced my hip for impact, still shielding my face. The moment I dropped my arms, he would strike.

He kicked me again.

And again.

And when he did it the second time, with a smile on his face, he forgot to outpace his kicks, and I ducked as he raised his leg, ramming him into his stomach and throwing an upper punch into his chin—teeth clattering and blood spraying.

He tried to hit my back with his hands clamped together but lost his balance, falling back against the ring's metal bars. The sound rang against all the little blades strapped to his body, and the crowd went wild. His anger slowly showed its ugly head. Just like I hoped it would.

I sprinted to him, throwing a punch that he blocked. He threw a punch that I cashed with my jaw. I kicked against his chin, and his face barely crumbled. He pushed himself forward, kicking his legs out in front of him in rapid succession. Impressive, but futile, as he lowered his hands to keep his balance while he switched feet.

I grabbed my chance and windmilled him.

He fell to the ground, but I wasn't the type of fighter to kick someone when he was down. It didn't seem like a fun way to win, even against Razor.

He scrambled to his feet and let his hands graze over his torso. He looked a little off, and I knew I was close to victory.

Slowly, he walked to me, and we circled each other again, our arms raised in front of us, upper bodies withdrawn. I threw a punch at the same time he did, his hand only grazing my cheek, which hurt way more than it was supposed to. Warm liquid dripped down my face a minute later, and the cut stung fiercely.

I saw something glint between his knuckles that he dropped quickly.

"*What the fuck*," I hissed.

He smiled with bloody teeth. Razor was clearly at his finish line.

I grimaced.

Stepping closer, he stepped back, and we repeated that dance until his back hit the metal bars again. When surprise took over his emotions, I pounced—throwing fist after fist, kick after kick, and the only thing he could do was protect himself—shield his body from my relentless attack.

I was pushing my limits as I kept kicking the fraudulent piece of shit.

I stopped and looked at the pathetic excuse for a human that hung against the metal bars. His eyes were now closed, but he still held on to the bars. The man didn't know when he'd had enough.

My hand curled into a fist, and I punched him straight into his unprotected throat, literally not caring if I killed this scum. I'd seen enough fights and heard enough stories about Razor over the last two months that I could only guess what he had done in a lifetime. "Choke on that, *asshole*," I snarled into his face.

His eyes rolled back into his head, and he crumpled to the dirt-caked ground in a wheezing heap.

The crowd went wild.

I stepped back, out of the ring, and let the mass swallow me whole. The fumes of sweat, smoke, and alcohol surrounded me. People clapped my back and hollered in my face, but I didn't care.

Something inside me had snapped.

I had seen my father, Hunter, and the rest of my friends now and then since coming back, but I tried my best to avoid everyday life as much as possible—avoiding *him*.

Even after three years, I still hid away in the shadows. And I was done being a coward.

# CHAPTER 3

After breakfast, I sat in the main room and stared at the white sheet covering Nigel Kent's body. We would leave early the following morning to return to base, without Hunter and the General, and I had noticed that I had been avoiding this space.

I memorized the image: the white sheet and the contours of a body underneath. I promised myself I wouldn't fail anyone like I had Kent—that I wouldn't let anybody die because of this gods-forsaken mutation ever again. So, I watched, until my palpitations subsided and the sweat on my neck and back cooled.

There was a time in my life when I wanted nothing but to be a dual function soldier. It was my ticket to this mission, 3B. But now, I somehow knew that my time as a dual function soldier was ending. I wasn't really exceptional at anything, and it made me feel useless. *Yes*, I had a talent for medical procedures—but I knew little besides the basics. And *yes*, I could fight and protect—my tactical skill was also fine. Only all to a certain extent.

I was a soldier who was exceptional at following orders. And when the person who gave the orders fell away, I panicked—hadn't known what to do.

The white sheet blurred, and I started blinking. If I had known what to do and had been *better*, I might have been able to save Nigel Kent's life.

"Lieutenant?"

I didn't react. To be frank, I didn't even realize he was speaking to me until he said, "Raven?"

My head turned sideways, and I saw Major General Locke, Jordan, standing beside me. I blinked again and rubbed my sore neck. I had lost all sense of time, especially since the rest of the group had been avoiding this space as much as possible.

"What are you doing?" he asked.

I turned to him fully. "Ever heard of exposure therapy?"

Jordan tsked. "Ever heard about self-destructive behavior?"

I squared my shoulders and arched a brow. "Call it what you want. It serves a purpose for me."

"What purpose is that?" he scoffed.

"To serve as an example."

"An example for who? You?"

"Just let it go." I turned away from him.

Jordan stepped closer and lay a hand on my shoulder. "Stop punishing yourself. You already have a hard time as it is."

"I don't have a hard time," I curtly replied and clamped my lips shut.

He raised a brow. "That would be alarming—if I didn't know you were lying."

Rolling my eyes, I tried to walk past him, but he took

hold of my arm. "Raven… Sorry, all right? I'll respect it if you don't want to talk about it. But please stop fooling yourself."

"What is it to you? You've known me for a day."

Jordan pulled a hand through his hair, frustrated. "Weird, huh? Wanting to help another person? To be kind?"

My hands started shaking, and I felt the pent-up frustration and fatigue coursing through my body. I couldn't meet his gaze. "You're right." I tried to pass him again, but he stopped me and pulled me against his chest.

Shock immobilized me, but I let my eyes fall shut when he laid a gentle hand on the back of my head. My body started heaving out of nowhere—tears were streaming down my face, soaking his shirt.

"Sorry," I choked, frustrated.

"Don't worry. It's all washable."

Even in my meltdown, I laughed. "I meant—"

"I know," he interrupted me, affectionately smoothing my hair. "I know."

## NOW

After the researchers found the serum three years ago, the army had made grand plans for the Special Shadow Unit. In the last few years, we have tried to push back mutant colonies with the help of the serum. The focus of the mission unit had been spreading the serum under mutant colonies. And because there was *finally* a new radar technology available that didn't get disturbed by mutants, they deployed hover planes to spread the food injected with the serum.

The research group, the army, the government, and the

leadership of this mission—including Nikolai Zaregova—all agreed to a cooperative plan regarding the future of the SSU. They had extended the mission for at least another five years. I had worked back on that base for half of those years, during which we had tried to push back the mutants and the shadow plains with them.

Pilots would fly over the areas with high markers of mutant activity and colonies, dropping the injected food there, hoping every mutant in the area would digest some of it.

There were also soldiers needed on the ground that went to these marked areas and searched for younger, surviving mutants to extract for research. Perhaps, one day, they'd get a chance at a semi-normal existence.

We also had to check whether all full-grown mutants were dead or gone. That's where I came in. I had overseen large parts of the teams that went onto the shadow plains—often going with them. But I'd grown tired of the monotonous task ever since the vaccine had officially been approved. The world was changing, and the army changed with it.

A rapid knock sounded on my door at the mission base, and I threw the letter I had just received on the coffee table. The rooms I'd gotten upon my return were three times as large as the ones I left the base from years ago.

Before I reached the door, it had already opened, and Kelian perched his head along the corner.

"Yo. What are you up to?" he asked, stepping into the room without invitation. He took in the place before looking at me and sighed. "I can't get over the difference in our rooms. Such hierarchic bullshit."

But when he *really* looked at me, his expression turned sour. He strode over with long strides and took my face between his hands as he tipped my head back a little. "What the hell did you do, Raven?"

I shrugged, a smile tugging on my lips. "You know, eating a little, getting some sleep, staying out of the sun."

"It is not *fucking* funny," he snarled. "Have you been going to that place again?"

"What place?" I asked innocently.

Kelian wasn't amused.

"What if I have?"

He dragged a hand through his wine-red hair, eyeing the bruises on my skin and the cuts on my arm and cheek. "Why the hell do you keep doing that?"

I chuckled. "You should've seen the other guy."

He didn't think that was funny either, and looked straight through me. "You're nervous, aren't you? Have been ever since you came back here."

I sat back down on the couch and broke eye contact. "What would I be nervous about?"

He connected his fingertips and raised both brows.

"*What?*" I asked him explicitly.

"You tell me."

I sighed.

"You know you can talk to me."

"I do," I agreed. Just not about *everything*.

"So, why don't you?"

He knew me too well. My best friend, now a lieutenant colonel, had been by my side for a large part of the last couple of years. I was forever grateful to him for that. But *man*, he could be an overbearing mother hen.

I scraped over the wooden side table with my nails, trying to leave a mark.

"Just spit it out," he said.

I dropped my hand in my lap and looked at him. "Ever thought about the possibility that I might not *want* to talk about certain things?"

"You've been absent lately." He tutted. "What happened, Raven? Why are you so dead set on hurting yourself?"

My gaze darkened as I glared at him in warning. I was *not* trying to hurt myself.

"I see I've hit a nerve."

My jaw clenched, and I narrowed my eyes. "Don't you always?"

Kelian threw his hands in the air and said, "Fine, I'll stop. But—"

I watched him from the corner of my eyes.

"You know I just want to help, right? I want you to feel *good*, Raven."

"I know."

"Then I'll shut up about it." Kelian clamped his lips shut and pretended like he locked them and threw away the key. "But you should stop going to that place."

I rolled my eyes again. "I'll think about it," I murmured, but we both knew I wouldn't.

"Right."

"Stop worrying so much," I said. "I'm *fine*."

Quiet settled in the room for a brief moment.

"On another note," I said, handing him the letter that I'd just been reading—glad for a change of conversation. "Our chief general has summoned me."

Kelian unfolded the paper. "He sent you a *letter*? Why wouldn't his secretary just message you?"

I shrugged. "Old school guy?"

He skimmed over the text, inhaling deeply. "Keep me posted?"

I nodded, taking back the piece of paper. "Sure. Why did you come anyway?"

"I came to check if you'd like to grab a drink tonight with the group?" Kelian shrugged.

"Can't," I sighed. "I'm visiting my dad today."

"Right." He stood. "Give him my regards. I'll get back to work then."

My smile was tight. "Thanks for stopping by, Kel."

He nodded, looked away, and clenched his jaw. Then he turned around and waved his hand in the air before opening the door and turning around the corner.

✫ ✫ ✫

I pulled into my father's driveway and parked the car. He lived just an hour's drive from the capital in a small village that still had a water tank. It was colder there than in the capital, where sunlight lamps burned bright at all moments of the day.

My father lived in a charming one-story house I bought for him short of a year ago during one of my breaks: small, with a white fence and a bed of flowers in varying colors in the garden designed to survive colder climates. Perfect for him on his own.

I rang the bell. I hadn't told him I was coming, so it would be a surprise.

The door opened, and my father's face lit up. His skin seemed to have wrinkled since the last time I saw him. But that was the only sign of his age because he had remained the same man from twenty years ago—full of life and vigor.

"Raven!" he said and pulled me into a bone-crushing hug.

I felt Benji jump against my legs, and I let go of my father to give him some attention. His tongue hung limply from his mouth, and he wagged his tail playfully as I rewarded him with a rub behind the ears. "You've been good to my papa, haven't you?"

"He has," my father agreed solemnly. "Come in, come in," he said as he pushed me inside. He whistled at Benji, who had already disappeared further into the street.

Once inside, I got tea with bucket loads of sugar. Just how I liked it.

"How are you doing?" my father asked as he sat down with a bowl of homemade cookies.

I picked one and took a bite, relishing the familiar taste. "I'm doing well."

"Life back at the capital already chafing at you, my dear?"

I took a bite of a cookie that said I didn't want to speak about my return. I also didn't talk to my father about the missions I went on—especially regarding the shadow plains. He knew, but I spared him the details. It could be… a lot.

He chuckled. "You need to get a life outside of work. Stop going on these long missions. It can't be good for the soul."

"I was on a mission with friends," I said around a mouthful of cookie. *If you counted having Kelian over for a year and Cardan for half of that.* "Besides, I have more responsibilities now that I'm a general, Papa."

"I know, I know, and I'm so proud of you. But work isn't everything."

My mouth pursed. "It is to me." What else did I have anyway, besides my father?

"Well," he said. "Let's start by not going away for years on end."

"All right." I wasn't planning to, anyway.

I looked around the house, spotting the only picture of the three of us that had survived the trip to the west: me, my father, and my mother. The memories of her seemed to fade with each passing year, but the afternoon we took that picture was etched in my brain.

"I miss her," I told him as I looked at it.

My father nodded gravely, and I felt my heart soften as he said, "Me too, every day."

There were some women in his town, widowed like him, that he could build a happy life with. And he had *tried*. But his love for my mother seemed to cast too big of a shadow over anyone trying to take up space in my father's life.

I didn't worry, though. Together with Benji and his bazillion other hobbies, my father was never bored or unhappy.

Looking at the other pictures of the two of us, I smiled. My dad was my best friend—never stopped playing with me like life was one big adventure and treasures could be waiting just around the corner. He gifted me a normal childhood amid chaos.

Some time later, I hugged my father tightly and promised him to visit soon. My father was the most important person in the world to me, and I hadn't seen him nearly as much as I wanted.

Now it was time to go back to Barak. For *real,* this time.

I looked at the star on my jacket. I was tired of hiding in the corner. It was time I started acting like the general I was supposed to be. Show them why I earned my title.

It was time I stepped back into the light.

# CHAPTER 4

## 3 YEARS EARLIER

My hands were covered in the blood of multiple wounded soldiers.

I didn't know how many I had treated so far, but the number was high enough for my hands to get numb. I held them under the freezing cold water, scrubbing away the blood, and bit the inside of my cheek as they cramped. But there was no time to feel pain: only people to help.

Looking up from my hands, I noticed General Zaregova walking into the medical center, scanning the room. Going by his face, which was covered in a layer of dirt and blood, he had been well off. But when I noticed the dark spots on his uniform as he walked closer, I stopped him in his tracks. "Hold on, General."

He turned around wearily and raised a bleeding eyebrow. "What is it, Lieutenant?"

I quickly stepped closer and gestured to one of the tables. "Let me check your wounds to ensure no stitches have loosened."

Even though impatience radiated from him while he

kept searching the room, he sat down. He sighed, studying his hands as if he looked at them for the first time that day.

As I opened his uniform, I immediately noticed a few of his newer stitches were torn. He was lucky his wound had already healed as much as it did—because an opening of this size could have cost him his life.

I was cleaning his wounds when he finally opened his mouth. "I want to thank you for what you did in the field." His dark eyes were sincere.

"Of course." I smiled at him.

General Zaregova looked back into the room again. He cleared his throat and *finally* asked the question that I had been anticipating. "Do you have any idea where Major Jameson is?"

I did my best to mask the smile blossoming on my face. "No, sorry."

The General gave me one of his impenetrable gazes.

Then, I noticed Jordan entering the building. He, too, looked through the space like he was searching for something—someone. His gaze crossed mine and slid to the General in front of me. He immediately came our way, but instead of the General, it was me he wanted to talk to.

After I changed the General's gauze, I stretched my back and swam in a sea of stars for a moment. I had to grab the table in front of me to keep my balance. Exhaustion and dehydration weren't an optimal combination.

I quickly smiled, so neither of the men would notice. It worked on at least one of them—because *his* thoughts were somewhere else... with *someone* else. The other man frowned deeply at me and lay a hand on my back while he guided me into an empty office.

The moment the door shut, I let myself lean against a

wall and closed my eyes.

"You have to take care of yourself, too, Raven."

I rolled my eyes. But *that* wouldn't make a difference. I made a difference by helping other people. Okay, I might be more able if I also took care of myself. But… what did they say about desperate times again?

"What do you need?" Jordan asked forcefully while he pushed me into a chair.

I opened my eyes, leaning my head into my hands. "Are you wounded?"

He shook his head, and his frown returned. Why did he always frown so much?

"Because you're not answering my questions."

Oh, shit. Did I say that out loud? "I think my brain spews rubbish when it's parched," I joked, but Jordan didn't appreciate the humor.

"So, water." He stood and walked out of the room but returned with a glass of water a moment later.

"Thanks," I said carefully, while taking the ice-cold glass from him. It was a miracle that my nerves still worked because I thought I'd lost all feeling in them a couple moments ago.

Jordan sat next to me and watched as I put the glass to my lips. After the first sip, I realized how thirsty I was. My body suddenly felt like it hadn't drunk in days, and I gulped down the water as if my life depended on it until it was empty, resulting in a brain freeze.

"Fuck," I said and pinched my eyes shut as I put pressure on my head.

Jordan took the glass from me and refilled it. I let my head bounce to the side and inspected him again. His ash-blonde hair was dirty from a substance that had found its way in there—and I didn't want to know what that was. His face, neck, and uniform were just plain dirty. But his eyes… His eyes were a vivid contrast to the rest of his appearance, which made him incredibly attractive.

*Dear gods.* I wasn't doing well.

"Why?" I whispered to him.

Jordan knew what I meant. "Because someone has to care." He walked to me and handed me another glass. "Slower this time," he said, but he didn't leave.

## NOW

The cut on my cheek hadn't fully healed yet, and a sickly yellowish color still marred the skin on my jaw. But walking around on an army base had its pros, as no one questioned any wounds or looked at them twice.

I was taking the scenic route to the main building. Chief General Domasc's assistant had paged me to come to the office. The Chief wanted to speak to me himself, so I had too much fun with stalling time. *It sucked, didn't it—people not coming when you asked them to?* But I couldn't push it for too long, because I cared about my career—and if you learned one thing in the army, it was to be punctual.

I saluted as I finally entered his office and waited for his nod before I sat down.

"Brigadier General Renée, glad you could make it," he said and looked at his watch, raising an eyebrow almost imperceptibly.

I sat in one of the chairs opposite his desk as he looked at the papers before him. His grey hair and beard made him look older since the last time I saw him, three years ago—when his dark hair had been laced with silver instead of swallowed by it. But I guess he did have a lot to worry about.

"You're being assigned a new mission."

That's one way to break the news. "What mission, *sir*?"

"We have detected some strange activity on the shadow plains indicating non-mutant behavior—which is classified information that will not leave this room. I've decided to send a specialist group to investigate. You're going to the shadow plains—to Damruin. A minor off-the-books operation."

My whole body locked up.

*Damruin?*

I recovered, barely, and swallowed. "The shadow plains, sir?"

He finally looked at me. "Yes?"

Clearing my throat, I tried to gauge how far I could push him. "I've been there for the past three years."

"Your point, Brigadier General?"

Wasn't it obvious? "I would prefer to get some new experience, preferably somewhere else."

That was one way to put it—the civilized way.

"And I would like my generals to accept their assigned missions without rebuttal, but apparently, we don't always get what we want." The Chief General looked at my jaw and cheek, noticing the discolored cut with distaste.

My jaw clenched with the effort of swallowing my retort.

"You're one of the few soldiers with the necessary amount of experience in the shadow plains, which makes you the best fit for this mission. But would you rather I send someone else? Someone less experienced?"

*Well, yes.*

"You don't want to be a *deserter*, do you, Brigadier General Renée?"

I had two years left before I was free from my contract, and to do whatever I pleased. Until then, I was obligated to do the jobs I was assigned.

He sat back, one hand perched on the table. "You have worked so hard to earn that star." He inclined his head. "Here's the thing, Miss Renée. If you disobey me, I will send you off immediately, discredited, dishonored, and stripped of your hard-earned rank."

"Is that a threat, *sir?*" I asked carefully, not letting the hissing enter my voice, trying to stay calm. Soothing myself proved near impossible with this man before me.

He chuckled. "Of course not. We're all friends here, aren't we?"

I kept my mouth shut.

"So, what do you say?" he asked like I had a choice in the matter.

I stood, saluting him. "*Yes, sir.*"

★ ★ ★

Domasc's cruel smile embedded itself in my brain like a tick. Something about the way he had threatened me felt crucial. Something was going on—I *felt* it.

Storming out of the main base, I finally got a gulp of fresh air inside my lungs. I kept walking the streets lined with tall buildings made of glass, until I found myself on the large square in downtown Barak—the lights reflected on the wet stones.

Posters of delegate candidates adorned the buildings. A couple of weeks ago, the voting for delegates had been held. The people chose mostly the same delegates until said delegates retired, but now and then, a new face emerged from the voting—who would shake up the way things had always been done and create something better.

The poster that caught my attention was that of Kenneth Locke, one of the more well-known, public figures in Barak. It was common knowledge that he was popular—and with good reason: his ideals matched that of the progressive majority. I, also, had voted for him. I just couldn't look at his posters for long. His face was too familiar and... confronting. It felt as if his piercing blue eyes looked straight through me.

The chief general voting would come up shortly, and it seemed Domasc was still running ahead—the only candidate at all so far, which sucked.

I walked into a somewhat deserted street and yelled, "Ben!" as soon as I saw him.

The man in question turned around, eyes squinting until his eyebrows tipped up. "Raven Renée? In the flesh?" he barked as he stepped from his stall.

When I reached him, he took my hand, shaking it wildly, and planted a kiss on my cheek. "Dear girl, it has been such a long time."

He walked back to his stall and stepped inside. "If I had known you were coming, I would have held back the finest hotdog for you."

Grinning, I shook my head. "We wouldn't want you to play favorites, now, do we?"

He smiled while he cut the bread and the smells coming from his stall made my mouth water.

"The last time I saw you was, how long ago? You were still together with Jordan back then."

"Jordan?" I asked him, breath hitching.

Ben sighed, looking up to the sky. "You were such a handsome pair."

My cheeks turned red. "We were just friends," I said.

With narrowed eyes, Ben shook his head and applied sauce to the bun. "Are you certain? If one of my supposed friends looked at me that way, my wife would be worried. You looked at each other like you were one of my hotdogs."

I burst out in nervous laughter.

"Anyhow," Ben continued, who was now pulling the sausage from the hot water, holding it up, "that new girlfriend of his, *Ashley*, she's nice, but she's got nothing on you." He pointed the sausage at me before he put it in the bun, applying some more sauce.

My smile froze. "They come here?"

"Sometimes, but she always chooses a pretzel. Says she doesn't eat meat and stuff. Can't appreciate the *haute cuisine* we're making here. Boring, if you ask me." He shrugged.

I hadn't.

Nodding, I took the hotdog from him, and handed him the money. "I missed your stall, Ben."

He smiled proudly. "It missed you too."

Stepping backward, I took a bite, held my thumb and index finger together in a circle, and kissed the tips. "Perfection."

He winked and said, "Don't be a stranger!"

# CHAPTER 5

## 3 YEARS EARLIER

I stepped out of my tiny room—an upgrade compared to my previous accommodation—and left the hallway to immerse myself straight back into the chaos of everyday life at the main base.

The talk with my supervisor earlier that week had gradually turned into a conversation about my future in the army now that mission 3B was over. He had read the psychologist's report, and together we had come to the conclusion that I was ready to do something else within the army.

I had to continue the conversations with my psychologist to process everything that had happened. But now that my official promotion to major was approaching, it was equally important to get tasks that fit this new position.

I had decided to stop working in a dual function, and my commanding general had given me the assignment to look around this week to find what I wanted to do—something that made my heart palpitate.

Dodging the larger crowds, I left the hall and held my

pass in front of a scanner that granted access to the training halls. I knew what I wanted to do, but didn't have the guts to ask for it yet. Not while I missed the skills for someone in my position in a function like that.

As I walked past one of the open doors to the gyms, I inhaled the musty, sweaty air that greeted me. Sweat gathered in the lines of my palm. Even my cheeks warmed. I wasn't a naturally nervous person, but being a beginner, doing something for the first time had been long overdue.

Chin high, I entered one of the locker rooms, changed into some comfy, fitted training gear, and found my way back into the hall. The tension in my body immediately evaporated as I told myself that this first step could save lives in the future.

It was crowded, chuck full of infantry soldiers. This, infantry, was the division I wanted to be a part of. Full-time.

I'd been partially trained as an infantry soldier, so fighting wasn't new to me. I even had a knack for it. But for the first ten minutes, I acted like a fly on the wall, watching others attack the punching bags and each other.

During the army program, they said on more than one occasion that you're in only *one* competition: with yourself. *Not* with your fellow soldiers, because you needed to count on each other in the field. However, something about competition unleashed a drive within me. I wanted to be the best, which I could only be if I measured myself to my peers.

I wanted to set the standard to which others aspired.

To do that, to be that person, I first had to learn what I did wrong and what others did right. Especially other people that were better than me.

A boy wiped the sweat from his forehead with his wrist,

and his eyes crossed mine. He pointed to the bag, his smile amiable. "You want to have a go?"

I returned the smile, eyebrows pinched. "If you could show me that set you were doing one more time."

"You're new?" he asked curiously.

Shaking my head, I stepped closer and bit my lip. "I look *that* innocent?"

He laughed out loud and placed a hand under my elbow while he positioned me in front of the punching bag, unnecessary, but not unwelcome. Slowly, he led me through the sequence of punches and kicks until I memorized them.

I completed the set five times in a row, going through the last one without any comments from the boy, and gave him an exciting look. He winked and opened his mouth as if he wanted to say something, but he got cut off by someone behind me.

"Her kicks weren't balanced enough, and at least three inches too low, Sergeant. Or did you not notice because you were too busy staring at the Major's ass while she was doing them?"

The boy saluted to the person behind me and hurried off to another punching bag, refusing to look at me again.

I turned around with a hand on my hip. "Officially not a major yet," I said, but clamped my mouth shut as I saw who was standing before me.

Major General Locke.

One of my eyebrows went skyward as I saluted him.

"You look good, Renée," he said, which made me feel all sorts of things.

"And here you just scolded that guy for checking me out," I said.

He rewarded me with a lopsided grin. "How are you

doing?"

"I'm fine." I shrugged. "You just came back?"

"Yeah." He pulled a hand through his ash-blonde hair. "Been back for a couple of days now. It's been taking some getting used to. My soldiers here seem to have forgotten who I am."

"So that's what that was? Asserting your dominance?"

Jordan chuckled. "Something like that."

I had to adjust after only a couple of months; I could only imagine what it must feel like after a couple of years.

"Why *are* you here, Raven? Not that I don't find it absolutely riveting to have you stop by. I presume you have other reasons to visit than to give me a warm welcome or distract my soldiers?"

My eyes nearly rolled out of their caskets. "I didn't even know you were here."

"So you're here for my soldiers?"

I snorted. "I want to join the infantry full-time, so I came to train. At least, I was researching different techniques to refine my own."

Jordan crossed his arms on his chest and tilted his head a little. "You're serious? You want to improve your fighting?"

I nodded eagerly. "I hope you don't mind an extra soldier popping in here. I promise I won't distract anyone, at least, not on purpose."

Jordan chuckled and shook his head. "If I had known you had such a smart mouth on you, I would've tried to find you a lot sooner at 3B."

My heart somersaulted, and I felt a tingle run through my body.

"I'll tell you what," Jordan said on a serious note. "Ever since coming back, I've had it easy compared to the last couple of years, and I'm kind of bored. I wouldn't mind training you for an hour every other day after dinner."

My jaw dropped. "*You* want to train *me*?"

He shrugged. "Why not?"

"Okay," I immediately said and grinned at him, because this was an easy decision. One of the best infantry generals in the army wanted to help me train. Of course, you accepted.

Duh.

"First lesson." He stepped behind me, taking my arm in his large hand, and positioned my elbow at a perfect angle. He let his other hand curl around mine, folding my fingers to make a fist. "You punch with these two knuckles," he said, his finger trailing over the knuckles of my index and middle finger.

I rolled my eyes again, but suppressed a shiver. "Har har. You should really up your game if you want me to keep considering you as a trainer."

He dropped my arm and turned around, grinning. "I'll see you tomorrow after dinner at eight sharp. Don't be late."

## NOW

The front door opened before I could knock, and Hunter pulled me into a fierce hug. She and Nikolai had moved into a gorgeous country house close to the city, and I spent the first minute after arriving just taking in my fill.

"Oh Raven, I'm so happy to see you again," Hunter exclaimed into my hair. She had put her curls up and wore a white sweater paired with her light blue jeans.

"I'm happy to see you too," I said as she stepped sideways and held open the door for me. "The house looks beautiful, Hunt."

Hunter inspected my face. "Why are you always covered in bruises when I see you? Last time I heard, they weren't allowed to use weapons during training."

I smiled. "They still aren't."

Hunter pursed her lips as we walked further inside, where Nikolai was cooking in the open kitchen. His smiles were rare, but I always got one. "Brigadier General Renée. Lovely bruises."

I raised my nose and moved my head towards a grinning Hunter. "General Zaregova." I mock saluted. He snorted before his gaze shifted to Hunter beside me, and I could almost *smell* his affection. It was infectious.

It was still crazy to see Nikolai Zaregova being a normal human being. After the serum had been found and we were all sent home, Hunter and Nikolai retreated for some time. And I had already returned to the SSU a few months later.

I kept in touch with Hunter while I was at the mission, and I even returned from the SSU to attend their wedding. But except for now-and-then appearances and a brief conversation, I hadn't spent time with him since mission 3B.

"How are you doing? At work?" I asked him when Hunter pushed a glass of red wine into my hands.

Nikolai sighed deeply as he turned the meat in his pan. "The upcoming elections make Domasc nervous, so the man is trying to get into the good graces of any delegate that has yet to form a clear opinion of him. Rumor has it he even plans to join the delegation going to Borzia in a couple of days."

I perked up. "Borzia?"

Borzia and Ardenza's relationship was strained, as in, there hadn't been a relationship with the other continent since the start of the crisis. Borzia had bought our sunlight technology and spread it across their continent. They, at least, the royal family, were wealthy. But when the shadow plains had spread over the world, and largely across Ardenza, we had asked them for help as we shared large parts of our border with them. But apparently, we had already served our purpose. And instead of sending aid, they barricaded that border and continued living like nothing had happened, sending all the mutants our way during the crisis.

Ever since then: radio silence.

"You're sure?"

Nikolai nodded. "They want to negotiate about the vaccine."

"I'm surprised they didn't already find the vaccine and kept it from us for years," I scoffed. Ardenza and Borzia had been ignoring each other's existence for *years*, but they had always tried to get the upper hand. "Anyway, I'm not surprised about anything Domasc does. Especially after the shit he pulled at 3B."

Nikolai grunted his agreement, and Hunter tipped up her glass of wine.

I swallowed. "I had a meeting in his office the other day."

Hunter looked up, concern framing her beautiful face.

"About what?" Nikolai asked grimly.

"He practically forced me to go on a mission back to the shadow plains. *Classified*, he said. Some activity has been detected, and he wants me to investigate it with a team. He even threatened to discharge me if I refused."

A frown had etched itself between Nikolai's brows. "I have heard nothing about the activity."

I laughed sardonically. "Well, there's Domasc for you. A real pain in the ass. Anything you know to get me off this mission without deserting?"

He shook his head. "But I will keep an eye and ear out for information on this. Domasc tries to hide as much as possible from me, but I'll find out what this is about and get some trustworthy people in the monitoring rooms when you're in the field."

His tone left a dent in my breezy attitude, realizing how serious this could be. "Thanks," I replied gratefully.

Hunter cleared her throat, giving Nikolai a look as he sat down. "Yes, we live in a semi-shit world that we have to share with semi-shit people. Let's forget about that tonight, all right?"

"Good idea," I murmured as I took my drink from the table.

Hunter and Nikolai's gazes met, and I paused the glass I brought to my lips. "What?"

Hunter seemed to glow as she stood to take something from a cupboard—a velvet purple box. "Nik and I had something made for you to celebrate your promotion. It's for tomorrow's gala."

"You're serious?" I put the glass down.

Hunter lay the box in front of me and sat back down next to Nikolai, who had draped an arm over her chair. His mouth grazed her shoulder as I reached for the box.

I opened it, and I felt my throat close up. In the box was a golden band adorned with a single golden star.

"It's an arm cuff. Nikolai told me that all generals were expected to wear their stars at gatherings like this, and most of them just use a simple pin. I like this better," Hunter explained. "Your dress doesn't have long sleeves, does it?"

I shook my head, then smiled at them. "You have no idea what this means to me." There was a moment of silence as I adored the piece of jewelry, letting my finger skim the elegant metal. I swallowed.

"Is Kelian coming with you tomorrow?" Hunter asked.

I nodded. Only generals were invited to this gala, but everyone could bring a plus one, and, of course, I would bring Kelian. I don't know if I would even go without him.

Hunter cleared her throat. "Jordan's coming, too."

Nikolai stood as if on cue, and walked back over to the kitchen, finishing the food.

"Oh?" I said carefully, feigning surprise. Seeing him at the gala was *all* I thought about.

"He and Ashley have been engaged for six months."

I evaded the look Hunter was giving me and tried to nod indifferently.

*Jordan. Engaged.*

Memories I had so desperately tried to escape bubbled to the surface. Unprocessed emotions filled my throat, and I suddenly couldn't breathe.

"Let's go outside." Hunter touched my arm, and I was startled by her proximity.

I shook my head. "No, I'm okay." The corners of my trembling lips pulled into an uneven smile, but I was still trying to catch my breath. "It's time to eat, anyway."

"The food can wait," Hunter said sternly as she grabbed my arm and forced me to leave the house.

Outside, I leaned against the wall and looked up at the clearly visible stars. I closed my eyes and felt tears escape. "Fucking hell."

Hunter pushed a tissue into my hands, and I wiped away my tears as I inhaled.

"What happened between you two, Raven?"

I turned my head to her, and my eyes filled with silent tears.

"Did you know Jordan drove out here after you left? To ask me if you were really gone? I had never seen him so distressed," Hunter said.

A shaky breath left my body.

Hunter handed me another tissue. "For whatever it's worth, Raven, he isn't happy with her, not in the way he should be. The way he looks at her pales in comparison to the way he used to look at you."

My heart spasmed painfully, and I tried to keep the pieces together with all my might.

"That only makes it worse," I whispered. "I don't want him to be unhappy."

"I know, smartass. I didn't say it to comfort you." Hunter arched a brow.

I dried my tears and sniffled. "Too late, Hunter."

"It's never too late."

For the second time that evening, I looked up at the stars, which were all twinkling brightly, like they were emphasizing Hunter's message. But I had clung to that hope for too long. So long that it had slowly turned into desperation, and I had sworn never to feel that way ever again.

"In this case, it is."

# CHAPTER 6

"Right," Jordan said.

A breath left my body as I punched my fist into his hand.

"Higher," followed almost immediately.

He meant my elbow. It had the tendency to drop when I got tired. I raised it and punched again, which won me an approving nod.

My arms and legs trembled from the past hour. Every training with Jordan was a carnage with only one victim: me. However, I had gotten much better because even Jordan couldn't stop a laugh from escaping his mouth—the kind of laugh that surprised you.

After some more kicks and punches, Jordan finally gave the redeeming word, and I let myself fall backward on the mat.

"Hell," I said as the world spun around me. "I feel sorry for your soldiers."

"You'll soon be one of them if you keep this up." Jordan grinned and brought me some water—which he always seemed to do. I thanked him. "You're better than the majority, so I think I'll have to be stricter with them."

I threw him a sarcastic look. "Because my skills are so disappointing?"

He pushed me back down as I tried to stand up, which made me laugh. "No. Now that I see what results can come from my hands, I'll have to get my other soldiers up to par.

"Maybe it has something to do with the student." I winked from where I leaned on the mat.

Jordan smiled. "Maybe."

I straightened and wiped the sweat from my face. He only had a few drops on his temple. Extremely unfair.

Jordan's stomach growled ferociously.

I tried to rein in my laughter. "You're *still* hungry?" I asked him with wide eyes. I couldn't believe this guy.

Lately, we've been having dinner together in the canteen more often. I had loads of questions, and he didn't mind answering them. Most of Jordan's friends had gone home for a while after all those years at the Special Shadow Unit, and they lived outside of Barak, so he had plenty of time for me.

*My* friends were scattered about, and I didn't run into them often. Kelian had been called away a week after I returned from the mission to serve temporarily at an outpost as an operating assistant. Cardan was in Barak, but always busy. I sometimes talked to him and Tania, but they were usually indisposed. And Hunter... she was still on her minor break with Nikolai. I would see her in a couple of days at the ceremony.

So, besides work, it was nice to have Jordan around—a friend. A friend that had five stomachs because I had no other explanation for how he could eat like a giant.

I narrowed my eyes at him while I stood and gestured for

him to follow. "Come." I put a sweater over my head and pulled my brown curls from the braid they were in, into a topknot.

"Where are we going?" Jordan asked as I opened the door.

"We're going to get some food from the best food stall in all of Barak."

Jordan peered at me from over his nose and held open the door. "Then I definitely know of it."

"I doubt it," I said on a serious note. "It's not exactly *your*... environment."

Together, we walked through the abandoned hall when Jordan, too, put on a sweater—the fabric stretching over his muscled shoulders. His breath sounded indignant. "My type of environment? What do you mean by *that*?"

I waved away his words. "You know, the my-dad-is-a-delegate type of places."

"What are you saying, Renée?" he asked and turned around, facing me as he walked backward. "You're all talk for an almost-major. I think you'll do good with some penalty training."

I rolled my eyes. "Like you're not already drilling me enough."

He winked.

When the distance between us increased, I smiled at him. "Where are you going? You can't get there without me."

"You mean to Ben?" he called and smiled widely as he noticed my stunned face. "I wonder how many hotdogs he'll have left at this hour." He looked at his watch and tapped it a few times while he looked back at me—dimples on full display.

That *sneaky*—"I dare you!" I warned him, but he turned around, and I started sprinting after him through the main base's exit.

When I finally arrived at Ben's stall a couple of minutes later, heaving from my sprint, Jordan was already paying for the last three hotdogs.

"Hey, Raven!" Ben waved. "You know each other?" He pointed from me to Jordan.

I sighed as I approached them. "I wished we didn't."

"Really?" Jordan said dramatically. "Because I just wanted to share my hotdogs with you, but if—"

I punched his arm.

"The hotdogs!" Jordan yelled and acted like he scrambled to keep them in his hands. He looked sideways at Ben, who was grinning at us. "This woman is dangerous, I tell you."

Then, he started walking back the way we came. "Nice evening, Ben!" He said cheerily.

I quickly followed, waving to Ben, who started to clean his stall.

Jordan put a hotdog in his mouth and held one out for me. He smiled with his mouth full at my narrowed eyes, but carelessly draped his free arm over my shoulders and pressed me close to his side as we walked back to the base.

By the time we returned, my cheeks hurt from smiling.

## NOW

I carefully stepped out of the car and ensured my green velvet dress was wrinkle-free. The wrap dress had spaghetti straps and fell to my calves, which elongated my legs— especially combined with the high, golden sandals I wore. And finally, the golden starred arm cusp I had gotten from

Hunter and Nikolai adorned my right arm.

I had pulled my hair into a low bun, and a few strands were hanging free and framed my face, making the low-cut back of my dress a feature.

Kelian offered me his arm with a slanted smile, and I grabbed onto it nervously. His dark red hair was styled fashionably, and the smoking he was wearing had been carefully selected. Even his pocket square matched the fabric of my dress.

He looked great.

Once inside, I quickly checked my reflection in one of the floor-length mirrors we passed as Kelian brought our coats to the cloakroom. It was the first anniversary gala I attended, and I had to confess I was excited.

"Ready?" Kelian asked from behind as he put his hands on my shoulders, and our eyes met in the mirror. Mine were kohl-lined, making them pop, but my gaze was uncertain as I took in the rest of me. I knew I had nothing to be unsure about; dressing up, and wearing a certain outfit, also counted as armor. And I was heavily packed this night.

I nodded and took hold of his arm again before entering the room.

It was the third time they held the gala in honor of the serum, but it was the first time I could attend since only generals were invited.

We walked around the space for a bit, chatting with several people. I had almost forgotten how to be a normal human being, but my social interactions were fine—great, even.

Finally, I spotted Hunter. She wore a beige, strapless, tulle dress adorned with pearls. It looked mesmerizing on her.

Yesterday, she had offered that I could stay the night at her and Nikolai's house, but I had wanted to train for a couple of hours in the morning. After I returned, Hunter sent me a message saying I could always talk to her, which had made my heart clench. We had the type of friendship that didn't need maintenance *every week*; when we saw each other again, it was like nothing had changed. She was my favorite type of friend.

As we stalked closer, she noticed us and smiled immediately. A group of soldiers surrounded her and Nikolai, but she smoothly excused herself to come over to us. Nikolai looked at her in a way I now recognized as mild irritation. He clearly *didn't* want to be left alone in that group.

Nikolai's gaze shifted to mine, and he nodded, his jaw softening.

I winked at him as I hugged Hunter. "Gods, I'm glad you're here," I said earnestly. Earning me a curious look from Kelian as he, too, hugged Hunter.

"You look good, Hunt. How's married life?" he asked her.

Hunter radiated joy. "It's great. But look at you! I almost didn't recognize you."

"Is that a good sign?" he asked semi-sarcastically.

Hunter chuckled. "You look great, Kelian."

Kelian stalked closer to my side and poked at me. "Do I not always?"

I snorted, brushing his arm affectionately. "Of course you do, honey."

His gaze was indecipherable, and he suddenly returned to looking around the room.

Nerves crashed through my body at the thought that I'd

be seeing Jordan again. After an entire year. Even more so now that he was engaged, the reality of it probably shoved into my face for the rest of the evening.

"I'm happy you two are here, too," Hunter said. "It's fun to see familiar faces from 3B, but it's unreal how many people are kissing Nik's ass on a night like this." She laughed and turned around to look at her husband. "He looks absolutely miserable."

I laughed with her and felt some of the tension leave my body.

"Jordan and Ashley have arrived." Hunter looked behind me and smiled.

"What?" I asked, a little shaken, and I felt my cheeks burn.

Hunter's eyes focused on something behind me. "They're coming this way," she said. "I'll do the talking."

"Why wouldn't we talk?" Kelian directed his question to me, genuinely baffled. But his brain seemed to catch up quickly as he watched me. He cleared his throat.

"Is it too late to walk away?" I asked, and Hunter mouthed a curt *yes*. I didn't want to keep standing there, but this moment was inevitable. As we turned around, I grabbed Kelian's arm and took in the couple before us.

"Raven—" Kelian started, but Hunter interrupted him.

"Jordan! Ashley!" she said.

I plastered the biggest smile on my face that I could manage, which wasn't much at all.

"Hunter," Ashley reacted just as enthusiastically, albeit a bit modestly, and kissed her on both cheeks. Hunter immediately started talking to her, but I couldn't hear what they were saying. Instead, I shifted my focus to the man in front of me.

Jordan was already taking me in. His eyes whirled from my dress to the hand clasping Kelian, and back to my face—staring. He was definitely staring.

I stared right back and swallowed—my throat suddenly parched.

His ash-blonde hair had grown a little. His black suit was perfectly tailored to his body, and his stormy blue eyes told me everything he didn't dare to say himself.

Hunter quickly lay a hand on his shoulder as she kissed him on the cheek. The movement finally tore his eyes away from me, and the tight band around my chest loosened a little. I inhaled sharply, testing the restraints of my dress.

I moved my gaze to Ashley, who Kelian introduced himself to and who then smiled at me. "Raven, right?" she asked. "Ashley. We met at Hunter and Nikolai's wedding last year."

"Of course," I nodded and smiled back. She was beautiful. "I remember. You looked just as amazing as you do now."

She smiled with the confidence of a woman that knew she looked good. "Likewise." She winked. "I think I dreamt of your golden dress that night. You should pass me the details of your designer."

I couldn't answer with, *well, funny you mention that! I dreamt about your man that night. Want to trade?* So I settled with, "I will." Although I couldn't remember the name even if I had wanted to.

She smiled a little wider. "I'll keep you to it."

Next, Kelian greeted Jordan, nodding in recognition as they shook hands.

After an awkward silence, I finally let my eyes glide to Jordan, who was staring at me again. Why couldn't he just say, "Hi" like a normal person?

"Congratulations," I told them and smiled at Jordan before looking back at Ashley. I refused to look at the ring. I also didn't ask them how he'd done it. I didn't want to know the details—didn't want to hear anything about it.

"Thanks," Ashley answered, and frowned at Jordan. She nudged him.

He scraped his throat and said hoarsely, "Yes, thanks."

A shiver ran through my body. What that voice did to me, even after all this time, you'd think there had passed none at all.

Ashley rolled her eyes and gave me a sympathetic smile. "He's been that way all night," she told us, but directed it at me. Ashley looked like she knew there was some history between us, but I highly doubted she knew *what* kind of history. She spotted someone in the room and excused herself as she left our group.

*Yeah*, she didn't know.

Hunter also turned around and folded her lips. "I'll check on Nikolai to see if I can save him. We'll see each other later, okay?"

I knew what they were doing.

They were giving us time and space to talk. I watched as she hugged Jordan, threw him a look, and disappeared into the crowd.

Kelian lay a hand on my arm as he picked up on the cue. "I'll be at the bar if you need me," he whispered. Jordan followed the movement, jaws clenching.

I knew I could go with him, but I needed to get this over with. I dipped my chin and watched him retreat into the crowd.

Reluctantly, I tore away my gaze from Kelian and met

Jordan's eyes. He looked pained—like I was a puzzle he couldn't solve.

"Hi," I finally said, and kept holding his eyes. I had the distinct impression I was burning—the urge to move closer and farther away at the same time was just as strong. He looked incredibly handsome in smoking. I wanted to scream out of frustration.

Jordan still hadn't smiled, but his forehead smoothed—the first sign of the man I used to know. "Raven."

"It's been a long time," I said.

"Too long," he agreed. He clearly wanted to skip the small talk. Or did he want to end this conversation as much as I did?

I swallowed and broke eye contact. This was easily the most awkward conversation of my entire life.

"You already met Ashley?" he asked.

My eyes returned to his. "At Hunt and Nik's wedding. You're a lucky man, Jordan." My compliment sounded hollow, even though I meant it.

"Yeah," he said flatly, and rubbed a hand over his throat.

"How are you doing?" I asked him, but I didn't know what answer I hoped to get. My feelings ran rampant.

He shook his head.

I felt my throat constricting and my eyes burning. I hadn't been ready for this conversation, this moment, the rejection—to *see* him again. My hand clasped my arm, fingers playing with the cuff, and I was just about to turn around when he stepped closer and—

"Wait," Jordan breathed. "Wait. *Shit*, Raven. I don't know what to do either."

I stopped moving, but I couldn't meet his eyes.

"Look at me."

Breathing was difficult.

"Raven," Jordan let his warm hand caress my chin and tip it back up to him. I inhaled sharply.

I saw a million things in his gaze. His eyes trailed over the healing cut on my cheek. He tipped my chin farther back, eyes glued to the make-up-covered bruise his keen eyes had spotted. His eyes trailed down, taking in the freshly healed cut on my arm. He did not comment on them, though I could see a storm of questions brewing in his eyes.

His hand trailed down to the golden cuff on my arm, and he smiled slightly as he let his finger roam over it—the touch, his eyes, *intimate*. "You're a general now," he said, and I swore I detected pride in his gaze.

I nodded and found my voice, "Brigadier General."

"That's amazing, Raven." Dimples appeared on his cheeks. "You'll be able to take over my job in no time if I'm not careful," he teased.

My smile was instant. "I think I would like to sit around all day and do nothing." The comment had left my mouth before I could think about it, and it felt so natural, *so* normal, that it stung.

I wanted to crawl out of my skin, run away, and never return.

Jordan barked a laugh, and I realized it had been too long since I heard that sound. "I forgot you've got quite the mouth." Stars shone in those eyes. "Maybe we need to fight it out on the mat sometime. I've heard tall tales about your skills, so I'd like to see how you compare to your teacher."

My lips pulled into a challenging grin, and I raised my brows. "You've *no* idea what you'd be getting yourself into, Locke. The time of you teaching me has been catching dust in my brain."

*That* was a big, fat lie.

"Oh," he answered and changed his gaze to the movements of my throat as I swallowed, "I think I do."

I didn't know what to do with my body or what to do with the smile on my face—which was blossoming just as the dimples in his cheeks deepened.

When a group of people behind us burst out in laughter, I was sucked back into reality. The clanging of glasses, the voices, the music—it all rushed back to me. I remembered where I was again, who I was, and why this, whatever this was, could never be.

His eyes, which had been full of warmth a moment ago, had once again frozen over as he seemed to realize the same thing.

"Well," I said after a while, and my throat felt bone dry. "I'm going to get something to drink. I'll see you around." I hoped, *not*.

But before I could run off, he had captured my elbow.

I searched his face, which was closer now than it had been all evening.

"Don't disappear on me," he breathed, the words only for me, his eyes boring into mine. "Not again."

My heart froze and burned up at the same time. I shook my head because I didn't know what else to do.

It seemed sufficient because he let me go, and I backed away, hurrying off to whatever destination my brain had decided on before I forgot my own name. I cursed my trembling hand as I opened and closed it again.

On my way to the bar, my gaze met Ashley's from across the room. She looked behind me and back—not angry, but more… somber? I returned her gaze with the only smile I could manage, because I *knew* Jordan's eyes were still trained on me. I *felt* them.

And Ashley finally figured out what that meant.

# CHAPTER 7

## JORDAN

Jordan placed his hands flat on either side of the large granite counter and hung his head over the washbasin. It was way past midnight, and the rest of the world had been fast asleep for hours.

His life was perfect: he had a beautiful family, his career was going the way he hoped, and his relationships with the people surrounding him were great.

But something was off. And he knew what the reason was.

Jordan looked in the mirror.

*Who*.

He had been staring at the ceiling in bed, only able to think of one thing; how it must feel to strip that golden cuff from Raven's arm, the metal heated by her body, and slide it down slowly. Or better yet: take off everything *but* the arm cuff and—

Jordan shook his head. He shouldn't think about that. Ashley was sleeping in the next room, for fuck's sake— wearing *his* engagement ring around her finger.

He closed his eyes but could only see Raven, her dark lashes, her smile, her lips—those soft, soft lips—and his eyes opened wide again.

All evening, he'd done his best not to look in her direction too often or think about her. Six months ago, he had made a decision, and this wasn't the moment to reconsider. That moment would never come.

But she had stolen his breath away, just like a year ago.

He had always found Raven attractive—but *wow*. She had re-awakened the exact feelings he had felt before at Hunter and Nikolai's wedding. He nearly ended his relationship a year ago if she hadn't disappeared again so soon—if she hadn't felt like a dream from which he was woken roughly time after time.

Jordan didn't know who he was kidding; himself or Ashley. *Ashley*, who had been nothing but patient while he had been sorting out his feelings. Like him, she had worked on herself and made the readjustments to be a better partner than before. And now that they were finally engaged, their relationship had a renewed sense of direction. This was the time to commit fully—to work on the family they had always dreamt about.

But something held him back.

The moment he saw her again, the world had disappeared around them. And his heart had thumped painfully when he'd seen Lieutenant Colonel Rudolfs by her side. He knew they were good friends, but he recognized the way Rudolfs looked at her, which wasn't exactly *friendly*.

Jordan wondered if Raven felt the same way about Rudolfs. The thought appalled him, though he wasn't in a place to say or think anything about it. Jordan straightened his back as he turned to the door when he heard a sound.

"Jordan?" The door cracked open a bit, and Ashley stuck her head inside. When she saw him, she opened the door and lay a hand on his cheek. "Are you all right?"

"Yes," he whispered, covering her hand with his, guilt chipping away at his conscience.

Ashley didn't believe him. "Did you have trouble sleeping again?"

He shook his head.

"Did something happen tonight? Did—"

"No," Jordan replied firmly, cutting her off.

She was silent for a beat. "You know you can always wake me, right?"

Jordan nodded. "I know." And put his hand on the back of her head to press a kiss to her brow. "I'll be there in a sec."

He didn't deserve her. He didn't deserve to lie next to her while he thought about another woman.

It made him sick.

A few breaths later, he silently crawled back into bed, and Ashley nestled against him. He listened to her breathing, which soon slowed down and deepened. As much as he craved sleep, it took a while before his brain finally dragged him under.

✯ ✯ ✯

The doorbell rang while Jordan was making himself ready for work. Ashley had already gone to her office, so he walked through his apartment and opened the door—revealing Nikolai Zaregova.

"Nikolai," Jordan said, but his expression indicated a question mark.

Nikolai smiled a little, though his body seemed tense.

"I'm not staying—but I wanted to tell you something you might find *interesting*."

Rubbing a hand over his chest, Jordan said, "You could have called, you know? But *damn*, Zaregova, what a way to make a guy feel special."

Nikolai huffed a breath of amusement, but the emotion didn't linger, and he clenched his jaw. "Domasc ordered Raven to go on a mission back to the shadow plains. Something about irregular activity in the field—I'm still looking into it."

"What? Say that again." That morning, Jordan had woken up anxious. The thought of Raven leaving again burned a hole through his chest. Even though she had promised him she wouldn't.

"He blackmailed her into going, and it doesn't sit well with me—especially since it's Domasc."

Jordan's blood simmered with rage. "He did *what*?"

Nikolai just looked at him. "She's going, Jordan. But something about this feels wrong. That's why I'm coming straight to you. I suspect he's tapping the communication channels."

"Like *hell* she is," Jordan snarled. "Overrule his decision. Go straight to Domasc if you must."

He shook his head. "You know I can't. She needs to go to keep her job, and give me time to look into it."

"What if it was Hunter?" Jordan asked stonily. "Would you let her go?"

A muscle in Nikolai's eye popped as he grimaced. "Raven, like Hunter, can hold her own. Just thought you wanted to know."

*That she's going again, leaving again, but this time not of her own accord.*

73

"That's not an answer to my question."

The General cocked his head at his tone. "She means that much to you?"

Jordan took a deep breath. "Thanks for letting me know." Before he slammed the door in his face.

He walked back into his apartment, collecting his things before he nearly ran to the building's underground parking lot. His patience was running thin, and his whole body itched to take this matter into his hands and *fix* it.

After a drive that went by in a blur, and the slamming of several doors, Jordan barged into Domasc's front office at the main base, his secretary standing in a hurry. "Lieutenant General Locke."

Jordan looked at the Lieutenant. "I'm here to speak with Chief General Domasc. Please let him know I'm waiting for him." He had no time or patience for pleasantries; he was single-minded.

"The Chief General has no time," she quipped, but Jordan wasn't so easily deterred.

He shrugged and kept standing in the room, a pillar of restraint. "Tell him I'm waiting here." *Let's try this the professional way first.*

The secretary seemed distressed. Clearly, Domasc had given her direct orders not to interrupt him. Eventually, she rang the phone and called Domasc. She spoke softly. "Sir—yes sir, I know, but—"

Jordan could hear Domasc's low voice booming from behind the door, but he kept his gaze on the secretary the whole time. Making a call was better for everyone.

"Lieutenant General Locke is here to speak to you... It seems urgent. He's very persistent. Sir." She hung up the phone, and Jordan stepped closer to her. Her lips folded into a firm line. "I'm afraid he really can't—"

Before she had finished that sentence, Jordan blew out a frustrated breath and barged into Domasc's office—under a loud shriek from the secretary.

He was greeted by Domasc's blasé expression, although he detected a slight twitch in his eye. The Chief General looked back to his paperwork, scribbling something before he lay down the pen and leaned back in his large leather chair—fingers lacing together.

"Lieutenant General Locke." He made a clicking sound as he pronounced Jordan's last name. "What is so urgent that you ignored a direct order from your commanding general?"

Jordan couldn't help the anger flaring up as he beheld the general. He hated the man. So. Fucking. Much. There weren't many people he despised more than him. "I received word about a classified mission set for the shadow plains."

Domasc's expression betrayed nothing.

"What is it, and why are you sending my soldiers there without my knowledge?"

"Let me stop you there." He waved a hand in front of him and leaned forward in his chair—resting his hands on the desk. "I get the feeling you forget your place, Lieutenant General Locke. As you mentioned, the mission is classified, so I can't speak on it. Nor should your soldiers have been blabbing about it."

"They didn't."

"What do you want, Lieutenant General?" Domasc asked, and Jordan knew he had hit a nerve.

"I don't think I have to remind you who my father is, Chief General Domasc." Jordan hated using his father, but in this case, he didn't feel like beating around the bush. "It would serve you to just put my fucking name on that list and make me the commanding general of this mission."

Domasc's face nearly exploded with rage. "Are you threatening me, boy?"

*How about returning the favor?* "Just stating facts, sir. That's all."

The Chief General stared at him; fury engraved in the lines of his face.

Jordan stared right back. The times of respecting this motherfucker had long since passed.

The moment seemed to stretch while Domasc shifted in his seat, and Jordan recognized the moment the General decided not to fight it.

"Consider it done."

The moment those words had left his mouth, Jordan nodded. "Sir." Before walking out of the room, leaving behind a seething secretary.

# CHAPTER 8

Jordan reached a hand for me. "You almost had me at the second turn."

"I *know*," I groaned.

He chuckled and brushed my chin with his knuckle. "You'll get there."

We sat down on the bench to take a break, and I looked sideways at him. A strand of blond hair had escaped from his usual perfectly styled hair and clung to his forehead.

"Ever miss 3B?" he asked.

I pursed my mouth, surprised by the question. "In some ways, I think I do. At least there, I had the feeling I was doing something useful. Here..." I shrugged.

Jordan nodded. "I was there for such a long time that it started to feel like normal life. Being back here has proven quite the change—to not constantly have to worry or look for signs of danger."

"The mission made me realize how insignificant I am," I said, raising a hand as Jordan opened his mouth to contradict me. "I don't mean it like that. It's just... humanity is so *fucking* fragile. We think we're so indestructible, but then the sun goes dark, and we go *boom*: half of the world wiped away. If there's anything we should take from this, it is that we are vulnerable, more so than we even realize, and we should find a way to fix that, you know?"

Jordan stared at me and rubbed a hand over his face. "Something keeping you awake at night, Renée?" he deadpanned, but grinned at me.

My cheeks burned.

"I mean," he continued, nudging my shoulder, "You make a good point. Increasing our chance for survival is valid."

It was silent for a moment, and we both stared ahead.

"What was it like to be attacked?" I asked him softly. He'd never spoken to me about it apart from the moment we shared on the shadow plains.

He looked at me, brows furrowed.

I cleared my throat. "I'm sorry, that's a very personal question—just ignore me."

Jordan's frown disappeared, and he chuckled, the deep sound reverberating through my bones. "Don't be silly, Raven. You can ask me personal questions." He bumped my shoulder. "I was just surprised that you asked."

Our gazes locked. "Why?"

He raised his shoulders. "Just that you would want to hear about it."

"What do you mean? Of course, I do." I sipped from my drink.

"Well…" he started, and seemed to look for words. When he looked at me again, I raised my eyebrows patiently. "My parents are incredibly busy, so I never wanted to burden them. I know they would want to know—to help me—but

I just... *No.* And then there are the people I *can* talk to here, but they go through the same sort of shit as me." He inhaled. "It would have been nice to have someone, a partner, that could share the load with me sometime, you know? Someone who would want to hear about my day."

"You *never* had a relationship with someone that did?" I asked. I couldn't believe it.

"I had a serious relationship once. We had talked about marriage, kids—that sort of thing. But we slowly reached this point where if I came back from a mission and someone close to me had died in front of my eyes, I couldn't tell her about it."

"You're serious?"

Jordan lay a hand on his neck and looked up at the ceiling. "I shared everything with her. I process my emotions and trauma by speaking about it. But after some time, she couldn't take it anymore, and I usually had to comfort her instead of the other way around. She told me she couldn't deal with all the hardship, and we agreed I would stop sharing."

"What a selfish—"

Jordan cut me off with a warning flashing in those stormy blue eyes. "That *was* the last drop. We separated. But we were still young, and I loved her immensely. Everything we went through together didn't suddenly disappear."

I cleared my throat. "She was your first love?" I guessed.

He nodded. "Always thought she was the one— sometimes I still do."

"*Please,* Jordan," I snorted.

Jordan looked at me, confusion marring his handsome features.

I elaborated. "*The one* will take you as you are—every

broken part of you. All of it. She should have given you the time and space to mourn for your friend and support you through it."

He blinked. "She didn't even know he had died."

"My point exactly!" I exclaimed. "Because she didn't care about you enough to see you weren't doing well."

Abruptly, he stood. "Why are you making this such a big deal?"

"Why are you still defending a girl that clearly didn't give a shit about you?" I followed, heart racing.

Jordan stared at me for a long time, silence bridging the gap between us, and I *knew* I had said the wrong thing. "You don't know what you're talking about, Raven," he said calmly. "You don't know her, and you don't even really know me, for that matter."

Before I could open my mouth again, he swallowed, grabbed his stuff from the floor, and left the training hall.

### NOW

I tiptoed to look over the queue I joined to get a look at the food they served at the canteen that day when I heard a familiar voice behind me. "Raven."

My mind immediately shifted to the blue-eyed man that stalked my mind no matter what I did, but as I turned, I spotted Kelian. Ever since the gala, my nerves had been going haywire. Seeing Jordan again, combined with my impending mission, was enough to make me crazy.

"Hey," he said as he joined the queue behind me.

I smiled, though I wasn't in a smiling mood. I couldn't help myself—it was Kelian, after all. "Don't you have work to do instead of pestering me?"

"Jeez," he scoffed while the queue shuffled forward. "I wanted to speak to you about something, and I guessed you would be here."

"Oh?" I said absentmindedly and tried to decide what I wanted to eat as the food shifted into view.

"Did you hear about Domasc? Rumor has it he went to Borzia this morning to negotiate a deal for the vaccine."

I raised my brows at him. Of course, I heard. It was all over the news. When we finally had our food, we walked over to a table and sat down together. "That's what you wanted to talk about?"

Kelian cleared his throat and looked at me directly. "What's going on, Raven?"

I looked at my food. "What do you mean?"

"The way you act, it's not like you. The other night, too—at the gala—your behavior was so strange."

Alarm bells rang as I did my best to hide my surprise. "Stop speaking in riddles, Kelian. Just spit it out." I put down my cutlery.

"*Jordan Locke*," he said slowly, pronouncing every syllable of his name. "What did he do?"

I swallowed. "It had been a long time since I last saw him." I tried to keep a stammer from my voice.

"Cut the bullshit, Raven." Kelian exhaled irritably.

I tried to gauge his intent as I looked up at him—but found only my friend's earnest expression.

"He was the reason you were hesitant to return, right? Why you suddenly signed up for that mission all those years ago, even though you were glad to be back home finally?"

I wanted to say I didn't flee, but I kept silent. It wasn't true, was it?

His hand curled into a fist as he looked at me. "What

BRITT VAN DEN ELZEN

did he do, Raven?"

"Nothing," I said, poking the food I suddenly wasn't craving anymore.

"Tell me what he did," he repeated in a dangerously low tone.

Under the table, I splayed my hands on my legs and forced myself to meet his eyes. "He didn't *do* anything."

Kelian's expression softened, but his posture was still tense. "He's clearly in love with you."

Those words shattered my composure and threatened to break the pieces of my heart I had glued back together again. "No," I whispered, denying those damning words. "He's not."

My friend's laugh was humorless. "Trust me, Raven. He is."

I looked at him with tears in my eyes. Gods, I hated those tears. They always came in the moment I least wanted them.

"I don't know what he did or what made you leave—but he's a fool for letting you go."

It had been *my* choice.

"Do you have feelings for him?"

When I said nothing, he took hold of my elbow. "Raven? Look at me. *Do you?*"

I said nothing, but to Kelian, that was answer enough.

"Then do something about it."

★ ★ ★

I wanted to drown my emotions. Squash them under my foot. Obliterate them.

The crowd's chanting in the Sewers heightened my aggression, and I knew this would be the perfect outlet for my rage.

*You're going to the shadow plains—to Damruin.*

*Don't disappear on me. Not again.*

*Then do something about it.*

This was as close as I ever dared to do something about my feelings. Here, I shut them off—had them punched from my system.

I always hoped I forgot they even existed.

Fighting in the ring with Tania was one of my favorite things. Every fight surprised me—taught me something new. We didn't hold back. And that meant something because Tania was one of the most skilled fighters I knew. She wasn't in the infantry. She was a special ops soldier—a breed of soldiers that were so kickass you hardly heard anything about them.

Tania had been the only of her kind to join mission 3B. We still didn't know why, but she said she had craved a change of scenery, and there had been a shortage of qualified soldiers to send. Like she'd woken up one day and decided, *why not?*

With every fight, I came closer to beating her. And this time, I finally did.

"Damn, Raven. You've become something else," Tania gasped, taking my hand so I could yank her up. She approached her girlfriend, Alina, in the audience, a short girl with long blonde hair. Tania kissed her straight on the lips, the blood running down her nose now smeared across Alina's face. Neither of them seemed to care.

"This round is on me," I said, and made a beeline for the bar.

Another way for me to bury my feelings. I ran my tongue over my split lip as I leaned forward on the sticky counter. I let my gaze travel freely over the assortment of drinks they poured and held an inner debate over which one would soothe the pain, both internal and external, the fastest.

"Hey, little bitch."

My head snapped to the side, finding a grinning Razor. The man was unhinged. I almost shattered his windpipe; now he looked at me like we'd been rolling through the grass together.

"Haven't you had enough yet?" I spat, which only seemed to encourage him.

His fingers trailed over my arm as he stepped closer, his chiseled features still bruised from our fight. "Nah, darlin'. You free tonight?"

I shrugged his hand off my arm as I glared at him. *The hell?* "Almost killing you didn't send a message? Find someone else to leer at."

Razor scoffed. "What—"

The crowd went wild, their roaring cutting him off and luring me in. I watched fragments of the fight as it was happening. Movement at the edge of the room captured my attention. A whisk of ash blonde hair caught my eye, and my heart started beating a hundred miles an hour.

I pushed away from the bar—away from Razor—as I made my way through the crowd. But when I finally arrived at the place where I had spotted the blonde man, no one was there. Walking back, I ordered four shots. Tipping back two of them, I grabbed hold of the others and walked back to Tania and her girl—trying to shake the feeling that Jordan was there.

He couldn't be.

Right?

I looked around again, inspecting the room.

Someone put a hand on my shoulder, and I jolted, turning around to find Tania behind me with a surprised smile. "Wow, Raven. Are you okay?"

I pushed the two shots in her hand and yelled over the crowd's roaring, "I'm going home. Not feeling well."

Tania nodded. "All right. See you tomorrow?"

I shrugged. "Maybe." But I squeezed her arm and waved to Alina in the back.

On my way out, I tried to stop myself from looking around like a stray cub looking for its mom. *I was doing fine. I was so fucking fine.*

Shit.

# CHAPTER 9

## 3 YEARS EARLIER

Hunter had come to the infantry department to have lunch with Jordan and me. We had declared we didn't see each other enough, so she came over during one of her hospital breaks and asked us where we were hanging out.

Jordan and I had been at the canteen, where we spent most of our spare time lately—if we weren't walking through Barak, training, or joining another meeting. It seemed like we were always together.

Which felt good—being near him.

Neither of us had talked about what happened a few weeks ago, and I preferred it that way. Jordan came to dinner the day after, like he always did, and had pretended nothing was amiss. We slid back into our routine easily. I was grateful to him for that. He quickly became one of my best friends in the short time we had spent together, and the last weeks had propelled our bond to new heights. The last thing I wanted was to fight with him.

Jordan and Hunter were looking at me expectantly.

"Sorry, what?" I asked as sounds rushed into my ears.

"Are you having fun at the infantry?" Hunter repeated.

Jordan grinned, and my heart pounded uncontrollably. I nodded. "It's everything I hoped it would be." I looked back at Jordan's soft smile. Heat crawled into my face.

A week ago, I officially switched to the department and secured a position as an infantry major—a proud moment. Jordan had helped a lot, although he hadn't been allowed to be part of my entrance committee because of our friendship.

"She's doing really well. By far my best student," he added, and I realized he was sincere. That glittering in his eyes only appeared when he was passionate.

Averting my gaze, I focused on Hunter, who squeezed my arm lovingly. "I'm happy for you," she said.

I smiled at my best friend. How far we had come kept blowing me away. "The only downside is the infantry's canteen. It's always so damn cold. My hands freeze into lumps of ice whenever I'm here," I joked.

Jordan grabbed my hand from the table and harbored it between his own warm hands.

I froze.

Burned.

He had touched me before; we had hugged. He had taken my hand one time to show me something. All familiar gestures… Jordan was a physical person, so it was nothing out of the ordinary.

But not this. This felt different.

How he held my hand between his own, and curled his fingers securely around it—felt different. It was intimate. Did he feel it, too?

Chuckling a little, I tried acting as if nothing was out of the ordinary, but I felt my cheeks turn an even darker red.

I was glad I wore my curls free, so my hair concealed parts of my face. And that I didn't have such a pale complexion, like Hunter, which would have immediately alert them to my blushing.

Hunter waved at someone at another table, but I was trapped in this moment.

"It feels warmer already, thanks," I told Jordan, and tried to take my hand back.

His head tipped to the side like he wanted to say something, but eventually he let go.

I nodded and let my trembling hand glide underneath the table. With a confident smile, I asked, "Can't you pull some strings as a general? Some radiators wouldn't hurt this place." The smile didn't reach my eyes.

Either Jordan played along, or he was unaware of my predicament as he narrowed his eyes. "You aren't already insinuating that I abuse my position now, are you, Renée?"

My eyes trailed to Hunter. "What other reason would I have to be friends with him?"

Hunter chuckled, but I still felt his eyes trained on me.

"I would be wary of tonight's training if I were you," he warned, a dimple appearing.

Then he focused on the food in front of him. Hunter grabbed my still trembling hand underneath the table and squeezed it—grounding me—as the realization hit me.

I was falling for Jordan Locke. And I was falling hard.

NOW

The cobblestone streets of Damruin were just as I remembered them. The terraced houses were a dull grey, lined with rows of flowers in all colors that had survived the darkening. This part of town was called the *flower* neighborhood for a reason, and it seemed everyone in the street had taken part in this year's gardening competition.

"This sight warms my heart, darling," my father beamed at me as I clutched his arm a little tighter. We made our way through the streets, greeting the people—all *so* familiar.

My heart filled with warmth, and joy flooded my brain, overriding any sense I had. I tilted my head to the sky, feeling the sun's heat on my face.

Suddenly, my father stilled beside me, and I opened my eyes again, following his gaze. The house he was staring at rang a bell so loudly that I gasped, my feet trailing forward.

"Can it be…" my father stammered.

I was holding his arm, throwing him a sidelong glance, and I realized he wasn't looking at the house at all. A woman sat on her knees in the dirt, a beige sundress pooling around her ankles, the fabric streaked with earth. We walked into the front garden lined with orange, pink, and blue flowers— all maintained in perfect condition and taken care of by expert hands. Hands I had watched working in that garden a thousand times. Hands I had never forgotten.

I now looked at them once more. I followed the path from the woman's hands and arms to her long brown hair that hung over her shoulders and draped onto her back. A straw hat shielded her face.

"*Natasha?*" my father asked, and as I looked at him, I shrunk, and the world enlarged. Suddenly, I had to look farther up, my hand tiny compared to his—my father, younger.

The woman looked up and shielded her face against the sun as it dipped below her hat. Her eyes widened, and she pushed herself from the ground, rubbing her hands on her dress. "*Leon*?" she gasped.

My father let out a sob. He stepped forward and dragged her into an embrace. He cupped the back of her head and buried his face in her neck. Her body heaved with silent sobs as he said, "I thought I had lost you."

"Mama?" I asked, biting my trembling lip.

She let go of my father and crouched before me, taking my head between her hands and kissing every part of my face before dragging me to her chest.

"You're better?" I asked her.

My mother laid her hands on my shoulders and squeezed me reassuringly. "I kept the house clean for when you would return to me. Where you belong." She flicked the tip of my nose as she had often done, and a smile blossomed on my face.

She walked forward and opened the front door. *Our* front door. A gentle hand rested on my back. Looking up at my father, he nodded for me to follow her. My tiny heart squeezed, hope filling the empty spot it had once occupied. Light shone through the opening, and I stepped toward it, squeezing my eyes at the brightness.

The door shut behind me, and all the light vanished. A chill crept over my spine at the sudden change. Shivers wreaked their way through me, and I wrapped my arms around myself to shield my body against the cold. "Mama?" I spoke. "Papa?"

"Here, dear." My mother's voice came from the back of the room. It took some time for my eyes to adjust to the dark. I could only see a large, dark shadow in the corner— where the voice had come from.

My lips started trembling. "I'm afraid, Mama. Where are you?"

The shadow in the corner started moving forward, and fear paralyzed me, rooting me to the spot. As the eerie shadow stalked closer, it reached out a hand.

Now, my body was trembling, and I slowly started crying.

"Mama's here," her reassuring voice came again, but this time, I closed my eyes, afraid of what I was about to see.

"Look at me, sweetheart."

I shook my head, pressing my eyes and lips as close as possible, shielding myself from the world.

"Look at me." More demanding now.

I didn't.

She yanked my arm. "Look at me!" she yelled.

Tears kept streaming down my face as I wished for it all to stop.

"LOOK AT ME!" she screamed in my face, and all I could do was scream with her.

My throat burned as I pushed myself upright in bed, my hair wet with tears and sweat.

"Not real," I whispered to myself. "*Not real. Not real. Not real.*"

It had been over ten years since I last had that nightmare.

Ever since my father and I had fled from Damruin, our hometown, I had lived through many nightmares about the place. It haunted me—how it had once been my home, and is now a forgotten place draped in shadows. Nothing left of it but the memories and the ghosts of our past that no doubt haunted it now.

With one hand on my chest and another on my belly, I regulated my breathing and tried to calm my raging heart. Not in a million years had I pictured myself going on a mission to Damruin. It was fucking with my head.

The place where I was born, where I grew up, and where

BRITT VAN DEN ELZEN

I had seen my mother for the last time. My mother, who had been sick because of the mutation, and—

*No.* I couldn't think about that now.

I won't.

My throat was still sore by the time I had freshened up and walked toward the mission briefing. With every step I took, I cursed Domasc for making me go. It had already proved taxing on my mental health, and I wasn't even on the mission yet. The little girl within me was terrified at the prospect of going back to Damruin.

I rounded the corner and walked into the briefing room.

"Brigadier General Renée?"

I looked up at the threshold. Colonel Keano, who I recognized from the SSU, was already sitting inside with a couple of others. She and I had been in the same extraction group on more than one occasion, and I remembered her as very capable.

"Hey!" I said, glad to see a familiar—and friendly—face.

I walked into the room and greeted the others: Major Britton, also from my time at the SSU—and the other two I didn't know yet: First Lieutenant Gabon and Colonel Kilich.

I sat down, finally relaxing a little. This group was capable, and the people seemed chill, which helped with my anxiety. *Gods*, it felt like a weight lifted from my chest.

But then Jordan stepped into the room, and our eyes met.

My lips parted. What was he doing here?

I was the first to speak. "Lieutenant General Locke. I think you're in the wrong room."

Jordan put down the folder he was carrying. "I'm in the right room, Brigadier General. Thank you for your concern."

I was under the impression that Domasc would do the briefing himself. Hadn't thought about it, really. I had been too busy forcing the mission to the back of my mind from the moment it was assigned. But this... I hadn't expected *this*.

My feet were glued to the ground, forcing me to stay put.

"He's hot," Colonel Keano whispered to me.

All I could do was clench my fists, letting the frustration of Jordan's presence dissolve, and resist the urge to rub my temples—to soothe the aching headache that had started the moment I arrived.

The emotion in his eyes perfectly matched mine. Neither of us voiced it, though. We never did. The consequences would be catastrophic.

Jordan broke the tension by laying down the folder and taking one of the digital markers. His eyes left me as he blindly closed the door.

"So, how are you?" I asked Keano, but I looked Britton's way, too.

Britton cupped his jaw as he cocked his head to the side. "Great. Got a nice promotion—more pay." He rubbed his fingers together with a lopsided grin, as if that explained everything.

"Cool," I responded and locked eyes with Keano, who rolled hers at me.

I bit my lip to keep from laughing. "And you?"

"I'm okay. Not sure what the fuck this is, but I decided to go with the flow more, so I'm trying to keep my cool."

I opened my mouth to respond, but all chatter died

when Jordan clapped his hands together, wringing them. I turned around. Jordan leaned on one of the larger stools, half sitting down, half standing up, with one foot firmly planted on the ground.

"This is an unusual mission," he started, "but it's also an unusual situation. You all know that unknown activity has been detected on the shadow plains. Damruin is on Ardenian soil and there are no missions stationed there, which is why we will investigate. All we know so far is that we are *not* dealing with mutants."

*We?* As in, he was coming with us?

He tapped the screen with his marker, opening a file that contained multiple aerial photos showing activity and movement through the plains over the past few weeks.

It was hard to focus on his words while looking at him, so I tried to focus on the photos on the screen.

Jordan went through the information Domasc had given us, which wasn't a lot. We were only investigating, but still… I had no idea why a group of SSU soldiers already on the base couldn't go, but I was a long way from wanting another *chat* with the Chief General.

He was the holiest of assholes.

The rest of the briefing was vague. But again, so was the mission. Before returning to the shadow plains we would have a couple of days at the SSU mission base near the wall—formerly known as the 3B mission base. Jordan promised us, a group of six people, including him, that more information would come before the start—because of the sensitive nature of the mission and the fact that we didn't even have all the info yet. Which meant the situation was a lot worse than I thought.

Pushing myself off the chair, I nodded to a few people

as they left the room.

"See you later, Brigadier General," Keano said.

"Yeah," I responded, smiling at her.

I waited until everyone had left the room before walking over to where Jordan was already looking at me, his arms crossed as if they posed a barrier between us.

He was wearing the same uniform as me: dark green cargo pants and a fitted long-sleeved shirt of the same color. But where there was only one star embroidered on my breast, he had three.

"Are you stalking me, Jordan?" I asked, forcing as much playfulness into the words as I could muster, but it came out cold.

"What? No 'Locke'?" he asked, scanning my face—his eyes lingered on my lips. Going by his expression, not in the romantic sense. "You've been keeping yourself busy, I see."

"Yeah," I drawled, brushing a finger over my split lip. "Rough lover."

His eye ticked. Jordan looked as if he wanted to say something else, but decided against it.

I inspected my nails, avoiding eye contact. "So, are you going to tell me why you're here?"

"I volunteered to be the leading general on this mission," he said.

*What?* "You volunteered?" I repeated.

He nodded, eyes dipping to my lips again.

"Why would you do that?"

Jaw clenching, Jordan turned off the screen.

"Jordan?" I tried. My heart thudded viciously as I added in a whisper, "Don't tell me you're here because of *me*."

Blue eyes found their way to mine, emotions lingering there. "I won't."

Clearing my throat, I stepped closer. "Why, Jordan?" The silence crackled with the tension between us.

He looked at me for a long moment, a storm brewing in his beautiful eyes. "You know why."

Goosebumps erupted from his admission.

I forced myself to nod and hurried from the room before I could say or do anything I would regret.

# CHAPTER 18

I'd let Jordan know I wouldn't be joining him for dinner and canceled our training for the night.

My mom always used to listen to classical music during my childhood. She would play the strings in the air, hum the tunes while gardening, or sway to the notes while making dinner. The music made me feel closer to her, and tonight, her favorite orchestra played at the Barak opera.

I was wearing a black satin dress that fell smoothly over my curves, the fabric at the neckline plunging, and matched them with high-heeled black sandals. I had straightened my brown curls, which made my hair look a couple of inches longer than usual, and several golden rings adorned my ears.

The large entrance hall was packed with people by the time I arrived. The building was breathtaking. My mother would have loved it. Extracting the entrance ticket from my clutch, I walked toward the cloakroom to store my coat.

Looking up at the mirrored ceiling, I smiled. A request for people to enter the theater sounded through the speakers, and I joined the long queue, which shuffled forward at a steady pace.

"Raven!" I heard from behind, and I turned around, looking through the many people facing me.

A familiar voice sounded. "Pardon. Excuse me." I noticed people parting for someone, a hand seeping through the crowd. I caught a glimpse of blonde hair while the voice bearer made his way through the masses until he stood right in front of me.

My lips parted, a hesitant smile playing around my lips.

"Raven," Jordan said. His eyes met mine. I had never seen the look that crossed his face before—like it was the first time he saw me. His chest rose, but it was the only sign of turmoil. The rest of him, well…

He wore a black suit and a white blouse underneath, the top buttons undone. His hair was carefully but loosely styled—like he had been in a rush, in a good way. And—*hold on.*

"Jordan? What are you doing here?" I stared at him.

He reached his hand out to me as he said, "Come. I'll explain."

I took his hand, which he pulled to his side as he excused himself to the people behind us, and let him guide me through the entrance hall, away from the theater. When we arrived in a secluded area, he turned around.

"After you sent those messages with no explanation whatsoever, I called Hunter to ask if she knew what was going on. Keep in mind that I was clueless—I'm not a stalker, I promise. She told me you went to this opera because of your mom and warned me you *wanted* to go alone. But…" he said, catching his breath, "my father has a balcony at the theater, and I thought you might like to see the opera from there."

I was speechless, in shock. "You've come all this way to offer me a seat on your family's balcony?" Why would he do that for me? We had rarely met each other outside an army setting.

He nodded reverently. "Yes. You can go alone, or I can come with you. I mean—"

"*Gods*, Jordan. Are you serious?"

Jordan looked confused. I raised my brows as a laugh bubbled up.

"Yes," he breathed and made a fist. "Listen, Raven. I didn't think this through."

I burst out laughing. "Jordan, *you idiot*! Of course, you can be there."

Jordan's eyes widened. "You're sure?"

"Yes, I'm sure." I took his arm. "Where's the balcony?"

He turned around and walked us through the small hallway to a set of stairs where a guard was stationed.

"Mister Locke. Miss." He nodded to both of us, and Jordan didn't have to show anything before the guard let us through.

The balcony was beautiful. It had two sets of chairs, all facing the podium. The velvet curtains and chairs glinted slightly in the theater's warm light.

"I'm impressed, Major General," I whispered to him, grinning. Part of me still couldn't even believe he was here.

"All credits go to my father," Jordan said, a dimple appearing. "But I use it now and then."

That made me pause. "You go to the opera?" No doubt it impressed the women he dated. *Did* he even date? I hadn't seen him with anyone since we started hanging out.

He shrugged, but looked directly at me. "When I'm in

the mood. Why not? It's a welcome contrast from the work we do."

Surprised and maybe a little shy, I smiled at him in the dimming light. "I guess it is."

Half an hour into the concert, tears were streaming down my cheeks. Jordan grabbed my hand and squeezed it gently. I looked at him, but he just angled his head as he sat closer and entwined our hands, weaving his fingers through mine.

He held them there throughout the entire show.

My heart beat in a maddening rhythm while I studied him underneath my lashes and caught glances of him whenever he wasn't looking. His cheekbones and jaw matched the perfect cut of his nose and lips. Jordan's features formed sharp contrasts in the theater's light. A lock of his blonde hair had sprung free like he had run a hand through it without thinking.

I was immensely grateful he was here—grateful he'd gone out of his way to make this evening more special to me.

A tight band wrapped around my chest. I tried to deepen my breaths, but they kept coming in short bursts.

If I hadn't already been in love with him, this would have been the moment I tipped over that edge and started falling. So far and long that even as I went to bed that night, my body still felt weightless.

## NOW

Kelian and Hunter were standing in front of my door with two bottles of alcohol, and Kelian pushed one of them into my hands. I had already taken a sip before I locked my door.

For my last 'free' night before I returned to my personal hell, the emotional rollercoaster that was Damruin and Jordan, we hit the Sewers. Tania and I had been trying to get the rest down there because that part of town was way too much fun to overlook, and now we finally went.

Cardan would love it. Hunter would, too. But Kelian... he always discouraged any possible and *unnecessary* discoloration of my skin.

We walked into a vacated-looking street, the wet stone road reflecting the city lights. "It's freaking deserted here," Kelian muttered as he draped an arm over my shoulders.

Hunter exclaimed, "What the fuck?" As Tania opened the metal doors in the ground that led to the Sewers. It was just a name. We didn't fight in the literal sewers. Thank the gods.

Cardan grimaced. "If you bullshitted about this party..."

"It's giving underground sacrificial offering party vibes," Hunter groaned.

"Relax your tits, both of you," Tania snapped as she unlocked the doors and gestured inside. "You especially," she said to Cardan, who, in turn, pointed at himself in question, "are going to love this."

Walking down the crappy metal stairs, loud music greeted us in the distance. Only people who were invited knew where to go. These fights weren't against the law, but most of the people coming here *were*, so it remained low key.

Tania followed and closed the doors after us with a bang.

I smirked at Cardan. "Now I *am* curious, Car... What exactly would you have done to poor Tania?"

"Poor?" Hunter snorted, looking at Tania, who just rolled her eyes at no one in particular.

I was grinning as we continued through the hallway—the music drifting closer with every step. Bringing the rest of the group was so much more fun.

Cardan slowly shook his head, like his brain was doused in liquid. Then took another sip from the bottle in his hands. Going by his dilated pupils, his blood was already swimming in alcohol.

Kelian looked at what I was doing with quiet contemplation. "What are we going to do? Join a cult?"

Batting my lashes, I smiled up at him. "Funny."

"What the hell are we doing?" Kelian asked again as the music drifted closer. His eyes shot to Tania, who looked at him like she had ascended from heaven.

I arched a brow. "Pretty vague question, Kel."

The fumes of stale air mixed with the stank of sweating bodies assaulted my nose. Sounds of people cheering battered my ears. But the only thing coursing through my body was a buzz of excitement. I started wrapping my knuckles, hands, and wrists for a fight.

Kelian pulled a hand through his red hair, scratching his stubbles, and sighed dramatically.

I shook with laughter, and pushed open the bar's doors.

Whatever they said next was drowned out by a loud bass and cheering. Inside, I got caught up in the sweep of people and sweat. We worked our way through the crowd until we stood on the outskirts of the current ring fight. The competitors were both regulars I had fought against.

"Don't tell me you're next," Kelian muttered behind me.

I kept looking at the fight before us, but a shit-eating grin took over my face. "Will you cheer for me?" I asked him, as I finally turned to face him.

Kelian's mouth set, but his eyes crinkled in the corners.

He shook his head in a way that meant he would. His finger moved to the side of my head in a playful gesture.

I looked for Cardan, who was already talking to a girl. The guy was unbelievable. He had been inside for less than twenty seconds and had already found someone to flirt with. I guess that explained how he brought someone else home on a weekly basis.

I hadn't heard of Kelian bringing anyone home, *ever*. He never talked about it, either. I looked at my best friend. He was handsome; he had great hair, teeth, dark lashes… Not to mention a winning personality.

I noticed a girl looking at him from across the room, and I nudged his shoulder, gesturing her way. "Your type?"

He looked at the girl and back at me, searching my face. "She might," he said eventually.

"Find out," I encouraged him. "But be back in time for the fight!"

He took a long swig of his bottle and then nodded as he strode off.

The most beautiful thing about Kelian was his character. He would go to hell for the people he loved. He would go to hell for *me*. He made me feel special and *always* listened to what I had to say, no matter how boring it was. He was the kind of friend that would bring up something tiny you mentioned months ago because he cared. Because he was genuinely interested in others.

"So," I bowed closer to Hunter. "You think Nikolai knows this place?"

Hunter laughed as she kept looking at the crowd in front of us. The dirty fighting ground was getting dirtier by the second. "I wouldn't be surprised if he did. But I do know he won't like me being here one bit."

I laughed. "No, I don't think he would."

As the fight before us wrapped up, and the winner was riling up the crowd, Tania stepped close to me, speaking in my ear. "I bet you my throwing stars, that you won't last three matches in a row."

Damn. I've thought about those throwing stars of hers more than I liked to admit. My fingers itched when I thought about using them. But three matches in a row… That was a lot.

*Fuck it.* "You're on."

I needed to blow off some steam, anyway.

Tania grinned.

I stepped inside the ring, and all eyes fell on me, including the pair of the previous match winner. As our eyes locked, I winked at her and saw her face grow determined with pugnacity.

The match was over in two minutes.

Walking up to our little group, Hunter offered me a sip of her ice-cold water, the glass slippery with vapor. "Well done," she commended.

I made a little bow, and Kelian tugged one of my braids, pulling me closer. "You're fucking crazy," he exclaimed.

"Thanks!" I yelled back and stuck out my tongue. "She wasn't your type?"

Kelian shook his head.

"Where's Cardan?"

He pointed to one of the back corners, where a dark head was being mussed by hands that belonged to a girl with fiery red hair. They were eating each other's faces.

"Next match!" the announcer called, and I dashed back into the ring.

Moments blurred together, and the second match wore

me out more than I wanted to admit. I wouldn't usually fight so much back-to-back, but I couldn't back down now. I desperately wanted those throwing stars.

My head rang with the roaring of the crowd as I won again.

Cardan approached, love bites bruising his neck as he took me in. He gave me an approving look. "Looking good, Raven."

I rolled my eyes, though I had to admit that I *did* look good. The black crop top, black jeans, and black boots flattered me. My curls were wild, with two braids keeping the hair out of my eyes—my eyeliner pitch-black and lips a bold red. I fit right in with the crowd.

His mouth dropped open as he looked at Kelian. "I was being nice, wasn't I?" but the latter squeezed my neck playfully.

"Next!" the announcer called again. I swallowed a groan—I couldn't let Tania see this was getting to me. I needed to get a fucking break and regretted this stupid bet.

Cardan's interest was piqued as he looked up and brushed his curls away from his face. "I'll go next."

Kelian immediately put a hand on his chest to stop him. "Dude, no."

"Why not?"

"You're wasted."

"Besides," Tania stepped in as Hunter rubbed Cardan's shoulder to console him and his dramatic pout. "I wouldn't want Raven's third fight to be too easy. We've got a bet going."

Cardan's mouth dropped open as he started sputtering in indignation. "What—" But the rest of his words were cut off by the crowd as I stepped back in. His grumpy face lit up as the redhead from before stepped into his periphery, beckoning him closer with a sultry look.

I mouthed to Tania that she was going to lose the bet.

"You see this, folks? She wants to go *another* round!" the caller said.

The noise grew louder. At first, I thought it was because people appreciated my tenacity. And maybe some did. But then Hunter's smirk fell from her face, and she cursed, staring behind me. Kelian's eyes widened, then turned to me, and I knew something was off.

I turned around, and the laughter died on my lips as I saw who the next contender was. There wasn't yet enough alcohol in my blood to dampen my heart's reaction.

"It looks like we have a new contender joining the fight," the announcer said while my blood turned to ice.

*Jordan.*

Jordan found his way through the crowd and into the circle—shaking his head while he did it. Though he was smiling a wolf's smile, eyes trailing over me and my every move.

No. I barely shook my head.

No fucking way.

The crowd went wild as he circled me, but his voice pierced through the chaos. "I heard generals are forbidden to take part in these fights."

Swallowing past a big lump, I needed some time before I could respond. "I heard that too."

Jordan's eyes swirled with shadows. He wore casual clothing like the rest of us. Black or dark blue—who knew—pants, with a white shirt. Both fit him like they were made for him, which was probably the case.

"How about that fight you promised me?" he asked, a

dimple on his cheek and a challenge lighting up his eyes.

In silence, I said goodbye to the throwing stars—but most of all, my frail ego.

"No." I walked back into the crowd, under loud protest, because that was against the rules. Once you stepped into the circle, you stayed inside until the match was done.

There would not be a match.

Kelian lay a hand on my shoulder and asked me something I couldn't catch. I was frozen to the spot, ears buzzing while I held Jordan's smirking gaze. People tried to push me back in, but I shrugged off their advances until I took hold of someone's arm and turned on my heel to punch the person in the face—the attack blocked by Kelian. I growled low in my throat at the surrounding people, and they shrank back.

Jordan had taken off his shirt, his lean muscles bulging in his torso—even more pronounced since the last time I saw him bare-chested.

"Anyone else?" he bellowed.

I backed away into the crowd until my senses were free of him, working my way to one of the far walls, refusing to turn around and look at him.

"Why wouldn't you fight him?" Kelian asked as he and Hunter caught up with me.

I swallowed as I watched a new contender walk into the ring from the corner of my eyes. "I've already been fighting him for too long."

My best friends shared a look and followed me as I dragged myself up the stairs just as the crowd roared.

I didn't look back.

# CHAPTER 11

"Yes!" I yelled, punching both fists in the air.

Jordan was staring up at me from the ground.

I had just kicked him to the ground.

*To. The. Ground.*

He had wanted me to train through another grueling sparring session tonight, and I had kicked his ass.

I still stood with my arms raised, bowing my head to the fake crowd that was giving me a standing ovation.

Jordan and I had gotten into a routine where we'd spent half of our days in each other's company. We did almost everything together, especially now that Kelian was on a mission and Jordan had pushed my training to another level.

Jordan lowered his head to the ground but kept his eyes firmly on me.

*Holy shit.* I had just beaten Jordan in a one-on-one fight. If you'd told me this day would come, I would have declared you crazy. Yeah, I'd been kicking ass the last few months, but *so much ass* that I beat Jordan?

Rising from the ground, he kept staring at me before he grinned like a maniac.

I bowed to him. "You're very welcome."

"That was good." He chuckled. "But don't get used to it."

A laugh escaped my throat. "Fuck," I said.

He frowned. "What?"

"I'll have to find another trainer now," I sighed like it was the worst of my problems.

Jordan pushed my shoulder. "Don't let it get to your head, Renée. Next time, you're mine."

I chuckled, but the air stuck in my throat as my whole body tensed up. My heart thrashed inside its cage.

His laugh faltered as his eyes searched mine. He noticed what had happened and swallowed visibly. Was he thinking the same thing? Did I have to voice my feelings? Would it ruin our friendship?

This moment was taking too damn long.

Carefully, I cleared my throat. "It meant a lot that you came last week."

He nodded. "Of course." It was silent for a moment before Jordan asked, "How old were you when your mother passed away?"

I swallowed.

*Passed away.*

"Eight."

Jordan's gaze slid back to mine. "So young. Was she sick?"

Words failed me. I tried to take a moment to organize the thoughts in my brain.

He lay a hand on my shoulder and squeezed. "You don't have to talk about it if you don't want to."

I waved a hand. "No, I need to talk about it. I haven't for a long time. It's always been something I processed by myself—am still processing."

He stayed silent.

My breath caught. "My mother was sick, in a way." I looked at him, forced myself to meet his gaze, open myself up. "I wasn't born in the West of Ardenza, but the East."

Understanding filled his gaze.

"She got sick and had to be brought to the hospital. It was the protocol when the mutation first surfaced. My father refused to for a long time because he knew we probably wouldn't see her again. Nobody with the mutation had come back. But eventually, he didn't have a choice anymore. We never got to know if she passed before the fall or—" I wavered, but he nodded.

"I've had nightmares for years; from the moment I understood what was happening in the world. That my mother—" I swallowed, blinking rapidly. "That she is looking for my dad and me," I added in a hoarse whisper.

Jordan grabbed my hand and squeezed it.

"I've never told anyone that—not even my father." We didn't really talk about what happened before we came to Barak—not knowing where to start or how to tackle the subject.

"That must have been incredibly hard on you," he said softly, his voice like a balm to my painfully throbbing heart.

Finally, I could breathe again. Like a heavy burden had been lifted, one that I could now shoulder with someone else.

"Sorry, I'm such a downer." My smile was forced.

Jordan let go of my hand to take my face between his hands. He brought his head to my level, looking me straight in the eye. "Raven, you never have to apologize for voicing what's on your heart. Especially to me."

He only let go when I nodded, brushing his thumb over my cheek.

I looked away. "Maybe we could go out tonight? Go somewhere fun to balance it out?"

He smiled, but it was a sad smile. "I'd love nothing more than that, but I promised my parents I would eat at their place tonight."

I felt a stone sink but shielded my heart from any rubble—trying to ignore the feeling I experienced at the thought of not seeing him tonight. It frightened me, that level of attachment.

Jordan clenched his jaw and brushed his thumb across his chin. "Soon, okay?"

"Sure." I smiled through my somber mood because how could I not? "Enjoy your evening. Meet up tomorrow, same time?" The desperation that clawed its way through my body had no place in it.

He grabbed his stuff, a slanted smile on his face. "Looking forward to it, Renée. Won't want to miss my hour of charity."

I stuck out my tongue at him, and he winked. I was glad for this moment of normalcy between us. My love for this man increased daily, but I didn't know how to tell him.

Not *yet*.

## NOW

The punching bag was unforgiving, and my knuckles were hurting.

Last night, I had left the Sewers with my friends after

I told them I had to get rest for my last full night—minus Cardan, of course, who had run off with the red-haired girl.

I'd planned on resting for the entire day. We were leaving at night, and I needed the break. But I was on edge, which had led me to the gym—blowing off some steam.

Damruin sat in the back of my mind like a predator on the prowl, so silent I could almost forget it was there, but it would eventually catch up with me. It *was* happening. I was going there in a matter of *days*.

Vivid memories of the streets, the people, and the life I had lived flashed through my thoughts. Those memories would be tainted the moment I stepped foot into the city. Nothing about the once vibrant town would be the same for me.

And I just couldn't deal.

I had been strolling through the main base earlier that day when I walked straight into a newspaper stand. It was stocked with a newspaper that showed a large photo of the asshole sending me on this mission. He was smiling on it—a fake smile, of course, because Domasc wasn't capable of a real one.

The photo showed King Sergei and General Zander with Chief General Domasc. It had been a long time since I last saw a picture of the Borzian royal family, and they had gotten older. King Sergei now truly looked like an old man compared to the photos they had shown us at our history lessons, while General Zander had grown into a fully mature woman, face slightly wrinkled—from all the scowling, no doubt. Early on, rumors about her had surfaced in Ardenza, and if any of them were true, she should be put into a straitjacket.

I studied the photo once more before stepping away

from the stand. The article used the words *Chief General Domasc*, *making history*, and *peace* in the same phrase. My eyes had nearly rolled out of my head.

I punched the bag even harder as I pictured it was Domasc I beat to a pulp. I had never been a particularly aggressive person, *but man*, he made my toes curl.

The doors to the gym opened, and the other reason I was in here walked in. I stopped attacking the bag as if it had personally done me harm and let my hand rest on it until it stopped swinging.

Finally, we looked at each other. Stared and stared and stared.

He had a minor cut above his eyebrow, but his eyes told me he hadn't lost a match yesterday. They had the glint of a winner.

Jordan walked closer and gestured his head to my bruised knuckles. "You weren't kidding. Hurting yourself gets you off nowadays?"

I narrowed my eyes. "Not nearly enough."

He raised a brow and laughed. *Actually laughed.* The sound infuriated me to no end.

"Why were you at the Sewers?" I fired back.

Cocking his head, he replied, "Do you want me to be honest?"

That was answer enough.

I looked away from him, inspecting my bruised knuckles. "How many fights did you win?"

"Not nearly enough," Jordan parroted.

I met his eyes, which had darkened, and I suppressed the urge to cast mine down.

"You promised me one, you know," he drawled.

I arched a brow. "That was *all* you, if I remember

correctly."

He brushed it off. "I see you're still too afraid to take me on." He stepped closer, and the room seemed to shrink. Other sounds and sensations were cut off.

"You know I can't resist it when you're baiting me."

"You resisted just fine last night."

I wrinkled my nose at him. Why was he even here? Couldn't he just leave me alone?

"So?" he insisted.

"Fine," I snapped, crossing my arms and keeping my voice steady through sheer will. "But under one condition."

Jordan inclined his head, eyes glinting.

"I need a couple of hours in Damruin."

Stars swirled in those blue eyes. "You *need* a couple of hours in Damruin?"

I nodded. "If I win, I'll get them."

He was silent for a moment.

"It's non-negotiable," I added.

"Tell me why."

"I need to search the hospital for my mother's files and get answers. I don't mind going alone, but I have to try." I didn't see the point of lying.

Jordan looked at me for a long moment. "*I mind.*" He pinched the bridge of his nose and shut his eyes while he crossed his arms.

I knew it was a risky move, throwing this in the mix *hours* before we went.

Finally, he nodded. "Deal."

"I won't be too hard on you." I rolled my shoulders back and threw him one of the blunt training knives lined up along the center of the room. "The mission needs at least one competent general."

Jordan barked a laugh. "And you're not?"

"Cute." I rolled my eyes.

Stepping onto the mat, he beckoned me closer. "Show me your worst, Raven."

I twirled the knife in my hand as we approached each other—both on high alert, willing the other to attack first. But I wouldn't. Only if—

Jordan veered forward, and I stepped sideways to block the brunt of his attack. The metal still slapped against my thigh, and I groaned. He just stepped back, lips curved. I pushed forward, knife swinging towards his head, legs, shoulders, *anywhere*—but he blocked attack after attack until he stepped off the mat and lost his footing.

I didn't stop attacking him. I hooked my foot around one of his ankles, forcing power into the move as he fell to the ground. Surprise lit his face.

We hadn't set any rules, so he couldn't say anything about it.

I used his momentary distraction and dropped to my knees to wrap my legs around his torso as he rolled away, pinning one of his arms to the ground as I pushed the knife to his throat. But Jordan shoved a hand between the two just in time. He moved his other arm to my neck, which he missed by a hair as I moved away from him. It made it possible for him to sit up, though, and he threw his weight into dragging me underneath him.

Jordan moved his knife to my abdomen, but I raised a knee to block the attack, grunting as metal collided with bone. I punched him in the chest, and Jordan gasped for air. He had to recover by taking a deep breath. I used that time to plant my foot against his torso and kicked him away from me.

Rolling to the side, I pushed myself upright. Before I could stand, though, he had already grabbed my ankle and pulled me back. I grunted as I freed my ankle and tried to kick him between the legs, but Jordan dodged the attack by turning away. Taking anything over a kick to the balls, I guess.

The moment he turned, I wrapped my arms around his neck and yanked him back. Instead of stumbling, Jordan grabbed my arms and shoved both of us to the ground, crushing me beneath his weight. He rolled over and raised his knife at the same time I did.

We grabbed each other's arms before our weapons made impact—halting the fight.

I stiffened as we were trapped in this cage of our making. His chest raced, and I noticed my own chest doing the same. I looked at him. His eyes searched mine and moved to my lips.

Abruptly, I let go of my knife and stared at him—watched his thoughts pace as fast as mine. Jordan, too, dropped his knife, but had yet to let go of my arm. Instead, his fingers pressed into my skin insistingly.

I tried to pry my arm from his grip to make him move, to get off me, but he wouldn't let go.

"Jordan," I whispered, emotions conflicted.

His eyes roamed my face—trailed the seam of my lips. "Hm?"

"Let go."

Gazing at the hand still holding mine, he opened it, granting me room to climb off the ground. Time seemed to stretch while he stayed put and stared at the ceiling. He rubbed his eyes with one hand and shoved it through his hair.

"Tie?" he rasped, pushing himself off the ground.

I smiled tentatively—glad he said nothing else. "Tie," I agreed.

"I'll adjust the route to go past the hospital, where you'll have ten minutes."

I reined in a surprised breath.

"An hour," I countered boldly.

"Twenty minutes."

"Forty-five."

"You won't get more than thirty from me, Raven, and you're already pushing it."

"Deal," I blurted.

He shook my outstretched hand with a resigned smile. "I hope Nikolai gets us some info about this mission soon. I don't have a good feeling about it."

My face fell as I leaned against the weapon rack and clenched a water bottle between my hands. "Me neither. Though, if he gets caught snooping around, Domasc will try to strip him of his rank—me, too."

"And if Domasc finds out in time, he could," Jordan agreed, but a smile played around his lips. A genuine smile this time.

"What?"

He raised his brows at me, his smile widening.

I gasped. "*Not* if Nikolai becomes chief general at the next election."

"Bingo."

"Is he planning to, then?" I hadn't heard anything about it from Hunt or Nik. "Does he even want to?"

"We're still working on that, but I can't see how he has a choice. I think Nikolai realized it himself during 3B." Jordan swallowed.

I nodded as I bit my lip.

An awkward silence hung between us. It made me long for the simpler days *before* this whole shitshow.

"Well," he said on a lighter note. "How are things between you and *Rudolfs*?"

Raising my eyebrows at his tone, I said, "Kelian?"

Jordan raised his brows.

"What do you mean?" I asked carefully.

His body screamed nonchalance as he shrugged, but I saw right through his act. "Are you dating?"

My lips parted. I really couldn't believe this guy. Shaking my head, I pushed myself off the rack and walked over to my bag.

"What?" Jordan asked, frowning.

I gave him a look before putting a towel around my neck. "And what if we *were* dating, Jordan? Would it change anything?"

Jordan clenched his jaw. "You know it does."

"Oh, yeah?" I asked him. "In what way? That you'd *actually* do something about it this time?"

Frustrated, he pushed himself forward. "Damnit, Raven. You know it's not that simple."

He walked my way, but I raised a hand. "Don't bother. I'll see you tomorrow."

With that, I turned around and left the training hall.

# CHAPTER 12

JORDAN
11 YEARS EARLIER

"I can't do this anymore, Ash."

Tears filled her eyes. "You can't do *what* anymore?" Her bottom lip trembled.

Jordan looked at her through burning eyes. "I'm tired of always treading lightly around you. We don't have fun anymore, *barely* talk, and I—frankly, I'm just exhausted."

Ashley cast her eyes down, and tears rolled down her cheeks. She wiped them away frantically, leaving black streaks underneath her eyes. "You're breaking up with me?"

Jordan nodded, wiping at his wet cheek. "I have a hard time doing this, Ash." He gestured her way. "You're all I want, but our relationship costs me too much. More than I want to give."

She closed her eyes and covered them with her hands. Her whole body shook.

Reluctantly, he stood and kneeled in front of her chair. "*Fuck*. Ashley, Look at me." His voice was hoarse.

"No," she whispered.

He lay a hand on her neck. "Please, Ash."

Finally, she did, her eyes reddened.

"I don't do this lightly."

"Why are you doing it at all?" she asked and pulled a hand through her blonde locks. She sighed deeply and leaned her head in her hands on the table. Distraught.

"I can't be myself when I'm with you—I can't even talk about the shit that haunts me without having to console *you*... It's just too much. You don't know how badly I wanted this to be different. But we have tried too many times. We're just not meant to be." He sighed and bit his cheek to keep it together—be the voice of reason for both of them. "In time, we'll both look back at this and know it was the right decision."

Again, she shook her head in denial. This time, she stood, grabbed her purse from the table, and walked out of the room. Jordan straightened and forced everything in himself to stay rooted to the spot—to not go after her. It was better this way.

He knew it was.

## NOW

"How is work, Jordan?"

Jordan blinked and shoved away his distracting thoughts as he looked at his mother. Her diamond earrings glimmered in the candlelight.

He lay down his cutlery, swallowed his food, and smiled. "Fine." He cleared his throat. "I'm actually leaving on a new mission tomorrow."

A new companion entered the room—his name was silence.

"Tomorrow? What kind of mission?" His father asked, laying down his fork, the utensil clattering on the ceramic plate.

Ashley, too, had paused eating, and looked at him like he had told her he wanted to start a world war. Jordan met her gaze.

"It's a short mission. Off the books," he explained.

The doors opened and a servant walked in with more food. The table was already loaded with it; silver platters had been served like artwork—the carefully coordinated food contrasting with what they served at the main base. But Jordan preferred that over all this nonsense. Luxury had surrounded him his whole life. He understood the meaning of wealth in this world and *was* thankful to his parents for the life they offered him, but he didn't care for it much. Privilege at its finest.

Ashley *did* like the luxurious lifestyle—also the only life she'd ever known—but she wasn't spoiled. The legal profession had thickened her skin, and she was a hardass when needed, especially for her clients. Jordan admired how she put her resources into her work as an attorney and advocated for the lesser privileged by mostly doing pro bono cases.

Ashley swallowed. "When will you be going?" She placed her hand on his arm, and he gave her a weak, apologetic smile.

"Tomorrow."

His mother looked from Ashley to him, narrowing her eyes ever so slightly. Jordan knew his mother. And she knew him. She could look right through his bullshit.

Suddenly uncomfortable, Jordan shifted in his seat.

The glass of wine on the table suddenly looked extremely

attractive, and he deliberately took a sip as he focused back on the food in front of him.

His father asked Ashley a question, and they started talking, tearing her attention away from him. Jordan wiped his mouth with a napkin and inspected the room. His parent's dining room looked more like a ballroom. It was bigger than any of his main base quarters when he lived there. After returning from mission 3B, he had chosen to stay at the main base. But after Ashley and he had gotten back together, they'd quickly moved into an apartment of their own, one his parents had already owned. They wanted to give it to him for his achievements, but he didn't want to take it like that. So now they rented it. The salary of a general was generous, so it wasn't a big deal.

"Are you all right, Jordan?" his mother asked softly while the conversation about Ardenza's politics at the other side of the table continued.

Jordan glanced at his mother and forced a smile as he took hold of her hand. "There's just a lot on my mind."

His mother raised a brow, but his father overheard what he said. "He's doing well for himself, our boy," Kenneth said, oblivious to the situation at hand if he had to go by his mother's face.

Ashley smiled again, a tad awkwardly, as she sipped her wine.

He hadn't told her anything about returning to the shadow plains yet.

Jordan avoided his mother's prying eyes for the rest of the night. They bid his parents farewell before they stepped back into the car. He started the engine when Ashley asked, "When were you planning on telling me about the mission?"

Clenching his jaw, he drove down the gravel path away

from his parent's mansion. "I wanted to tell you, but… I only found out recently and it's a classified mission. The fewer people that know about it, the better."

"I am more than just your fiancée, Jordan," she said.

Jordan looked at her and noticed the deep frown between her brows. "I know. I'm sorry."

She crossed her arms but remained silent. She was clearly running the words he'd just said through her head, dissecting them, looking for fallacies.

"Do you think getting engaged was a mistake?" Ashley asked out of nowhere.

His head turned to the side, and he blinked twice before looking back at the road. He grasped the steering wheel a little tighter. "What?" he asked, clearing his throat.

Ashley glared at him through a narrowed gaze. "Do you regret getting engaged?" she spelled out for him, loud and clear.

He inhaled sharply. Licked his lips. "Our engagement?"

"Yes, Jordan," she replied, agitated. "*Our engagement.*"

When he remained silent, she laughed cynically and shook her head. "Really, Jordan? That's how you feel?"

"Ashley, you know I—"

"Don't sugarcoat it. Just be honest for once."

He nodded. "I think…" *Gods, he needed to tell her about Raven without hurting her. How? Without being a gigantic douchebag? Impossible.* "I don't think I can love you the way you deserve to be loved."

Her red lips parted, staring at him. "How long have you been thinking that?"

"Ash," Jordan's heart pounded in his throat. "It's not that I don't love you; it's just—"

"I asked *how long*, Jordan," she hissed, tears brimming

in her eyes.

Jordan opened his mouth and closed it again. He couldn't find the words.

"I see," she said. "I think it's a good idea that we don't see each other until after the mission—however long *that* is. Drop me off at the Westeria. I'll get a cab to drop me off at my parents'."

"At least let me drive you there," Jordan said.

She didn't respond, but didn't refuse either. They continued the rest of the drive in silence until they arrived at her parent's home.

Ashley still didn't look at him. "I'll pick up some of my stuff tomorrow when you're at work."

"Ash, please—"

"I'm done getting hurt by you, Jordan, even if that isn't your intention." With that, she shut the car door and walked up the driveway. Jordan couldn't muster the will to fight for her.

Which made him hate himself even more.

# CHAPTER 13

I had decided today was the day.

Yesterday, Jordan had left for dinner at his parent's house, and I had missed his presence so much that I'd simmered through our shared memories. Realization had hit me. I couldn't do this any longer—pretend like we were just friends. I had taken the whole day to gather the courage to tell him about my feelings. Darting around this conversation would not cut it anymore. I had to get an answer to move on with my life. If I prolonged this, my feelings would drown me.

Jordan had feelings for me, too. Of that, I was sure. I wasn't stupid. There had always been a certain pull between us. I wouldn't *ever* profess my feelings for him if I was sure he saw me like a little sister.

My heart raced a thousand miles per hour as I walked through the halls toward Jordan's rooms. By the time I arrived, I was short of breath, which had nothing to do with my endurance.

I knocked on his door before I could second-guess myself,

and it opened almost immediately.

"Raven," Jordan said, his eyebrows hiked up, and a faint smile appeared on his lips. He was wearing green cargo pants and a light grey shirt, his muscles shifting underneath it as he moved his hand higher on the door.

I forced my eyes upwards. "Yeah, hi. Can I come in?" I pointed into the room behind him.

"Always." He stepped back and opened the door wider.

As I made my way inside, I put one foot in front of the other. It was neat, even for military standards—like no one was living here at all. His clothing hung wrinkle-free on a rack and lay neatly folded on the shelves. The bed I could see in the adjacent room was made with folds I had only ever seen at high-class hotels—again, wrinkle-free.

When I turned around to face him, butterflies fluttered through my body.

"Make yourself comfortable," he said and gestured to the chairs surrounding a round wooden table. "Want something to drink?"

I shook my head. *Gods, no.* I wouldn't get it past my throat. "I actually came to talk to you about something."

"Yeah," he said as he sat down with a heavy sigh. "I have something to tell you, too." The light left his eyes as his expression turned grave.

I wanted to make that look disappear from his handsome face, so I asked, "What happened?"

He shook his head. "You first."

There was no way I would profess my feelings for him while he was struggling with something. "Jordan, tell me. What's going on? Can I help?"

After a while, he said, "I don't know."

I signaled for him to speak, and he rubbed his throat.

"A couple of months ago, the week I just got back from 3B, before—" his eyes pleaded with mine "—before you and I saw each other again in the training hall, I went to this club in the city. I drank way too much. Partied too hard. There I reconnected with my ex, Ashley, the one I told you about."

"*The love of your life*," I murmured, not liking where this conversation was headed.

Jordan's mouth opened like he wanted to say something, but decided against it. "She's a successful attorney now—all grown up. I almost didn't recognize her. We…" His eyes found mine again, gauging my reaction to the confession that wasn't said out loud—as if he was ashamed to admit it. "It shouldn't have happened, but I don't know; she was familiar, we were drunk, and it was all too easy." *Falling back into each other's arms.*

I did not want to hear about who he slept with.

I *really, really* didn't.

"As you know, I had this dinner with my parents yesterday. Turns out, they had invited their friends—Ashley's parents—without giving me a heads up."

My brows furrowed. I held my breath and tried to calm myself.

"Her mother is my father's colleague-delegate, and our families have known each other for *years*. That's also how Ashley and I first met." He paused, biting his lip. Jordan sighed as he focused on his hands. "And Ashley was with them, too."

I could not care less about Ashley. "What happened, Jordan?"

He looked up at me with those stormy blue eyes. "She's pregnant."

Air leaked from my lungs like someone had punched me

square in the chest.

*Pregnant?*

"She is?" I asked him, practically choking on air. "It's yours?"

Jordan nodded, his eyes shattering as they held mine. "Before I knew it, she had asked me for a second chance."

I had to remember to keep breathing and keep talking to him. "What did you say?" I insisted as I clasped my hands together in prayer.

"I told her I had to think about it." He swallowed. "*Shit,* I don't know."

My mouth dropped open. "You're considering getting back together?" I don't know why I was so surprised about the fact. They were getting a *child*.

He nodded again, slower this time, and I wanted to run from this room.

"I don't know what to do," he confessed, looking at me like I could help him figure it out.

He might as well have stabbed me in the heart.

What did he want from me? *My advice?* Didn't he fully grasp how I fucking felt about it yet? "You know my opinion."

"She has changed," he countered, pleading for his case.

"Then don't ask for my opinion if you don't want to hear it. Do whatever you want to do."

His eyes softened, face contorting. "Raven, I'm—"

"No," I raised a hand to stop him. "I understand this decision is hard on you, but I can't help you make it. Just follow your heart." I didn't know how I managed the words, but I felt the walls build up behind them—the fortification closing me in.

"But a child—" I choked on the words. "*A child* is not a reason to be together."

A cynical laugh escaped him. "My mother said the same thing."

"And what did you tell her?" My voice was small.

He pulled a hand through his hair. "That *no*, a child isn't a reason to be together. But it's a reason to try." He avoided looking me in the eye. "Everyone deserves a second chance, right?"

I tried blinking away the tears filling my eyes because I knew that if I said any more, my voice would surely break. How do I get the fuck out of here? *I need to be alone.*

Jordan still wouldn't look at me as he started nodding to himself. "*Yes*," he said, like it was the only thing to keep his life from falling apart around him. "There's too much history between us *not* to try."

Everything in me wanted to hurl at him; try to get it into his thick skull that he deserved better. But where would that get me? I wasn't unbiased in all this. Who knew? Ashley might be able to make him happy. She had done it before. Maybe she truly had changed this time. And a child... A family... That's huge.

It would be *everything* if they could make it work.

Tears pricked in my eyes, but I blinked them away.

"Sorry," Jordan said, finally looking at me. "I didn't mean to burden you with my problems."

I shook my head. "No, Jordan. Don't apologize. That's what friends are for." My smile was unsteady. "This—this is just a choice you have to make on your own."

He nodded. Then he asked, "What did you want to speak to me about?"

"Oh," I said and cleared my throat. "Nothing. Only that I'll be taking a step back in the coming week. I don't feel quite well."

Jordan's eyes turned worried. "We can do something else. Something more relaxed?"

I smiled. "No, that isn't necessary, but thanks." My pager went off, and I looked at the screen, thanking the gods for this timing.

*Battery level low.*

"Well, duty calls." I held up the pager to emphasize my point. "Talk later?" I asked and didn't look back as I stood and stormed from his room.

I turned a corner in the hallway, tears already streaming down my cheeks, and I finally gave my heart permission to break.

NOW

It was freezing cold in the middle of the night. The alarm had been set early that morning. I hated waking up so early, but it was part of being in the military; we had to be ready at all times of the day.

I had called my father the night before and told him I would be gone for another week or two, deliberately leaving out the part about returning to the shadow plains, least of all to Damruin. I didn't even want to admit that part of the mission to *myself*. Thinking about it made me sick; talking about it would most definitely tilt me over the edge.

Colonel Keano was standing next to me and dropped her bag to the ground, her jaw tensing and her eyes puffy, like mine, no doubt. Her hair was fully braided, and I cursed myself for not thinking about that. She let out a long breath. The smokey clouds lit up by the large lamps attached to the building where we joined the rest of the group. Neither one of us was very talkative this early in the morning.

A large black bus drove up and stopped in front of the meeting place. A military driver stepped out, and we stowed our bags in the luggage compartment before joining the queue to get inside. Jordan was checking to see if everyone was with us.

I stepped forward after Major Britton and looked up at the Lieutenant General, whose chiseled face was more pronounced by the night's shadows. Keeping my voice low, I saluted, "Good morning, Sir."

He just looked at me, an unreadable expression on his face. "Pretty sure it's still night, but welcome on-board Brigadier General Renée."

I stepped inside and walked to the back, where Major Britton had pulled his hoodie over his eyes and seemed to have drifted off already. There was enough room for everyone to get their own row, so I sat down in the row in front of him, with my back to the blinded windows and my legs stretched out in front of me.

As everyone got in, the doors closed, and the bus started driving.

I watched as Jordan spoke to the bus driver for some time. Then, he walked into the bus and sat down in the front. Our eyes locked before the lights dimmed.

I pulled up my hoodie against the cold and closed my eyes.

★ ★ ★

Someone woke me violently, and one of my eyes cracked open against my will. Major Britton was smirking. "You're a deep sleeper, Brigadier General."

I wrinkled my nose in aggravation. "Fucking hell," I muttered under my breath as he walked off the bus.

The lights were back on, and I noticed almost everyone had already made their way out. The movement of the luggage compartment opening vibrated through my seat. I took a couple deep breaths before pulling off my hoodie and climbing out of the bus.

A year ago, a new airport was built some distance from the city—they needed the space for people to live. Now that they had found a vaccine, the government wanted to focus more on future developments instead of battling with the past. That's why they decided an army airport near the main base wasn't necessary any longer. Why would there be if there was no immediate threat?

That's why the army had received part of this newer airport, but it was a pain in the ass drive and took multiple hours from the main base.

We walked over to the hover plane while the cabin crew took our baggage away. I stepped inside, put on my seatbelt, and closed my eyes again, trying to squeeze in every moment of rest I could. If you weren't the type of person who could sleep when they needed to, you would learn to do so in the army.

Something bumped into me. A bag? A Person? I had no idea, but I didn't care and hoped they would just sit down quickly to let me rest. As another thing bumped into my arm, I opened my eyes and suppressed a sigh.

Jordan sat next to me and fastened his seatbelt as he looked behind and checked the people on board. We were complete because he turned back around and looked my way. His smile disappeared.

*Great.*

"What?" I asked him. "There weren't any other seats left?"

He clenched his jaw. "There weren't, actually."

I shrugged indifferently, but felt heat crawl up to my cheeks.

To my relief, I slept throughout the larger part of the flight. A little less soothing was that I woke up with my head on Jordan's shoulder. The body part in question felt heavy as I tried to lift it, but I soon realized that his head rested on top of mine. Not on purpose, though, because his posture stiffened as I straightened.

"I didn't—" I started.

"Yeah," he replied hoarsely. "Me neither."

And that was that.

# CHAPTER 14

After a week without seeing Jordan, I walked into the canteen. I had to admit I was nervous to see him again. Nervous about what he was going to say and what he had decided.

I glanced around the packed room, my stomach growling. The first day after the news, I cried so much that I hadn't been able to eat, which meant that after a week of avoiding the dining hall, the smells that greeted my senses were almost a little *too* stimulating.

Again, I looked to my left, back into the hall, where I finally spotted Jordan.

He was already looking at me—a close-lipped smile on his agonizingly handsome face. The rest of the hall didn't notice our exchange, but to me, he might as well have been shouting my name.

Butterflies fluttered through my stomach, and the hunger I felt moments before vanished. I had to hold myself back from running over to him like a fool. I was definitely *not* going to do that.

*He was going to be a dad.*

I held my ground as I got something to eat. Eating was important.

When I got my food, I walked over to Jordan and sat in front of him—never beside him. I loved looking at him. *Still* loved it, even though it hurt like a bitch.

"How are you doing?" he asked, studying me.

"Fine." I shrugged, which was decidedly not the way to make this less awkward. "You?" I tried putting a jingle to the word, forcing a smile on my face.

Jordan looked at me like he saw right through it. "All things considered... Okay, I guess." He took a bite. "I came by your room a couple of times."

He said it as he would comment on the weather—like we were two people having a normal conversation. But something in his eyes made me pause and think twice about my response.

"Yeah," I said casually. "Decided to take some time off."

"Ah," he said, clearly not buying that either.

The conversation flattened, and I tried to come up with things to talk about—something I had never done before. Asking him about Ashley and his growing family was possible, but a *hard pass*. Thinking about it made me want to scream. And that was the full extent of thoughts about him in my brain. *Ashley* and his *growing family*. Just lovely for my mental health.

Instead, I remained silent.

"Want to get back to training next week?" He hopped right over to the next subject, brushing off the rest of our conversation like it had never happened.

I took a bite and swallowed it. I smiled at him, although everything inside me cringed. "Sure."

It wasn't like I was lying. I *wanted* to get back to training—to *before* all of this had happened. But sadly, life didn't always go the way you wanted.

Instead, it went the way it was supposed to go. And I clung to that belief.

## NOW

The rest of the way to the mission base had been uneventful. And when the familiar lights had loomed up in the distance, they wrapped around me like a comforting blanket. I hadn't expected to be back so soon—a part of me thought I would never be back. But in a way, it felt like coming home.

After I dumped my stuff in my assigned rooms, I almost ran from the general's quarters, visiting the familiar halls that led to the canteen for some dinner. I passed many familiar faces on my way there, and some of them had even asked why I was back.

I picked up some food, keeping my back firmly to the rest of the room. But as I turned around, my traitorous eyes immediately looked for, *and found* Jordan before quickly looking away and gathering the courage to walk up to him.

It felt like a déjà vu.

After all this time, my feelings for him remained like they had never left—and I hated myself for that. Maybe it had been childish to storm off the other day, but I couldn't bear to be in the same room as him without either wanting to strangle or kiss him.

Being near him was so overwhelming that it hurt too much.

I wanted to believe I was over him, but seeing Jordan at the gala, I knew it was a lost cause. If, after three years, my feelings for him hadn't simmered, I would probably always keep them, just like the feelings he had for Ashley.

I noticed his eyes were still trained on me as I walked his way. He stopped eating as I sat down, and we looked at each other for a second before opening our mouths.

"Hi." *Awkward.*

His slanted smile was tentative. "Hey."

"I'm sorry," I said carefully.

Jordan smiled like he carried the world's weight on his shoulders. "You have nothing to apologize for, Raven. If there's anyone who needs to be on their knees, it's me."

I bit my lip and dismissed his comment. "No." Trying to clear the image of Jordan on his knees before me, I added, "It was very unprofessional of me."

"No," Jordan said. "I—"

"That's all I wanted to say. Please, let me. Let's agree to bury the hatchet, okay?"

Jordan nodded and swallowed the rest of what he wanted to say.

"How does it feel being back here?" he asked suddenly.

After a beat of silence, I looked around. "Weird, in a way. I hadn't been *planning* on coming back here." It was an olive branch of sorts.

He said nothing, but his eyes found mine, and the depth of emotions swirling in them was overwhelming. "You were planning on staying."

I felt my hand tremble as his blue eyes scoured my face. "Yes."

Eventually, he nodded and leaned back in his chair, his posture more relaxed. He pulled a hand through his hair, inhaling deeply. Why was he so impossibly handsome? "Good." A smile curved his beautiful mouth like he couldn't help himself. "But you should know, I would never have let you go back here. Not alone."

My uniform felt too tight. I cleared my throat. "I thought as much."

Jordan smiled at the table.

I prayed my thanks in silence as the loud ringing of Jordan's satellite phone shattered the moment. He picked it up with resistance, the apology in his eyes warming me up from the inside.

"Okay," he spoke through the phone and stood, jaw clenching as he gestured he needed to go. "I'm coming."

I nodded, indicating that he should.

He held the phone away from his ear and covered the microphone. "We'll talk later." He walked away, speaking again. Jordan casually put a hand in his pocket and walked off like he had no care in the world.

I checked him out from behind; his tall, strong legs, firm ass, and muscled back—the cords shifting beneath his t-shirt.

*Damn,* he was gorgeous. Mouthwateringly so.

My heart thrashed inside my chest and got even more distressed as Jordan—with the phone still to his ear—turned around and winked at me, dimples flashing. Then, he placed his hand on the door and pushed, disappearing.

Fuck my life.

I was way in over my head.

✯ ✯ ✯

After finishing dinner, I walked a little. It was weird to stroll over the grounds of the mission that had been my entire life not so long ago. I looked up, gazing at the sky, the forever night that was permanently littered with stars. The stars that had always brought me solace.

Ever since fleeing from Damruin, I have felt lost at sea. But here, at the mission's base, I had found a home—and although my story here had wrapped up; it *did* feel good to be back. It was a sanctuary, calming me like I hadn't been since I returned to Barak. Funny how such a high-stress environment could make a person feel more at ease than the capital, where people weren't even thinking about the shadow plains most of the time.

An hour later, I entered the dimly lit bar where I had spent a lot of my time preparing missions, drinking, talking, and… doing other things, too. I smiled at the memories that flooded me. And as I looked up, Jordan's eyes latched onto mine, inviting me to join him.

Somehow, I'd accepted my feelings for him, but that didn't mean I had to act on them. I knew I couldn't.

I felt a blush blossoming on my cheeks as I ordered a drink, leaning forward on the bar so it shielded me from his piercing gaze, and tried to forget that my body was ablaze from one look. I inspected the snacks on the menu this week—pinching my eyes as I tried to decide what to get.

"Hey, beautiful," someone whispered in my ear as a hand curled around my waist.

The corner of my lip hiked up at the sound of his voice. I turned to look at him.

*Vlad.*

He hadn't changed a bit. His skin was just as pale as I remembered, his features just as grave, and his angular eyes were still as dark as his buzz cut. The color contrasted with his skin like day and night.

"It's good to see a familiar face," I said.

Vlad drifted closer, his familiar scent entering my nose,

which had me biting my lip. "Want to show me just *how* much you appreciate it?" he asked smoothly, pulling me closer into his body.

"I'm not *that* glad." I grinned.

"I missed you, you know?"

I snorted. "You mean you missed me warming your bed."

"No one does it like you," he agreed.

I slapped him on the chest playfully, but he caught my hand—capturing it there. "You're sure?"

"Yeah." My eyes trailed past him to Jordan, who clenched his glass and looked at us like he wanted to smash it into someone's skull. Vlad's, specifically. "Not really in the mood right now."

Vlad's gaze followed mine, looking over at Jordan. "You're with the prince of Barak?"

"What?" I asked him, barking a laugh in shock. The laugh sounded dangerously close to being caught. "*No.*" I was such a shit liar.

"Jordan Locke, right? It's what we used to call him in training." He tipped up his chin to the general in question. Then he looked back at me, amused.

"I'm not." My chest vibrated with laughter, even though I bit my lip to halt it. I didn't want Jordan to think I was making fun of him.

"He seems under the impression that you are."

"Yeah, no."

"I heard he is a baby daddy these days."

My heart clenched violently. "Let's stop talking about him."

Vlad's fingers trailed close to the curve of my ass, skimming lower and lower. "Sure," he replied easily. "So, if it's not a who, then *what* has you all wound up?"

My fingers rimmed the glass in front of me as I sighed. "This bullshit mission Domasc has sent us on."

"Ah." He let his hand fall away, the mood changing. "I heard about that from Zaregova."

My eyes widened as I looked at him in surprise. "He told you?"

Vlad nodded. "Wanted to give me a heads up—needed me to be your eyes and ears around here."

That loosened the knot in my chest a little. I knew how skilled Vlad was. "Thanks."

He let his hand trail over my spine until it curved around my neck, squeezing gently. "Of course." For a moment, Vlad's depthless eyes looked back at where Jordan had sat. The place that was now empty. "Well, I guess that's my cue to go, too, before he thinks of ways to flay me alive," Vlad said, pushing himself from the bar with a generous smile. To the barman, he said, "All of her drinks are on me."

Before he went, he grabbed my hand. "Did you visit the Sewers?" he asked, his dark eyes warm.

"I did." I smiled.

"Good." He kissed me on the cheek before walking away at last. "See you *later*, Renée."

I tipped my glass to Vlad in salute and downed the rest of it in one large gulp before shoving it forward to get another refill.

The gods knew I needed it.

# CHAPTER 15

## JORDAN

Raven's laughter filled Jordan's ears as he rounded a corner and stepped inside the gym. There weren't many sounds like it—if any. It was the type of laughter *he* had been the recipient of years ago.

He was greeted with the sight of Raven fighting in a pleasantly revealing training outfit. The tight leggings and a sports bra she wore looked amazing on her. But an ugly thing bubbled up as Jordan realized her sparring partner was the cause of her laughter. And he wasn't just *anyone*.

It was Vlad *fucking* Minstrel.

The night before, Jordan had looked at Vlad smoothing up to her. They had slept together before, seeing how Raven responded to his touch—how easily her smiles came for him.

It had irritated him to no end. In the end, she had looked at Jordan, longing in her eyes that wasn't Vlad's—and the fucker had seen it, too. He had been ninety-nine percent sure she hadn't gone with him to the gods' know where. Though seeing them together now, he wasn't so sure anymore.

Though, if she had, he knew he couldn't do or say anything about it. He had no place to speak his opinion. He had no business meddling with her relationships—telling her what she could and couldn't do to spare his feelings.

*Gods.* Jordan was the most hypocritical person in the world. *He* was the one engaged to another.

Raven and Vlad looked his way, the latter smiling as Jordan nodded at them before returning to what they were doing, although Raven seemed a little less loud than before. *That* bothered him, too; being the reason her joy dimmed.

While Jordan trained, he looked at their fight on the mat.

Sparring felt like *their* thing—his and Raven's—not her and *fucking* Vlad's. He was weirdly possessive of it. Whenever he watched the man come close to her, touch her, and give her playful smiles, Jordan clenched his jaw at his irrational responses. He needed to focus on himself. Fix his own mess first.

But something in him made him continue to watch. He couldn't help himself admiring her technique, the way she moved her lithe body. The growth she had been through over the years when it came to fighting was astonishing. Jordan couldn't help but be proud of her. *For* her.

After an eternity, they finally stopped fighting and drank water together at the climbing wall. Vlad rubbed a towel over his face and threw it around his neck. Then he pulled her braid, and she pushed him away as he walked out of the hall with the biggest smile Jordan had ever seen on his face.

The hall was relatively big. Not as big as the hall at the main base, but still—the space seemed smaller now that the only two people left were him and her. Jordan pushed away from what he was doing and found himself walking over to her.

"Raven," he said, and she turned around with a bottle to her lips.

She stopped drinking and said, "Hey." A layer of sweat coated her face, and even her eyes gleamed more than usual. Jordan noticed her braid was still completely intact. He remembered that a curl or two would always escape when they fought together.

A tiny solace.

Jordan gestured with his head to the mat. "You done?"

"You watched me fight just now, right?" she responded, but her tone was teasing.

Jordan inclined his head. "Guilty." He let his gaze travel down her body, past her hips and long, strong legs, back up to her beautiful face and hypnotic eyes.

Raven played with the ends of her braid; her cheeks were tinted a little pink from more than just working out. "What do you want, Jordan?"

*Everything.* The word lay on the tip of his tongue.

"A rematch," he said instead.

Letting go of her hair, she seized him up. "I don't think so." And put the bottle back against her lips before wrapping a towel around her body.

Jordan stared at her and shook his head. "Where are you going, Renée? We're not done here."

Raven smiled but continued walking backward. "I'm going to get some rest, General. Tomorrow is an important day." She saluted him, but her lips hinted at a teasing smile.

Something in his chest moved like a rabid animal at that smile. But she had already left the hall by the time Jordan could get anything past his lips.

That was the moment he realized Raven was going

to be the end of him. He was *far* past the stage of mere infatuation. Staying away from her was like the ocean resisting the moon's gravitational pull.

*Impossible.*

✯ ✯ ✯

"Look, Sev!" Ashley said as soon as the call went through and showed her with Sev in her lap.

Jordan's smile was instant as he watched his son claw at the screen. They sat in the study of Ashley's parents' house, where she and Sev had been staying since their fight about this mission and the engagement. He knew it had been the right decision to go, but he missed Sev a lot. He didn't know how soldiers with children managed at 3B for an extended period.

"Hey," Jordan said, smiling from ear to ear, waving at Sev and Ashley. "Man, you're growing up way too quickly."

"He is," Ashley agreed, grinning down at Sev. She looked back at the screen. "He's doing well. He'll start speaking in coherent sentences in no time."

"Not before I'm home he won't. Right, Sev?" Jordan said, causing Ashley to chuckle.

Sev babbled something unintelligible, more interested in something offscreen as his blonde curls disappeared beneath the camera, but the sound of his voice warmed Jordan's heart.

Jordan looked at Ashley. "How are you doing?"

Ashley swallowed, readjusting Sev in her lap, and pulled a hand through his blonde hair. "I'm doing well, actually. Been doing a lot of thinking." She looked up at the camera. "You?"

"Yeah, me too." Jordan scratched his throat. "We should

talk when I get back."

"We should," she agreed, and he knew her well enough to see what lurked beneath the surface. Their relationship was broken. They had squeezed it for all its worth. They should end their misery, for Sev's sake, and they both knew it.

Jordan was done trying to squeeze himself into this picture-perfect version of himself. It hurt Ashley, Sev, and everyone around him, including himself. And it had taken him thirty-three years to figure that out.

# CHAPTER 16

Everything was fucked, but I chose not to think about that.

Instead, Jordan and I returned to our regular schedule and never discussed Ashley or their dates again. Maybe that's why I experienced the sensation of a train hitting me when I first saw them together.

Jordan stood near a black luxury car, talking to someone, and he was having the time of his life. His smile was broad, genuine, as he listened with the utmost interest to what the woman before him had to say.

The woman—Ashley—had light brown hair streaked with blonde highlights. She wore a light grey smart suit styled with high stilettos. Despite the height of her heels, she barely reached Jordan's shoulders. I easily reached Jordan's chin *without* them.

Not that anyone was counting.

When Jordan turned around, I could see her face. The only way to describe her was *beautiful*. She had a sweet, heart-shaped face—all soft features: big, round eyes and full lips. Only after he placed a hand over the curve of her belly did I notice the slight bump.

She had to be, what, two or three months along now?

Her feet must be killing her.

Jordan kissed her on the cheek after exchanging some words and turned back around, walking inside the main base—the dimples in his cheeks pronounced.

He looked happy.

Ashley stood outside, watching him enter the enormous building through the glass doors. She was beaming as she waved. It was apparent she was crazy for him. But it was equally clear that she truly made him happy. She could give him what he deserved: a family to love and cherish.

The image of them together *made sense*. Like Hunter and Nikolai, who radiated a certain sense of *yes*. Both couples looked natural—which was obnoxiously rare.

It was only after Ashley had entered the back of the car that I walked toward the building and tried to glue back the pieces of my heart that had shattered.

On my way to my room, I passed familiar faces, but an announcement on one of the communication boards drew me in and was the only thing stopping me in my tracks.

*Continued missions SSU. Pilots and soldiers wanted.*

I tapped on the announcement.

*Do you have experience at the SSU, or are you a glider pilot ready for a new challenge? We are looking for immediately deployable soldiers to enter or fly the shadow plains, preferably between the ages of 20 and 40 at the time of enlistment. Experience with and on the shadow plains is preferred. Leadership positions are available.*

I didn't hesitate as I filled in my information and applied. Anything to get me away from the front-row seat of watching the man I was in love with start a family with someone else.

## NOW

The shadow plains were just how I remembered them; a little less scary with every year that passed, but haunting enough not to trick me into thinking it was safe.

Mutants still dwelled here. *Yes*, their numbers had dwindled; most of them driven back by our continual effort to spread the serum through the plains and take back land that used to be ours. Even so, you were a fool to think the possibility of crossing them was zero.

Damruin would be the farthest we had ever gone on foot.

We hadn't built any more bunkers throughout the plains because we were planning to expand our borders soon. Besides, hover planes could now fly almost anywhere… Which meant we were inevitably setting up camp in places that weren't safe.

The highway in front of us was abandoned—the area surrounding it stretching out wide—leaving the periphery open. Not a place a mutant colony would settle. They liked to remain hidden in the musty, dark corners of the world. Not literal plains, ironically enough. And not this cracked asphalt road that went on for miles and miles and miles.

It reminded me of the highway my father and I were found on.

Yesterday, our team received the final briefing. But besides the route we were taking—including the minor detour and stop at the hospital, which no one seemed to mind or commented on—and our exact target destination, the information remained scarce. No one had been reassured. Even Jordan had been restless—his foot tapping the floor during the entire briefing.

The first day in the shadows went by in a blur. I hadn't

spoken to anybody, fully enveloped in my down-spiraling thoughts. I tried my best to rationalize with myself and work through it like I had learned in therapy as a teenager, but none of it seemed to help.

Shadows were closing in on me, and I felt like I couldn't breathe the entire time.

Exhausted from our fourteen-hour walk and crippled by anxiety, I excused myself under the scrutiny of Jordan's prying eyes and sought a space to do some breathwork. But I was too far gone. Panic had etched its way into my brain. And part of me wished I had taken up any invitation from Colonel Keano for joined meals and shared sleeping arrangements. I had declined too soon and was too stubborn—afraid of the possibility of waking someone with my nightmares.

Even Jordan had come to my door, asking me if I was all right, and I had said *yes, but I want to be alone* because I was ashamed.

I sagged down on the floor of some abandoned building, took off my helmet, and let my head rest on my backpack. I hoped that my body's exhaustion would be enough to help me drift off, but my mind remained wide awake.

Anxiety forced its way through my body every time I closed my eyes. I knew—just *knew* that I would have a nightmare if I slept. The closer I got to Damruin, the worse it got. I felt it.

Somehow, my brain had given in, and I had drifted off. It couldn't have been long because I woke up, still dead-tired, with my body drenched in a layer of cold sweat and my throat parched. I sat upright and forced myself to drink as much water as possible.

My whole body felt weak, like a newborn deer on

trembling legs.

I was having a panic attack.

My sweat-coated body was shivering as I looked up at the ceiling, searching for a focus point, but I was met with grim darkness. I ached for the night sky to soothe my raging heart, but there were no stars to be seen there. A knot formed in my stomach at the thought of the city we were heading to—the answers I could get, whether or not I liked them.

My breathing quickened, and I pushed myself upright on wobbly legs. I braced my hands on the wall as tears forced their way into my eyes.

I hadn't had a panic attack like this since I was seventeen. I knew how this worked. If I couldn't get my breathing under control, I would start getting sick, gag, and fall down a well I wouldn't be able to get out of for some time.

*Shit.* With shaking hands, I pushed my sweat-stroked hair from my nape and let my neck cool down while I regulated my breath. I clenched my jaws and ground my molars, forcing myself to stay calm.

When I couldn't take it anymore, I pushed myself off the wall and into the hallway. I opened a window and looked up at the stars for help, but none of them reached out to soothe my anxiety.

On autopilot, I walked down the hallway to the room Jordan had told me he was in. I tried to be as silent as possible so that I wouldn't wake anyone. My head was determined, but my heart was not. Before I could stop myself, I knocked on the door. I cringed at my stupidity. *He needs his sleep, Raven! What the hell is wrong with you?* But before I could walk away, the door opened, revealing a bare-chested Jordan.

Jordan's brows pinched; his hair sleep mussed. "Raven?"

"I'm so sorry, Jordan." I held up my hand to him, with tears streaming down my face. "So, so sorry." But I couldn't get my feet to move. Didn't back away.

He stepped out of his room and grabbed one of my wrists, seizing me and pulling me into him. Only then did I let go, clutching my hand in a fist on his shoulder, my voice hoarse and pitched—body trembling all over. "I'm so sorry."

"For what?" He brushed a hand over my hair. "What happened?"

I shook my head. "I shouldn't have woken you."

He took my shoulders in his hand and bent his head a little to look me in the face, wiping away some tears. "Don't worry about that. Tell me what's wrong."

Shaking my head again, I put a hand over my mouth as silent sobs heaved through me. Jordan guided me inside his room without fuss and sat me down on a wooden bench, crouching in front of me with his hands on my knees. "Raven, talk to me." His voice was soothing but stern. He wanted to know what had happened.

"*What if she is a mutant?*" I said, voicing my greatest fear. "What if she's still out there? In Damruin?" The pain-filled question that had haunted me almost my entire life was finally spoken out loud. Shame burned through me for having woken him to my personal drama.

His brows smoothed, and his eyes turned soft. He let his hand travel to my chin, tipping it up to his face, so he looked me straight in the eye. "We'll deal with that when it arrives."

My eyes kept filling with all the unshed tears accumulated over the years. "I'm so afraid, Jordan. I'm *terrified*." It was the first time I had ever confessed it. "And I'm so sorry I'm disturbing you with this."

As if he sensed I was about the leave again, he took my hand in his. He kissed each wrist—sending goosebumps down my entire body. "It'll be okay, Raven. We'll face this together."

I didn't know anymore. Thoughts were crippling. But I knew that being here, with Jordan, helped.

He leaned back, took something from one of his backpacks—water, always water—and unscrewed the lid to hand me the bottle. "Drink something."

With trembling hands, I accepted the bottle and put it to my lips, taking a big sip. "What if it won't?" I asked a moment later. *Be okay.*

"It will." He said it with such finality that I almost believed him. "Because your mother lives here." He pointed to my heart. "You get to decide who she is or isn't. *You,* Raven."

I gave a small nod and took another sip of water before giving it back to him. I inhaled sharply as I wiped my face clean.

"You know…" He looked at me like he was deciding something. "When Sev is crying," Jordan grabbed my head between his strong hands. "I kiss him here." He brought a finger to my temple, where a steady beat pulsed. "Here." It trailed to my left cheek. "And here." His thumb tapped my right cheek.

I smiled, swiping my nose. "It helps him?"

Jordan nodded. "Every time."

"I'm sure you're an amazing father, Jordan."

He smiled a little. "He makes the job easy."

For the first time in my life, I didn't mind talking about Jordan being a father or him mentioning Sev. On the contrary—I loved that he was opening up to me, distracting me from my devastating thoughts while he shared an intimate part of his life with me.

And this moment… This moment was utterly and completely *ours*.

One of his hands still cupped my cheek. "Are you okay?" he asked me.

"No," I answered truthfully. "But I will be."

His eyes bore into mine as he nodded, looking at the tears that still fell, and wiping away their existence. I had to shut my eyes at his closeness because I couldn't focus anymore. His scent wrapped around me, his breaths filling the space between us. Then his thumb grazed my bottom lip, wiping away a stray tear.

I was breathless for an entirely different reason. Mourning the absence of his touch as he let go.

"Sleep here tonight," he whispered.

I opened my eyes again.

We looked at each other.

I wrapped my arms close to my chest. I wanted to, *but,* "I shouldn't."

"You could."

Slowly, I stood.

*Pull yourself together, Raven. You're a Brigadier General now. Act like it.* Shaking my head again, I looked up to meet his eyes. "Thank you, Jordan."

Then I left.

# CHAPTER 17

## 3 YEARS EARLIER

I got a response the day after I applied. Two days later, I had an interview. And a day after that, I got my final acceptance call. When six days had passed, I decided to leave without saying goodbye to Jordan. I just *knew* that he would try to change my mind and that he'd probably succeed, too.

I went home to spend a few days with my father before I had to miss him for an indefinite amount of time. During the interview, the military personnel had asked me if I would be open to the possibility of staying for an extended period, like a year or more. I almost *screamed* yes. This new job was a possibility to further develop myself as an infantry soldier, just as it was the perfect way to forget all about my feelings for a particular infantry general.

Fact was that I had to move on with my life, and that wouldn't happen as long as I stayed near him.

On the way back to the main base, I visited Hunter and told her I was leaving. She made me promise I wasn't running away from something, and I said I wasn't, but I could tell she didn't really believe me.

I entered my room, turned my computer on, and logged in to the army's communication system.

My heart skipped a beat as I checked my inbox and saw I had some unread messages from Jordan.

Our online conversations were brief. We usually talked face to face.

**J. Locke: Renée, 1700 tonight? Hotdogs after.**

**Me: Yes, sir.**

I had some unread messages from the days I had spent at my dad's.

**J. Locke: You don't know what you're missing. \*file shared\***

An image popped up when I clicked on the message. The photo from his webcam showed Jordan tearing into one of Ben's hotdogs like his life depended on it. Chuckling, I shook my head, but that laugh died soon after.

I would miss him so much.

Somewhere, I hated myself for what I was about to do. I would damage our bond irrevocably. But he was starting a new chapter of his life—one that had no place for me. Not in the way I wanted.

I had to break my own heart.

**J. Locke: When will you be back?**

I grimaced and read the following message.

**J. Locke: Was it today or tomorrow? Anyway: asses will be kicked.**

The last message was from today. I knew that if I answered now, Jordan would know I was back on base, and he would pop up unannounced like he often did. To minimize the chance of running into him before I left, I shut off the screen and went to bed.

The following day, I woke up way before my alarm, anxious, and made myself ready to leave. Finally, I answered Jordan's message.

**Me: Hi, Jordan. I'm going on a mission. Sorry that I didn't tell you. I genuinely wish you the best.**

I cringed at the last phrase. The man was having a baby, for crying out loud. I was erasing myself from his life. It was such a dick move I almost debated not going and canceling the whole thing. But as I pictured myself sucking it up and watching him form a perfect little family, I bit my cheek and pressed send. Then, I logged off and left my room, permanently shutting the door to this life.

**(Unread) J. Locke: Funny! You know there are better ways to get out of training, right? So... still up for tonight or not?**

**(Unread) J. Locke: Are you fucking serious?**

**(Unread) J. Locke: You're at the SSU? When I asked about Major Renée at the main base, they asked if I meant Lieutenant Colonel Renée. Hunter confirmed it. What the hell, Raven?**

**(Unread) J. Locke: I'm so fucking pissed. Why didn't you tell me? I don't**

understand. This isn't you. But it's not like you're reading these messages or will reply to them anyway, so good luck with everything.

(Unread) J. Locke: I'm sorry. I'm trying to be angry but only feel disappointed. When are you coming back, Raven? This week was hard enough as it was. I don't want to do this without you.

(Unread) J. Locke: Please answer...

NOW

The memory of my hometown would be tainted for the rest of my life.

Damruin was nowhere near how I remembered it.

Part of me was glad, and the other part wanted to weep at all that was lost. I was young when I had to flee the city, so I didn't recognize most of the blocks. But I mourned everything I did remember. The buildings were decaying, overgrown with plants that had had free play over the last decades.

We had to be quiet and walk with one eye on our heartbeat sensors, as mutants still inhabited the city. From footage of our hover planes, we already knew that the three mutant colonies here weren't close to where we currently were, but they still hunted—and Damruin was a significant hunting ground.

The further we walked into the city, the more I recognized it. Especially the little things; a small fountain on a small square surrounded by untamed nature and houses, a supermarket I used to visit with my parents, or the large school building, where I had gone more times than I could count. Where I had made friends—friends that were probably dead. I didn't know. We never heard about them again.

All because of this godsdamned mutation.

There was one street, though, that I would recognize even if it had been buried under a mountain of dust. I hadn't expected to stumble upon it like this. The way through Damruin was blurry; even if I had wanted to go here, I wouldn't have known how.

I stopped walking. An aching pain gripped my chest in a vise. Tears clouded my vision, and I had to remind myself to keep breathing. Just keep breathing.

*Everything will be okay.*

*You got this.*

"We can set up camp here," I whispered, but everyone heard me.

Jordan turned around. I couldn't see his eyes because of the night vision goggles, but his mouth stretched into a grim line. "All right."

Tension cut the air as I lead the group behind me. None except Jordan knew this was where I grew up, and I liked to keep it that way. I didn't want their pity.

I couldn't distinguish color through the night vision goggles, but I was sure it was still there. Faded, yes, but definitely present. It *had* to be. Weeds had dominated the small gardens in front of the houses, and plants that could survive darkness had taken over and blocked most of the front doors from view.

Then, I spotted it. It was still some houses along, but I couldn't tear my eyes away.

My childhood home.

I quickened my pace and put one foot in front of the other as I made my way down the street.

The garden my mother had tended to so passionately was gone, destructed by more than just time. I inhaled sharply at the pain in my chest—my body. I stalked forward, finding the door ajar.

My heart thudded in my throat.

"Wait here," I told the others, but Jordan walked up right behind me, ignoring my command.

I pushed the door open a little further and looked inside. Destroyed.

The house was completely destroyed.

Nothing about it resembled my childhood home. Somehow, I had thought—hoped—the house would have still been like it was when my dad and I had closed the door behind us. But the aftermath of the crisis had wrecked through the city long after we were gone. People that hadn't been able to flee had probably stayed here. Mutants...

The house was a one-story home with only two bedrooms, a bathroom, and a living room. It would be big enough to rest with six people.

As Jordan walked over to check the bathroom, I opened the door to my parent's room and found the frame of their bed containing a mattress that had been plucked, as if it had stored gold inside. The shelves on the wall had all been torn down—glass littering the floor. The chest of drawers was havocked—most of the clothes inside either taken or destroyed.

I quickly stepped out of the room, my hand clenching the doorknob like it was a lifeline.

I opened the other door—to the room that had once been mine. It was a small space, and looking at it made me wince.

This had been my sanctuary; the four walls, the single

bed, the vanity mirror with the little desk. But now, the single bed had collapsed—the mattress gone entirely. The four walls had punch holes, and the vanity mirror was fractured.

I heard Jordan tell the rest to come in, but I just stood there, reliving how helpless little me had felt. Her life had been ripped away from underneath her in a flash.

Colonel Keano and First Lieutenant Gabon's soft voices filled the house while Major Britton was still installing safety measures outside in the street and in front of the house. If mutants got close, we would have enough time to get away. I heard Colonel Kilich get ready to make dinner in our makeshift kitchen, which comprised of a sole gas burner.

A hand landed on my shoulder, but I didn't react. Didn't turn around. I just stood there—frozen in the tiny space that had once been mine.

"Raven?" Jordan's voice sounded close, and I turned around to see that he had taken off his night vision goggles.

I did the same and waited for the rods and cones in my eyes to adjust to the dark. "Not now."

Jordan promptly left the room, closing the door behind him.

I let myself sink to the floor and clutched my frail heart as I looked at the stars through the small window.

★ ★ ★

I didn't know how much time had passed when Jordan opened the door and sat down beside me.

"How are you doing?" he asked, and my head lulled his way.

"Fine, considering," I answered truthfully. After seeing him last night, I had gotten a couple of hours of sleep between waking on and off and drinking a lot to compensate loss of sweat. That morning, I'd woken up hungry and quivering, but after a careful meal, something to drink, and a walk in the crisp air, I had been *fine, considering*. "You?"

"Me too."

We were once again silent and let the conversation die. I looked at the small room that had once been mine and back at the man in it. No doubt young Raven would have had a crush on him, too. Although I think calling my feelings for him a *crush* would be an understatement.

In the dim light of the stars, Jordan offered me a small, heartbreaking smile that felt so familiar that I wanted to run out of the house and pull him closer simultaneously.

"How are you and Ashley?" I asked, pointing out the elephant in the room. I wanted to know. I was involved now, whether or not I wanted to be.

Jordan's face changed, and part of me was relieved—the part that was smart enough to protect me against myself. He focused on his hands, unable to meet my eyes, moistening his lips before he replied, "Not well."

I sat up straighter as he looked at me, my heartbeat spiking. That wasn't the answer I'd been expecting.

His eyes changed, pupils dilated, and I sensed he was going to say something important. *Life-altering.*

Jordan exhaled—his intense eyes piercing me to the spot. "I made many mistakes, Raven. But *not* choosing you has always been my biggest regret."

I gave him absolutely nothing, keeping my face blank as I stopped breathing.

"Look." He wetted his lips, thinking about how he would put his next words. "I won't say I regret having Sev because I *don't*. But I would lie if I told you I hadn't thought about undoing that night with Ashley a million times if it meant you and I would have been together."

There was a pregnant pause in which my heart started hurting. Knowing *that*—hurt. The fact that he still hadn't chosen me—hurt. All that we had lost splayed out before me—hurt.

I wouldn't ask him to choose me. I would *never* ask him to pick me over his child or family. I was done. Too much time had passed. I had to get over it, and he had to let me do it.

Jordan wisely kept quiet as I stood from the floor and started walking out of the room to set up my sleeping arrangements in the living room with the others.

"Good night, Jordan," I said, unable to look him in the eye.

I wouldn't be able to bear the love I'd see there.

# CHAPTER 18

The digital screen buzzed as I tapped the map of the shadow plains and zoomed in on the area I wanted to investigate. We had mapped many mutant colonies in this area over the last couple of weeks and spread the serum throughout the region during the previous three flights. Five colonies were targeted, so we expected to find mutant children in these locations, and the main base wanted at least three.

"Lieutenant Colonel."

I turned around to a saluting soldier. "Yes?"

"The General is here," she said. "I've sent him to your office."

"Thank you." I turned back to the screen and turned it off.

Once every two months, someone from the capital came to check the mission's progress. This time, I'd heard from Hunter that Nikolai was coming to check if we were well on our way with the set targets.

But it wasn't Nikolai who awaited me inside my office.

It was Jordan.

I halted briefly as everything inside me wanted to turn back around. The two sides of me conflicted as I shut the door behind me. It was a weird contradiction; the butterflies fluttered at the sight of him, and my stomach wanted to empty itself.

"Lieutenant Colonel Renée," Jordan said, but I detected irritation in his tone.

I inhaled deeply before replying, "Jordan." I didn't feel like playing his game.

"Seriously, Raven?" he exclaimed; the words aggravated. "*This* is what I have to do to speak with you? Get a response?" He kept standing in the corner.

Carefully, I forced myself to sit down behind my desk, the movements of my limbs stiff. Seeing him after this time felt like a blow to the face.

"Why are you here, Jordan?"

"Why am I here?" He cocked his head like he was seriously wondering if I was sound in the head. "The question is, why the hell are *you* here? You think it's normal to disappear without saying a word?"

"I did—say something."

"You left me a fucking message!"

*And* I told Hunter. "Listen, Jordan, I don't know how you got Nikolai to let you take over, but let's just review the progress."

"I'm not doing anything before I get answers."

"That's it, isn't it?" I yelled suddenly, slamming my hand on the table as I rose. "You think you're owed answers?"

Jordan stared at me, clearly taken aback, but his rage was far from gone.

I walked up to him and pointed my finger at his chest. "I *owe* you absolutely nothing."

He was shaking his head in disbelief. "I thought you cared about me."

"That's the fucking problem, Jordan!"

He pushed a hand through his hair. "*Gods.* What did I do for you to hate me so much?"

My fury ebbed away, but the void was replaced with grief. I didn't desire this gap between us. Of course, I didn't. But I needed to protect myself.

I tried to hide my feelings. "There's still a lot to discuss," I said coolly—far from how I felt as my body was burning.

Jordan's nostrils flared. "I don't know where to start," he answered sarcastically.

"Then please don't." I turned away from him. "I can't do *this,* Jordan."

He touched my hand, his fingers grazing mine. "Do what?"

"Being near you." *It hurts too much.*

Jordan's eyes widened, and he dropped his hand in shock. I looked away from him. I couldn't handle the rejection in his face.

"You didn't have to go, Raven," he murmured. "If you had told me…"

"You're building a family, Jordan."

Jordan rubbed a hand over his face and folded his lips together as he stared at the ceiling. Then he bowed his face, his eyes finding mine.

"You think I planned for this to happen?" he asked. "Please come back. We'll be able to figure it out—together."

My laugh was cynical. "You mean we, as in, the three of us? This is hardly the moment to forget Ashley." *Who was carrying his child.*

Jordan swallowed. "No. I meant *us.*" He pointed between

us. "It doesn't make sense without you."

My swallow was visible. "I owe you nothing," I repeated.

"I would have picked you," he said, voice hoarse with desperation. "But I promised Ashley to try."

I cringed away from him. I tried to push back the floodgate of tears. He might just as well have stabbed me in the heart.

"Why are you here, Jordan?" I asked him.

Silence.

"To get you back."

"Do you even hear yourself?" I asked him, irritation flaring. "You say you would've chosen me, but you won't end your relationship with Ashley because you gave her your *word*. And I get it, Jordan, I do. But please don't ask this of me."

Jordan turned my way, and I saw I had hit a little too close to home. "I know that—"

"Please go back to Barak." I closed my eyes and fought back the tears swelling behind my lids. "Right now, I want nothing from you, least of all your excuses." I cleared my throat and straightened. "I'll send a report to Nikolai about the progress. You can go now."

We stared at each other for a moment and saw the truth mirrored in each other's eyes. Finally, he nodded and left the space.

I folded my arms around my body. When I was confident that Jordan had left the building, I let my tears flow freely. My heart throbbed painfully because the truth hurt. He still had the power to twist the knife in my heart even deeper.

And I still wanted *everything* he had to offer.

NOW

I woke up disorientated.

At first, I thought I was having a nightmare; my nightmares usually starred my old home.

But no. This was real life—and I was really there.

We ate a quick, dry meal and drank some water, careful about not consuming too much. We were already a third through our stock, and the mission wasn't over yet.

Our black field uniforms weren't the comfiest clothes to sleep in, but it had been unsafe to wear anything else in such an unprotected area. I redid my braid and noticed the golden star embroidered on my shoulder.

*I got this.*

I inserted my earpiece and turned it on. "Renée, checking in."

Vlad's voice sounded immediately. "Copy that, Renée." Only Jordan and I had a direct line with him, as he was the head of the monitoring room while we were outside. The knowledge that he was on the other side assured me. "We flew a hover plane over Damruin a couple of hours ago, and the mutant locations are still the same. Good luck."

"Thanks, Brigade General," I said, muting the line as my eyes locked with Jordan's from across the room.

After we had packed our stuff, I looked back one last time—my childhood home, the place that had haunted my dreams and nightmares. I wasn't planning on coming back here. Not even when the city is rebuilt. Things would never go back to how they once were. My Damruin chapter was closing, and I had no intention of ever opening it again.

Shutting the door behind me, I walked out of the tiny, one-story home where a small family had lived, loved, and lost.

"Ready?" Jordan asked me.

I nodded firmly. "Let's go."

Jordan gestured to the rest of the group to walk, and we made our way through the city together to the hospital, where the answer to the most pressing question of my life would hopefully be answered.

★ ★ ★

It took a couple of hours before the hospital finally loomed up in the distance, but we couldn't move faster because of the constant threat of mutants hanging over us. The rest of the group hadn't asked why we were going to the hospital—Jordan had informed them as if it was a pit stop along the way to our final destination.

The hospital was large. Larger than I had expected. Which made the half hour Jordan had granted me even less than I would probably need. I would have to scour the eight-floor building by running.

I wondered where they kept patient folders.

We stopped in front of the main entrance, consisting of a glass wall with glass doors that had almost entirely been destroyed.

Someone took my arm, and I jumped a little. Jordan took me aside. "You're sure?"

I nodded. "I'm sure."

He let go of my arm.

Colonel Keano stepped closer while the rest of them started inspecting the street. "You're going in alone, Brigadier General?"

"I am."

"I can come with you," she offered.

I shook my head. "You stay here. I will do this alone."

"*All clear*," we received through our earpiece as Major

Britton walked back out of the hospital. The others were scattered on the streets surrounding the enormous building.

Jordan was still looking at me, so I turned to him. "If there's any sign of danger, you leave me behind."

He said nothing.

I focused on Colonel Keano. "You copy that?"

"Yes, Brigadier General."

Jordan looked at his watch. "You've got thirty minutes. *Go.*"

I sprinted away from them through the broken glass, careful to make no sounds as I maneuvered my way around the shards on the ground. As soon as I was clear, I ran for the nearest floor plan I could find. What was I looking for? An archive of sorts? *Surgery*—no. *Orthopedics*—no. *Neurology*, no? *Genetics*, maybe?

*Hurry, Raven.*

Then I saw it; a sticker covering one of the departments, with *crisis* printed on it. Yes! I trailed a finger over the board to the right, finding it was on the fourth floor.

Stairs—there would be stairs at an emergency exit. There *had* to be. Noticing an exit sign, I ran to it.

I opened the door, inhaling sharply as I saw the stairs. Taking three steps at a time, I sprinted up, up, up until I almost jumped on another flight of stairs before I noticed the large four on the wall.

*Focus.*

I pushed open the large door and entered the abandoned hospital floor. Glass littered the floor here, too. Hospital beds stood in the hallway, and stuff belonging to people no longer here lay scattered over the floor like they had been in a hurry to get away from there.

To be fair, walking through a long-abandoned hospital

with no one there was scary as fuck. I grabbed my heartbeat sensor out of habit, checking if there weren't any mutants— or other living creatures—lurking around.

I continued walking, trying to ignore the dried blood and the remnants of a skeleton that had probably been there for *decades*. When I thought about it, this would probably have been one of the most terrifying floors to have worked at.

Just keep on walking. Keep on walking. Keep on—

I passed a door that said *staff only* and tried to push it open. It wouldn't budge. Taking out my silenced gun, I shot the lock, destroying the wood surrounding it. I found myself in a larger room with a small kitchen, but continued and looked at a glass wall that led into a small office containing archive drawers.

One of the archive drawers said *current patients*, but as I looked through the names, there was no *Natasha*.

"*Fuck*," I cursed, looking through the office—to no avail.

I rushed out into the hallway and ran the length of the hall, looking into most rooms, until I found another locked door with *staff only* on it. I tried the door, which was unlocked, and entered a storage room containing different devices, more tools to help the sick, and—more filing cabinets!

Opening the drawers, I noticed they were in alphabetical order, arranged by last name, and I gasped as I found hundreds upon hundreds of folders. Clicking on my light again, I clamped it between my lips.

I looked for *Renée*, but couldn't find anything. My heart hammered viciously in my chest. I checked the rest of the drawers in case the order had been tampered with or someone had replaced a file the wrong way. The last names were blurring into each other, so I started looking for a *Natasha* instead.

I was sweating now. Had my mother gone to this hospital? Damruin didn't have another hospital, *right*? I opened a Natasha's file, but the woman staring back at me wasn't my mother.

Gods-fucking-damnit.

"Raven, it's time to get back," Jordan suddenly bellowed in my ear. "*Now.*"

There was no need to panic.

I looked at my watch. Inhaled. I reminded myself to keep breathing. To relax. To Keep looking. I had ten minutes left. My fingers skimmed through the folders. Caution braced me for the disappointment that would no doubt come any minute.

*She wasn't there.*

A bead of sweat trickled past my brow.

"Mutant activity has been spotted two streets from the hospital," another voice boomed, and I took the flashlight from my lips.

"Vlad?" I hissed. "Are you serious?"

"Fucking hell, Vlad," Jordan's voice thundered. "I said not to tell her."

My fingers clamped around another folder that said *Natasha,* but I didn't care that the last name was *Bruna* as I opened it and saw my mother staring back at me.

"She has to get out of there, and she wasn't listening to you."

"Don't—"

"*Shut the fuck up,* both of you, or I'll mute you."

I had to concentrate on the words before me, and my eyes were getting tired.

It really was my mother in the photo. They must have messed up her last name. And her maiden name... The name was vaguely familiar.

No. That wasn't important right now. My fingers almost tore the folder open as I scanned the documents inside. It contained a birth registration, which I couldn't look at now—medical history and intake forms, including a diagnosis.

It had been the mutation.

And my mother—she…

She had died here.

She had *died* here!

My relief was potent. It wrapped a blanket of reassurance around my body like the one I had lost when my father and I had fled. I closed my eyes. *Thank you. Thank you. Thank you.*

"*Now*, Raven." Jordan's voice was uncompromising. Suddenly aware of my surroundings, I didn't care. My mother wasn't a mutant, and my heart thudded with renewed strength because of it.

I tore her picture from the file with the rest of the papers, stashed them inside my uniform, and got out of there.

# CHAPTER 19

(Unread) J. Locke: Raven... I don't know what to do, but I realize now that I made a mistake by visiting you. I won't bother you again.

NOW

We stopped at an abandoned warehouse that Vlad had cleared for the night. The rest of the group had already stationed themselves in one of the rooms downstairs, but I couldn't sleep. There was too much going on, and I had to be outside—see the night sky. Leaning down onto the railing of the old warehouse's rooftop, I looked at the darkened city. Trails of life still hid inside its corners: a packed suitcase in the streets; front doors left wide open in a hurry; a child's toy dressed in mold. All withered by age.

*Forgotten.*

Just like my mother had been. She had died alone in that hospital. Just another name—another patient they lost to the mutation.

My gaze was pulled upwards as a falling star soared

through the sky, leaving behind a trail of a bright, electric blue color before disappearing. The night sky was the only thing that had remained the same throughout my life. It had been my comfort zone, the place my eyes could wander when life on the ground became a bit too much. The tiny, sparkling diamonds always seemed to lure me in—beckon me closer.

If only I could. I would have found a home amongst the stars, somewhere else, far away from this wretched planet.

I stared into space, *wondering…*

"Raven."

The sound behind me dragged me back to the roof, and I turned around slowly.

I found Jordan already looking at me. He had been so happy for me when I had told him the news about my mother. Now he raised his chin a little and let his eyes wander to the sky—where mine had been—as he stepped closer and dropped his hands to the railing beside me. His eyes reflected the stars he looked up to, and I couldn't seem to tear mine away from them. Shadows formed in the hollows of his cheeks, and when his face turned to mine, the darkness seemed to swallow his eyes whole.

I kept looking—transfixed by him.

*Not choosing you has always been my biggest regret.*

Jordan reached out a hand and brushed a stray curl behind my ear. "You are so beautiful."

I turned my face away. "Don't."

"Stop fighting it," Jordan whispered as he stepped forward.

"Stop giving me reasons to."

His gaze burned into my face as he stood next to me, fingers curling into fists.

All my clothes felt too tight, too constricting. The creatures fluttering in my stomach were no longer butterflies but moths—the frantic animals thrashed inside me without finesse. They felt possessed. Wild. *Oppressed*. Like they didn't know what to do with themselves, either.

My breathing turned uneven as Jordan's fingers twined with mine—featherlight touches, exploring the boundaries I had set, which were none at all.

I looked at him again, his ash blonde hair turning silver in the starlight. The muscles in his cheeks moved beneath his skin, jaws clenching.

The truth was splayed out on the table. My lips parted a fraction, my heart hammering in my throat. The fight left my body, and the frown on my face disappeared as I whispered his name.

Jordan translated the message, his eyes searching mine for any sign telling him otherwise. He let go of a breath— one he had held for a long time—as he agreed, "Yes."

I turned to him fully, and he gripped my face, his fingers splaying. Thumbs caressed the corners of my mouth. He looked at my lips, shook his head once, and then captured them. Hard.

There was no room for argument.

I had imagined this moment a million times; how it would feel to be kissed by Jordan Locke. How it felt to be his sole focus, the receiver of his undivided attention.

But everything paled at this.

His soft lips were firm, demanding, attentive, sweet. I felt them curve into a smile when I wrapped my arms around his neck, pulling him closer, deepening the kiss, and sliding my tongue between his lips where it met his halfway.

Everything about him felt like a warm embrace. And

for the first time since arriving in Damruin, I felt safe. Cherished. *Home.*

His tongue fought mine as if his life depended on it—as if he had something to prove. As if he had been waiting all his life for this moment. To overpower me.

I knew better than to give in. My hands gripped his hair roughly, and I pulled him closer.

One of his hands went to my throat. He applied light pressure and pushed me back hard against a door.

A moan escaped me of its own accord.

His tongue seized mine, and it was the only thing in the world I could focus on at that moment.

Jordan pulled me flush against him, walking me through a door and into a room the gods knew where—I didn't care.

I found myself sinking into something hard, looking up at him.

Hoarsely, he said, "You don't get to regret this."

My thumbs found their way along his jaw, trailing a path upwards until they gripped his soft hair. A sound escaped his chest when I pulled him closer to me.

I was beaming up at him, but as my hands trailed to the collar of his shirt, grave emotions clogged my throat. My hands hitched at his buttons. It was almost too much to bear. As if Jordan knew I was faltering, he raised his own hands and started unbuttoning his shirt. His eyes were a dark blue as they focused on me with feral intensity.

"Do you—" he started, but I cut him off by pressing my lips to his because I knew I wouldn't dare to give him the answer he wanted. I knew that if I did, the moment would be over. Instead, I wanted to lose myself in it for the rest of my life.

His hands trailed to the hem of his shirt, which he pulled

off, revealing his bare chest. He consisted of hard, powerful lines with contrasting soft spots, but as I put my hands on his body, I knew that the softness was only an illusion. Everything about him was unyielding.

Before my hand could wander, Jordan covered it with his, making me look up. "I swear it, Raven." *Dare to regret it,* his eyes seemed to say.

My hands curled around him until my nails embedded themselves into his skin. "Stop talking, Jordan," I said hoarsely, burying his words somewhere deep, where I hoped I couldn't find them anymore.

He shook his head but didn't smile. This was as serious for him as it was for me. This moment was our story's beginning, middle, and ending—the only moment that mattered.

He put a hand on the nape of my neck and pulled me away from the wall, pushing me toward a wooden bench. Slowly, he let me sit down and lean back—all the while looking at him. His eyes were darker than they had been before, daring me to do something he didn't like. But I wasn't afraid of him.

How could I be?

Slowly, I took off my shirt while he was looking at me without moving. But as I took it off and stripped myself from my bra, the last layer before I was bared before him, something in him switched.

I had always suspected Jordan to be... *different* in the bedroom. All easy smiles and flirting until you stalked closer. Only then would you witness a version of him he let very few people see. But nothing could have prepared me for the primal look now visible in his eyes.

He bent forward roughly, covering me, chest heaving

like he had been running for his life. He wriggled a knee between my legs and let a hand trail to my throat like he was trying to get a scope of what he could work with. Like he wanted to see how far he could go.

I wanted to make sure he knew the answer was to go as far as he wished to, but before I could say anything, his hand was already caressing my breasts, my side, my waist, my hips, until he arrived at the edge of my pants. There, he let a finger trail underneath before curving it and pulling the pants down.

Seconds passed while more and more of my naked skin was revealed to him. It was unbearable, but I knew better than to interfere.

Jordan *clearly* knew what he was doing.

He pulled my pants down completely and let a finger roam over the seams of my panties—leaving a shudder in its wake. He sat between my legs, which were confined in the pants that hung at my ankles.

"Fuck, Raven," he sighed as he felt the damp fabric. He pulled it to the side and let one of his fingers rub over the source of my wetness.

He grabbed my hips roughly, pulling me to the edge of the bench as he sat on his knees before me, legs still locked firmly in place. There was nothing for a moment until he let one finger—two—enter me slowly, and the moan I had wanted to suppress slipped out.

I saw stars when I felt his tongue glide over my clit.

Jordan let me linger on the edge of madness and pulled back—pushing me to that edge and letting me shudder with the need to come before he pulled back again. He was playing me like a fiddle. Knew exactly which string to touch and did it over and over again.

"Come for me, Raven," Jordan finally murmured.

I erupted.

Jordan's hand clamped down over my lips as he tried to mute the moans I elicited. Remembering where we were, I tried to stifle them, too.

When I had finally landed, I said breathlessly, "My turn."

I let myself glide off the bench until I sat on my knees before him. He looked down at me, his hand cupping my chin, thumb caressing my mouth.

My hands rubbed over his legs, upwards, over the bulge in his crotch, to his fly, which I opened slowly before I pulled down his pants. Jordan tracked my every move.

His boxers were next, and I looked at his dick, moistening my lips as I took hold of his shaft.

Looking up, eyes meeting, I opened my lips and wrapped them around him. My eyes shut the moment I tasted him.

It felt so good.

*He felt good.*

Jordan growled like I was torturing him.

I took him all the way, my hands coming up to massage his balls as he slid in and out relentlessly. I, too, dragged it on for longer than necessary, and he burrowed his hands in my hair from the restraint he had put on himself.

The moment I opened my eyes, I could see he was close to his own release, and I moved even faster, harder, and more urgently—letting him know he could come. Our gazes locked the entire time. His hand wrapped in my hair and gripped it the moment I felt him swell even more. My nails pressed into his backside while his lips parted a little, and his chest moved at an urgent pace.

Releasing a loud groan, Jordan stilled and came in the

back of my throat.

I swallowed until only his taste remained, and I saw something change in his gaze now that the haziness of desire had subsided. Something I hadn't been ready to see: pride, possessiveness, and—

I remembered why we couldn't do this. Too late.

*Ashley.*

He was in a relationship.

A relationship I knew about. And we had—we had—

All the blood in my body rushed from my head, and I felt like I was floating. My cheeks burned wildly as I let go of him and cleaned myself up, putting space between us— avoiding his eyes.

Jordan clicked his tongue. "No, Raven." He stepped closer, but I moved away from him, flinching. "Raven, look at me."

I shook my head once and gathered my clothes, putting them back on.

He stood behind me and gripped my wrist. "Don't pull this shit on me right now."

I twisted my wrist to make him lose his grip, and he made a disapproving sound.

"You know better than to walk away, Raven," he warned.

An indignant breath left me. "That's what you think I do? *Walk away?*"

His gaze turned heated. "Isn't that what you always do when feelings get too real?"

I sighed, frustrated with him and myself, as I pulled my shirt back over my head and turned to grab the door handle to pull it open, but Jordan slammed his hand against it—keeping it closed. He loomed over me, and I watched as his nostrils flared. "You knew there was no going back from that."

"Let me out." I refused to meet his eyes.

He let his hand glide off the door, and I opened it to leave. But as I stepped out of the room, he said, "I warned you, Raven."

# CHAPTER 28

2 YEARS EARLIER

**(Unread) J. Locke: Congratulations on your promotion to lieutenant colonel.**

## NOW

I couldn't meet Jordan's eyes, but I had felt them on me the entire time.

I needed space to grasp what had happened and process the emotions it had left me with in its wake. But *not* right now. There was no room for it in the shadow plains. I had to focus. We had an important job today, and something in me told me it would be dangerous.

More than ever before.

The instructions were simple; get inside the building, find out who or what is causing the activity, and find out why they're there. Shoot to kill if the situation arises. And go back home.

We had packed and moved on quickly, making our way through the abandoned streets.

Before leaving the warehouse, we had to ensure the

mutants had pulled back a little before escaping the street. They had been close to the entrance, within hearing distance, so we had to be careful not to make too many sounds.

I walked out front, taking the lead.

Jordan was walking at the back, as he usually did, and I couldn't help but wonder what he was thinking. Did last night run in a loop through his head, too? Did he still feel my lips on his skin like I did his?

I was officially *the other woman* now—the woman I *never* wanted to be to him. I'd rather be a stranger. But we were never going back to being strangers, not after last night.

"The building is at ten o'clock," Vlad's voice interrupted my thoughts, and I halted, looking for the building.

Jordan had gotten the message and walked forward until he stood next to me. "It has a rooftop," he pointed out.

*Which meant we were going to climb it and enter from above instead of below.* The safer option.

In silence, we walked closer, slowly approaching the building, and the rest of the team lined up against the wall. I was the lightest of the group, so I started unclasping my backpack and gun, but kept my knives strapped to my body in several places. First Lieutenant Gabon and Colonel Kilich took my stuff, strapping it to their bodies instead. Major Britton brought me the rope and buckles, which I fastened to my uniform instead.

The climbing part was easy; there was a rain pipe going all the way up at the side of the building, and it was only three stories high. I could climb this. But climbing without alerting our arrival was the hard part.

Jordan walked over, anchoring me with one hand on my shoulder. "You got this?"

I looked up at him and swallowed. His touch ignited a

flame within me. Memories of last night flooded my mind and I forced my breathing to remain calm.

"I do," I said, and grabbed the pipe, pulling it a little to ensure it was secured and wouldn't collapse when I put my entire weight on it. With one last look up, I put my feet on the other sides of the pipe, and started climbing, pulling the pipe to me to create a good grip for my feet—one step at a time.

I moved my hands, keeping my body weight pressed back into my feet. The pipe groaned with the next movement—the metal bending beneath my hands. It better hold me, though, because I was almost past the first floor, and falling from a couple of feet wasn't exactly deathly, but it would hurt a whole damn lot if I fell on my ass.

Hand, hand, grip. Shuffle feet. Rest. Repeat.

As I continued my path upward, sounds came from the right, on the second level, and I looked in terror as I watched a window opening. I hadn't made *that* much sound, right? The pipe's groaning was just as loud as the wind that swooshed past the buildings and the trees whose leaves rustled.

Laughter sounded, and someone stuck out a hand holding a cigarette, which they tipped down so the ash made its way down to my group, who were still lining the wall.

If the person the hand belonged to would look down, he'd see them. If he looked up, he'd see me.

My muscles were burning from the effort to keep still.

The person kept tipping his cigarette—even blowing some smoke into the crisp air.

After what seemed like an eternity, they pressed the cigarette out against the windowsill and threw it outside, closing the window again.

*Thank the fucking gods.*

Inhaling sharply, I quickly continued on my way. I was almost there. I didn't dare look down at my group, afraid another window would open—or worse yet, they would get over to the roof and smoke there.

Arriving at the top, I had to reach one arm over the ledge and peek over it—but no one was there. I climbed over it and looked around to find an old roof vent protruding from the roof. Walking over to it, I unwrapped the rope from my waist and made a loop around the metal vent. I tugged it, testing the cylinder's strength. Fastened the string with a clasp, I let the rest of it trail behind me as I made my way back to the ledge.

I threw the rest of the rope down, being careful to fling it far away from the building. It would make a lot of sound if sturdy rope thudded against a glass window.

Jordan caught it, pulling it taut before it could fall back. He tested it, pulling his weight on it, and I looked back at where the rope looped around the metal. Nothing happened. Not even a groan. I stuck out my thumb, and he passed the rope to Colonel Kilich.

Swiftly, one after the other, they made their way up—not one window opening during that time. The last to come up was Jordan, who pulled up the rope but didn't unfasten it.

The door to the roof was locked, as we had expected. Major Britton started picking the lock, and in no time, the door popped open with a sigh—groaning slightly as we opened it halfway.

We descended into the building, making almost no sound. My heartbeat sensor showed life, about five spots, one less than us, but it didn't show what floor they were. Jordan beckoned us closer and signaled in different ways.

Britton and Keano remained on this floor, Kilich and Gabon would go all the way down, and Jordan and I would go to the middle floor—where we *knew* people would be.

We all went our separate ways, four of us descending. When we arrived at the second floor, Kilich and Gabon continued down the stairs.

When they were gone, Jordan held his ear against the door and listened. His large frame curved around it as he stuck his head around the edge, looking inside. With one wave of his hand, I followed him onto the floor—both of us going in different directions.

Before we parted, we looked at each other; a silent convey passing between us. His helmet and night vision goggles shielded half his face, but with a twitch of his lips, he turned around and walked away—gun out.

Although I preferred knives, I, too, had a silenced gun in hand and made my way through the floor. I turned off my earpiece to hear better and focus on my surroundings.

Many rooms were open and abandoned, but I heard someone speak around the corner. As the person started walking, I quickly dashed into the room opposite me, hiding behind the door. The footsteps faded into the hallway, and I darted across it to where the person had come from. At the door, I heard nothing, so I slipped inside the room and closed the door softly behind me.

After inspecting the room, I found a desk with a lot of documents on it. Not old documents, *new* ones. I tried to read with my night vision goggles, but it took too much effort. Carefully, I removed my helmet and night vision goggles and pulled a small flashlight from my pockets. I turned it on and shoved it between my teeth, taking the documents from the table and holding them closer.

My blood turned cold.

These documents were *Borzian*.

Making sure my recording camera captured all the papers, I quickly put them down again. Squatting, I opened more drawers, which contained even more documents.

Most of them were unreadable, all written in Borzian. But when I found some that were in Ardenian, my breathing hitched.

I recognized one name on them.

Domasc.

My eyes scanned the documents fervently. The more I read, the more the ice in my veins burned. I was looking at messages from Domasc and someone else, but I couldn't figure out who that was.

*You promised me three years, and they're almost over. The voting will be soon.*

*The bird is on its way. Don't threaten me, Ana. I have more important things to think about than your games.*

*I will be there soon.*

Then, from the last couple of weeks.

*The bird is coming sooner than I promised. What will I get in return?*

*A peacock has joined the package. The entire flock is yours. Don't return them. They are of no use to me.*

*Yes, all of them. A present.*

The messages made no sense to me. It was a conversation between Domasc and someone else—maybe even someone he had a relationship with. It had to have something to do with why they were here. Why we were here…

And the *bird*. Domasc kept going on about birds in all of his messages.

Light footsteps sounded behind me, and I turned around

in a flash, dropping the flashlight from my mouth. I saw the outline of a person walking through the door opening, but immediately lost sight of them. A beat later, my head was slammed against the wall behind me—and the person in question ripped off my body camera, tearing it off and shattering it with a weighted object.

Then, the person, a woman, started speaking, and the blood drained from my face.

"Finally, we get to meet," she said in accented Ardenian.

"Who the fuck are you?" I hissed, pushing her away from me and grabbing the flashlight from the table—directing it at her. She was of average height, just a tad smaller than me. Her black hair was pulled back into a ponytail, revealing a stern face.

She didn't have to answer. I recognized her.

"It's only fair I introduce myself, I guess, as I already know *your* name," she drawled, stalking closer to me like I was her prey. "I'm Tatiana Zander."

I said nothing.

"Won't you say hello to your aunt?" she asked.

*Zander.*

My stomach sank as it all clicked. My mother's maiden name. The bird. *Ana.* It all fit so well that I felt the need to scream at Jordan to get the hell out of here.

This mission...

It was all a set-up.

# CHAPTER 21

## NIKOLAI

Nikolai was watching something that could only be described as *disturbing* when his pager went off.

He ignored it—his eyes glued to the screen.

Chief General Domasc was fucking a woman against an elevator wall in the middle of the night. The woman had black hair and light brown skin, but that was about all Nikolai could see. Though it was enough to know that it wasn't Domasc's wife.

The elevator doors opened, and the woman snatched a gun from her pants that she fired two times, grimacing as a shadow in the open hallway dropped to the floor, and a puddle of blood seeped into view before the doors closed back again. She said something, and Domasc pounded into her like that would make her stop, but she only laughed harder—clawing at his hair like she was feral.

*We make cute tapes*, was all the message attached to the video said. It was one from a thread of messages—from Domasc and the woman in the tape. But there was nothing that gave away who Domasc was talking to. Skimming through it, Nikolai suddenly stopped as he found another attachment added to the conversation, a photo from a couple of months after the video.

It was a photo of a swollen belly, clearly of a pregnant woman. *You're going to be a daddy*, it said.

*Domasc has a child with someone else?*

Nikolai had finally found someone who had dared hacking into Domasc's network, digging up this peculiar conversation for him. The hacker had also figured out the footage was from the hotel Domasc had stayed at when he had gone to a military congress. *So, either he had brought the woman with him, or she had already been staying there.*

Nikolai didn't recognize her. But then again, he had little to go off.

His pager went again, and he finally tore his eyes away from the screen, cursing himself for forgetting it had rung before.

*SSU Monitoring Room*, it said.

"Shit," Nikolai cursed. Vlad would only call if it were urgent. He logged into the communication line, calling the monitoring room.

Vlad answered immediately. "Zaregova?"

"What's going on?"

"It's not looking good." Vlad's voice was strained, another thing that showed just how serious the situation was.

Nikolai received files in his inbox and opened them.

"Raven has been transmitting footage from the inside, and they need translating asap. Not all of it—but a sizeable chunk." Vlad wasn't wasting any time.

He clicked through the footage and noticed most documents were in Borzian. Almost all of them had been faxed from the royal palace in Ostra, Borzia's capital.

Nikolai cursed and immediately forwarded it to a translator he trusted to keep this information below deck. He told him to drop everything and report back with details on the contents as soon as he could. Some older generations spoke a bit of the language, but most people in Ardenza didn't. Younger people didn't have to learn Borzian in schools anymore. Not since the estrangement during the first waves of the mutation, when trade had stalled and bonds were broken.

"The detected activity is from Borzia?"

"Apparently. But that's not all. Did you read the pieces in Ardenian?"

Nikolai zapped through the video again, pausing when Raven did, too, and he read the words.

Messages from Domasc to *someone*—a certain *Ana. Didn't ring a bell. Could it be the same woman?* He reread Domasc's words. *A Borzian woman named Ana?*

Something was off.

"Tell them to pull back," he said to Vlad, who Nikolai heard was furiously typing on his keyboard.

"We're already trying to, but I can't reach Raven," he grunted. "And her camera stopped working just before you called."

*Fuck.*

"Did you get in contact with the rest of the group?"

"Yes."

Nikolai stalled as the first translated piece popped into his mail.

He skimmed the summarized text and turned dead still.

Nikolai put the pieces together in an instant. *Raven was the bird Domasc was talking about.*

This entire mission was orchestrated to get Raven into Borzian hands.

To kill her.

"They're there for Raven," Nikolai said. "Tell everyone she's in danger, and they need to go to her *right fucking now.*"

He heard Vlad's cursing as he yelled his orders to the rest of the room, and he tried getting in touch with Raven. "*Answer me, Raven, damnit,*" Vlad shouted, and a loud bang sounded, like something got smashed.

Nikolai kept reading the translated Borzian files and shrank further in his seat. Oh, *hell no.*

Raven was the daughter of Natasha Zander—older sister to General Tatiana Zander.

*Ana.*

Who, clearly, was seeing Domasc. And who, clearly, was the woman in the footage. She had been there, at the military congress. Even the physical appearances matched.

Tatiana wanted Raven gone because she posed a threat to her heritage.

*The Borzian throne.*

# CHAPTER 22

## 2 YEARS EARLIER

**(Unread) J. Locke: I miss you.**

## NOW

"What do you want from me?" I asked Tatiana Zander.

The woman huffed, muttering something in Borzian. "I see you're just as stupid as my sister was." She morphed the words into knives.

I had heard about Tatiana Zander—*General* Zander—but the little I knew about the Borzian royal family were mostly rumors.

"I think you got the wrong girl," I said, but felt the lie turn sour in my mouth. My mother had spoken to me in an unfamiliar language and had told my father not to go to Borzia for help. They had tried to tear me away from my father at the border as soon as they had realized who I was. They had my birth certificate. Probably had it all this time.

It all made so much more sense now.

Why hadn't my mother said anything?

"Oh, no. You're the spitting image of your mother," she sneered, and like me, wasn't wearing night vision goggles. Her sight couldn't be any better than mine.

She wanted to kill me; I felt it. And she was crazy enough to do it, too.

I flashed the light straight into her eyes and threw it right at her head. I ran toward her in a beeline and landed a punch to her chest, which made her double over. She crouched and jumped up, and I couldn't land the next blow I was anticipating—her foot colliding with my side, making me lose my footing.

"My sister *always* felt like she was better than us." The word got punctuated by her throwing a punch to my face that I barely blocked.

*Get a grip, Raven.*

"Getting into discussions with my father about how to rule the continent," she continued as I landed a kick to her side and dodged one of hers. "Scolding me about how I played with the other children."

"I'm sure you were a real sweetheart," I groaned, faking my breathlessness while she punched, and I blocked. I let her repeat that two more times. Just when she thought I was losing the fight, I jumped at her, trying to get her to the ground—but instead of going down, she bumped into a table. Twisting her body with a growl, she tried to slam my head against it, but I twirled out of her hands just in time. She tried to grab my hair, but I was already backing away—regaining my balance.

She was good.

"My mother tried shaping her into the vision *I* already fitted. The woman thought she could 'mold' her and felt betrayed when she finally ran off. But not me. I was glad to be rid of her. She had done me a favor." She stepped forward. I felt an unfamiliar object prodding my back, but I couldn't look back to see what it was.

"*So? You're* named heir now," I snapped, fumbling with my hands behind my back in the dark while she got closer. "What's your fucking problem with me?"

"Your blood poses a threat to my position," she said, grabbing my neck, and my back sank into the sharp object, which depressed the skin. I stumbled and then sagged to the ground, my left foot catching on to something as I fell.

My left leg ended up suspended in the air, and I tried wiggling my foot free, but it was *stuck stuck stuck.*

Tatiana Zander noticed my struggle and took her chance; she slammed her knee into my leg and leaned down with her entire body, bringing it down. A yelp left my throat as I heard a loud *snap.* I groaned as she climbed onto my broken leg, still leaning down on it with all her weight. I clenched my teeth as my leg twisted angrily and I groaned in pain. "You'll never get it," she snarled, clawing at my face, tearing it open with her sharpened nails.

"I don't fucking want it!" I yelled back in her face, voice hoarse from pain. I throat-punched her with every bit of rage I felt. Her head lolled back as she wheezed for air, and I pushed her off me to climb on top of her instead, my leg protesting in agony with every move.

I landed punch after punch until the blood that trickled down my face mixed with hers.

"*Fucking bitch,*" she spat, spitting blood from her mouth.

I grabbed her by the throat and *squeezed.* I growled in her face like an animal, and I squeezed as she wriggled beneath me.

In all my rage, I hadn't noticed her getting a knife, her

arm moving and slashing it into my side. I froze in pain, mouth open in a silent scream. She pulled it back with a choking shriek and rammed the knife into me again—my back this time—immobilizing me.

I kept squeezing as hard as I could through the pain that nearly suffocated me—until the woman beneath me finally fell still, and her arms slackened. She was out cold, her face a garbled mess.

Sitting back down as the world twirled around me, I tried to twist my body and get my arm to bend around my body but only grabbed onto the air behind my back. It hurt so much—like a million knives had been rammed into me instead of just one.

I clicked on my earpiece with trembling hands and croaked, "Vlad?"

"*Raven!* Holy shit, Raven."

No doubt my body scan was flaring all reds and blues on the screens in the monitoring room.

"They were here for me," I managed weakly. Black spots danced through my vision.

"I know." Vlad's voice was soothing. Unusually so.

The pain numbed my body. I couldn't even feel my legs anymore. "Tell Jordan I'm sorry, okay?"

"Tell him yourself," Vlad hissed. "Hang on. They're coming your way."

I looked at the blood pooling around me. Mine. Hers. It all blurred together.

Red swarmed my vision, and blood rushed through my ears as the world started swaying around me.

"You better hang on, Renée," Vlad warned in my ear, but it was the last thing I heard before I closed my eyes and let myself drift into oblivion.

# CHAPTER 23

## 1.5 YEARS EARLIER

### (Unread) J. Locke: Congratulations, Colonel.

## NOW

Borzians occupied the building.

Jordan had passed a room where two men had been speaking to each other, and he'd recognized the language immediately. It did not surprise him they were Borzians, but he wondered what they were doing here. So far, though, he hadn't been able to find any clues telling why.

He was inspecting a room as the monitoring room buzzed. He opened the line, and immediately, Vlad said the words that had him in a chokehold, "Go to Raven, *now*, she's in danger."

"Can you reach her?" he asked Vlad.

"No."

*Raven is in danger.*

From that moment on, Jordan was a single-minded machine. He ran from the room and into the hallway.

*She had to be on this floor somewhere.*

Jordan heard a loud thud, which sounded a lot like fighting. He scoured the hall, stalking closer to the sounds.

But so were the two Borzian men he had passed earlier. They stepped out in front of him. Jordan had the element of surprise and took his knife from his pocket, slamming it into one of their meaty necks.

The man reached behind him, trying to cover the wound in his neck where the blood was gushing from, but he couldn't. He let out a garbled sound and fell to his knees.

The other had immediately turned around, swinging fists at Jordan—blocking his knife attacks. The man wasn't wearing night-vision goggles like Jordan, but his eyes were adjusted to the dark.

One of his attacks hit the mark, and Jordan's hand splayed open, the knife scattering to the ground.

Jordan inhaled as another loud noise came from somewhere close by, followed by a piercing cry that was definitely Raven's.

Panic tried to seize him.

He faked a punch while simultaneously slamming his other fist from below into his chin—snapping the Borzian's jaws closed as he stumbled back a couple of steps. Jordan immediately kicked him in the stomach and, again, in the head. The Borzian fell to the ground, losing his balance for a moment, as the punch messed up his vestibular system.

Jordan grabbed the knife from the ground at lightning speed and jumped onto the man trying to get back up. He slammed his head into him, cracking something, and the Borzian's head fell back to the ground, his eyes blinking, trying to regain control over his body.

Jordan didn't let him. He swiped the blade across his

neck—slicing it open. While the man attempted to claw at his neck, Jordan continued running, searching for the place where the sounds had come from, but he heard nothing.

He entered room after room until he stumbled into a room where a flashlight lay on the ground, illuminating the window. He ran inside and found two bodies stacked on top of each other.

Heart throbbing painfully, he rushed forward. Both weren't wearing helmets or night vision goggles, so he immediately recognized Raven.

"*No*," he gasped.

Jordan dragged her off the bottom person and registered the wounds. Everywhere he could see skin, he saw blood. But as he carefully lay her down on her side beside the other body, she grunted a little.

*Alive*, he reminded himself. *That meant she was still alive.*

"Vlad, get a hover heli this way *right now*," he ordered.

"It was airborne ten minutes ago."

Jordan inspected her, his fingers roaming her body as the others barged inside. "They were blocking the staircase," Colonel Keano said to Jordan as if explaining why they were late, but he didn't care as he kept inspecting Raven's body. "They're dead?" he just asked, as his hand met a knife still protruding from her back.

*No, no, no.*

"If not, they're close to it."

Jordan knew they didn't have time to finish them; Raven's life was more important. "Find a plank—something that can pose as a stretcher. The rest, help me splint her wounds and stop the bleeding."

Colonel Keano crouched on the floor, ripping off her backpack for supplies. "What the hell happened?"

Jordan kept shaking his head. "I don't know."

They took off her uniform together—cutting away fabric around the knife—until she was only wearing her sports bra, the full expanse of skin covered in blood. First Lieutenant Gabon poured water over it, washing away any excess until a wound in her side became visible. A stab wound. Probably made with the same knife as the one still embedded in her back.

He opened the first aid kit Keano had taken from her backpack and started treating the wound, putting pressure on it as he bandaged it.

If most of the blood on the ground had been Raven's, Jordan knew she had little time left before her body would succumb.

Kilich and Britton returned with a large wooden door, and together, they lay her carefully on her side, making sure the knife was free. If they'd taken out the knife, that wound would start bleeding, and they had no way of knowing what organs it had hit.

Jordan prayed none of them.

"One minute out," Vlad said in his earpiece.

"Let's go," Jordan breathed, his voice hoarse.

They lifted the makeshift stretcher from the ground. Raven was covered by the remnants of her bloody and torn uniform to shield her from the cold. Jordan kept holding onto her, so she wouldn't fall on her back and pull the knife even deeper. But he could feel she was growing weaker with every moment that passed.

As they reached the third floor, they waited until the hover heli landed, the thudding and groaning of the building indicating that a heavy weight had landed, before they made their way onto the roof and into the vehicle.

# BRITT VAN DEN ELZEN

*Hang on, Raven.*
*Just hang on.*

# CHAPTER 24

They say time heals all wounds, but sometimes I wonder if that's true.

I looked out of the window to the world I had left behind some time ago. The choice of not returning to Barak during my time off had been deliberate—I only visited my father and Hunter, who lived outside the city.

With every lamppost we passed, my face was reflected in the window, and my shadow projected on the leather backseat of the car.

The early morning greeted me as the sunlight lamps in the distance turned on softly—mimicking a sunrise with its orange hues and rays of light. Kelian, who had been working at the SSU for the past half year alongside me, had already gone to Barak the week prior. He had wanted to extend the trip to visit his friends and family. I would only stay for the night of Hunter and Nikolai's wedding.

Work occupied my mind twenty-four-seven, which was the perfect distraction. As I rose in rank, so did the amount of work and responsibilities. I loved being busy with *actual* problems instead of making my own bigger than they needed to be.

Barak's skyline came into view, and a knot in my chest twisted tighter at the sight. It was beautiful.

I had missed it immensely.

A serene feeling washed over me as I let my head rest and closed my eyes.

Eventually, we arrived at the hotel I was staying at with the other guests from far out of town. I stepped out of the car and took a deep breath. It felt good to be back.

The driver opened the trunk and grabbed my bag. I tipped him royally. My SSU bonuses were as much as four months of pay combined when I first started in the army.

My mouth dropped open as I entered the Westeria. The hotel was *gorgeous*. Everything was gilded, just like the gold dress that was (hopefully) already waiting for me in my room. I was thankful to Hunter and Nikolai for hosting me in such a place. I wouldn't have minded crashing at the base for a night, but they insisted.

A girl approached me almost instantly. "Miss Renée?"

I smiled, "Yes."

"Welkom to the Westeria. You can put your belongings on the rack. We will bring these to your room. Please follow me."

I followed her, grinning from ear to ear, taking in the breathtaking space. Even the elevators were golden!

As we stepped inside, her eyes fell on my coat, where my colonel insignia was embroidered. I had a habit of wearing my uniform everywhere I went nowadays. "You work with the bride and groom?"

I smiled. "I did, a couple of years back."

Recognition flared in her round eyes. "At the shadow

plains?"

The lift pinged open, and I nodded.

"Thank you for your service." She bit her lips like she wanted to say more, but she pointed into the hallway and led me through it. We arrived at a door on the left, and she put a golden card in the little slit, opened it, and gestured for me to enter.

I walked inside, and for the second time today, I gasped. "Wow." I also noticed the rack in the middle of the room where my golden dress hung.

Then she suddenly asked, "Do you maybe have a tip?"

"What?" I turned around, confused.

The girl shook her head like she was clearing it. "For the army. I applied for the next selection round after I finally turned eighteen last month."

"Really?" I regarded her for a moment, thinking. "You want a tip for the selection process?"

She nodded eagerly.

I regarded her for a moment, cocking my head in deliberation. "The most important thing I can think of is your motives—your intrinsic motivation. It has to be strong. *Why* do you want to join the army?"

"To help people," she said immediately.

I smiled. "That's a great start, but you can help people in a million ways. Why do you want to help people specifically through the army?"

She had to think about that question a little longer, but the girl had an answer. "When I see soldiers, the sight of them brings me a sense of safety. And when I think about possibly being a soldier, I feel powerful. Not in a greedy way, but in the way that counts. I haven't always felt powerful in my own life."

Nodding, I bit the inside of my cheek. "Bingo," I said. "If you keep holding onto *that*, the rest will fall into place."

She beamed. "Thanks… *Colonel*."

I winked, and then she was gone.

★ ★ ★

The hall was beautiful, a perfect mix of old and new: one wall was made entirely of glass, and the other walls were decorated with a golden relief.

My golden, A-line dress, which I specifically bought for the wedding, was made from tulle. A strip of fabric was wound around my waist, creating the perfect silhouette for my body. The back was open, and the whole dress sparkled, reflecting the lights surrounding me. I wore golden sandals with golden straps that climbed up my legs, and golden earrings adorned my ears.

My hair was half pinned up, and the front braids pulled around my head to meet at the back like a halo. The other half hung loose, accentuating that my curls now fell to my waist.

The last time Nikolai came to check the mission's progress, he had brought me the marriage invitation. Hunter had added a personal note to it and asked me if I wanted to be her witness, and *of course,* I said yes. I hadn't been a good friend the last years, as I mostly spent my time on the shadow plains. But our friendship wasn't measured by the time we were together. Every time we saw each other, it felt like no time had passed at all—no matter the amount of time or space between us.

I walked through the hall and focused on anything but the mingling crowd. My eyes strayed over the architecture, the beautiful decorations—anything to distract me from finding someone I didn't want to see. I was glad when Hunter's mom walked out of a door into the large hall and beckoned me closer almost immediately.

When I got closer, I gestured approvingly to her wine-red wrap dress. "You look stunning, Mrs. Jameson."

"Dear Raven, didn't I tell you to call me Clara?" She smiled and planted a kiss on my cheek, then pointed to the semi-open door at the end of the hallway behind her. "Hunter is in there."

I gave her a knowing smile as I walked to the room. I pushed the door open and heard Hunter sigh deeply before she pulled me into a tight hug. "Raven! It's so good to see you. I'm *so* glad you're here."

Laughing, I took her hand and squeezed. "You look beautiful, Hunt."

"I regret inviting so many people," she confessed as she fussed with her hair.

I smiled at my best friend. "I'm sure that once you're inside the room, the only one that will matter is Nikolai."

Hunter bit her lip. Nodded.

"You ready?" I asked her.

She inhaled. Exhaled. Then she smiled. "Let's get this over with."

"I'll see you inside." I gave her one last hug and exited the other way I came in, straight into the ceremonial hall where all the guests had trickled in. I walked past Kelian, Cardan, and Tania—waving to them and gesturing I would meet them later, but I refused to look anywhere else. At the end of the aisle, I took my spot in the front row beside Hunter's parents.

His eyes had been boring in the back of my head during the entire ceremony. It wasn't just an illusion; he had been looking at me. When I was addressed from behind, my glance had drifted off to the left, and our eyes had locked.

The rest of the ceremony was beautiful; violins had played as Hunter walked to Nikolai, waiting for her on the dais. They were such a mesmerizing couple. And as their witness, I had to sign Hunter and Nikolai's wedding document at a small table on the dais beside them. When I lay down the pen, I once again felt the heavy weight of Jordan's gaze on me. I had tried to ignore the feelings that stirred up as much as possible.

Now I stood at the sidelines of the party, to which about two hundred people had been invited. But I only focused on Hunter and Nikolai, slow dancing together. I knew that if I didn't focus on them, my deceptive eyes would stray in search of a particular general.

I needed a drink.

Carefully, I let my eyes wander, finding the bar. My feet moved forward, and I tried my hardest not to look around to see if I could spot any of my friends. Where were they when I needed them?

I was ordering a glass of champagne at the bar when someone walked up next to me. At first, I was afraid to look to the side, but when I saw it was a woman, I physically relaxed. Not for long, though, because I recognized her blonde hair and delicate features.

Up close, she was even prettier.

She didn't look at me, but seemed to be deciding what she would get.

I pointed to the champagne in my hand. "This one's good if you love sweet drinks. I recommend it," I said, tipping my glass to the sky in emphasis.

*Cringe.*

What the hell is wrong with me?

"Then I'll take that one," she said to the bartender. Her smile was friendly, and it was directed at me. "I'm Ashley."

"Raven. You're Jordan's girlfriend, right?"

She nodded, a proud glint in her eyes. "You know him well?"

"Reasonably," I said carefully, "We worked together at mission 3B."

"Oh! Of course. *Raven!*" She facepalmed her forehead like she thought she was an idiot. "He mentioned you, but you went away some time ago, right?"

My chuckle was awkward. Strained. "Yeah... That's me."

"So that's where you all know each other from? 3B?"

"Most of us, yes," I answered. I gestured toward the hall. "Speaking of, I have some more catching up to do. But it was nice to meet you."

Ashley smiled broadly, radiating joy.

*I would be, too, I guess.*

"Yes, of course. Enjoy your evening."

I smiled at her before I turned around and hurried off. *Why the hell had I opened my mouth? Why, why, why?*

On the way to wherever I was going, I finished my champagne and grabbed another from a passing tray.

I found a door behind a curtain that led to a balcony, and I almost groaned in relief as I made my way outside into the crisp evening air. Walking to the railing with big strides, I leaned my body against the cool stone and took a few deep breaths. I placed my glass on the rim and gripped the balustrade with both hands.

The balcony looked out over the city—the lights complementary to the stars I could faintly see. At the SSU base you could see them all, their beauty unhindered by our light pollution. The stars were the only real thing in our sky that we hadn't fabricated. I stared up at them. They always calmed me down—the idea that we didn't matter all that much. That we were just a tiny blip in a sea of stars.

The door banged shut behind me and I jumped, causing me almost to drop my glass of champagne from the ledge. I spun around.

Swallowed.

And swallowed again.

"Jordan," I finally managed. My lips wanted to twitch into a smile at the sight of him, as if my body didn't care what happened in the past. But I *really* did not want to smile.

I wanted to cry.

"Hey," he said, looking me up and down. He cocked his head as he walked closer. Dimples appeared on his cheeks. Jordan wore a gray suit paired with a white shirt, the top two buttons undone. His tanned chest was visible and—

"How are you?" I asked him abruptly. My hormones were raging like I was a teenager again.

He nodded and reached a hand into his pocket. Leaning against the railing, he said, "I'm fine."

I nodded furiously. *Come on, Raven.* "Congratulations on your promotion to lieutenant general." I wanted to kick myself.

Jordan inclined his head in thanks. He looked at me again, his eyes searing a path over my body, goosebumps trailing in their wake. "You look beautiful, Raven," he said out of nowhere. His Adam's apple rose and fell. "You always do."

Blood flowed to my cheeks, and I blushed a deep shade of red.

He took another step forward. If one of us leaned in, we would be touching.

I met his dark blue eyes. I forgot everything. *What I thought, where I stood, who I was.*

Jordan, too, searched my eyes with an intensity that made me quiver. Then his eyes dipped to my lips, and one thing became abundantly clear.

If he kissed me right *now*, I would be his. If he chose me *now*, I would choose him back.

But he didn't.

Of course, he didn't. It was a fantasy he could never afford. One I couldn't permit.

"I think—" I took my glass of champagne from the railing, my movements slow. "I think this isn't a good idea." I wanted to slip away and get back inside before he could hurt me more than he'd already done. But before I got past him, he gripped my arm.

"Raven…" he said, his voice taking an apologetic tone that I absolutely couldn't stomach. "About when I—"

I nodded firmly as I looked up at him. "Let's not make this more complicated than it needs to be." My breath came in sharp, and I almost choked on it. "A lot of time has passed in which we both went our separate ways. *It's fine.*"

I was lying. None of it was fine.

Jordan stared at me, a crease forming between his brows. He seemed to want to say more, but I didn't want to hear his apologies or why he couldn't choose me.

I wouldn't put myself through that. Not again.

"Get it together, Jordan," I hissed. "You've made your choice; now stand behind it. That's what's best for everyone involved." *Including your child.* But I couldn't get myself to say the words. I hadn't been able to since the moment I left. It wouldn't be true if I just didn't speak it into existence. I knew it was immature, but it was a coping mechanism.

Imagining him with a happy family… *In love…* It hurt too much.

His eyes were unreadable, but eventually he let go of my arm and let me slip back inside, merging with the crowd.

# CHAPTER 25

## JORDAN

It had been two weeks since they returned from the shadow plains.

Two weeks during which Raven was in a coma.

The moment they had landed behind the wall, the medical team rushed Raven inside the medical center. Doctors and surgeons had been waiting for her, taking her to the operating room to treat her injuries. And as Raven had gone inside, Jordan walking next to her, he'd seen her wounds in the light. Her face had also been torn open by what appeared to be someone's nails—*claws* even.

She was taken to the operating room, where he couldn't follow, and the doctor came back after *hours* of surgery to tell him that her left leg had been broken in two places.

Jordan wanted to punish himself for not noticing her other wounds, but the doctor emphasized that they hadn't been life-threatening. When Jordan had asked him if it would heal well—if she would walk again, the doctor had said he couldn't tell yet. The stab wounds hadn't punctured any vital organs, except for the wound in her back, which had hit some nerves, which made it very difficult to say whether she would walk again.

Right now, she was kept in an artificial coma, so her more severe wounds could heal properly, and she wouldn't be conscious to bear it.

After a couple days of Raven stabilizing at the mission's base, Jordan made the transfer with her to Barak's hospital, where her father and friends could visit her, too. He got a private hover heli for the way back, and had stayed in touch with Hunter, who updated the rest of their closest friends. But Jordan had been the one contacting her father, and the man had taken the news like a champ. Leon had unwavering faith that his daughter would get better—that she was the strongest person he knew.

Jordan had liked him immediately.

When they arrived at the hospital, Jordan helped install Raven in her private room. Her father had already waited there all afternoon for her after Jordan had told him they would come.

"Jordan Locke," someone said behind Jordan said and he turned around. A tall man with greying hair—undoubtedly Raven's father—stood in the hallway, looking at him.

He approached him and held out his hand. "Hello, sir."

"Please, call me Leon," the man said, tired eyes crinkling at the corners. "How is she?"

"Leon," Jordan said, and swiftly stepped aside, gesturing to where Raven was intubated. Her heart monitor showed a steady rhythm. He would know; he checked it every ten minutes. "She's a fighter."

Leon's gaze shifted to the door, and he seemed unable to breathe as he approached it, fingers resting on the doorknob. But then he let go and looked at Jordan again.

"What happened?"

Jordan hesitated.

"You know what happened?" Leon asked.

"I don't know the specifics, but she will tell us when she wakes up."

"She will," he agreed. "You'll stay here?"

Jordan managed a weak smile. "Yes, sir—Leon."

"Want to get a cup of coffee downstairs in a bit?" her father asked him.

He nodded. "I would like that."

"Raven would, too, I imagine." Leon winked, then he disappeared inside.

✮ ✮ ✮

Jordan hadn't taken a good look at the person on the ground next to her, but when Vlad had told him it had been Tatiana Zander, he cursed himself for not making sure she was dead. As he was talked up to speed on why they wanted to get Raven and how quickly she had transmitted the documents to the monitoring room, he was proud—and scared for her. *Scared out of his fucking mind.*

Borzia was a powerful continent. They were rich, far richer than Ardenza. And Tatiana Zander... she had one crazy reputation. Knowing Raven had taken her on so well made his heart fucking swell.

A few days later, Jordan sat opposite Nikolai and his father and read the translated texts from the Borzian documents Raven had filmed and had belonged to Tatiana.

"It's more than enough to get Domasc sentenced," Nikolai said softly, looking at both Lockes as they read the evidence he had already investigated.

Even Jordan's father, Kenneth, had raised his brows at

the documents, and he and Nikolai shared an understanding.

Jordan was fixated on the text before him about the woman he loved. But when he reached a part that clearly stated that she was the rightful heir to the Borzian throne, he stiffened. "What the hell?"

"It's true," Nikolai said.

Cold sweat broke out on Jordan's back.

"You can't use this information on Raven in court," he choked, looking at the two other men. "*Everyone* will know."

"We won't be able to win without it. There has to be a motive, Jordan." His father tried to reason with him, but he wouldn't hear it.

"If this information gets out… You know just as well as I do that some Ardenians hate Borzia with a scary intensity. She would have a target on her back for the rest of her life."

Nikolai tapped a finger on the table. "That might not be true if we let her testify, and she tells the story of how she fought with Tatiana Zander and wants nothing to do with the Borzian royal family."

"For some people, it's only about blood. You know this, Nikolai," Jordan accused.

"It's Raven's choice," his father jumped in. "She can look after herself, as she has proved many times over."

"We all know she would jump to the rescue if you asked her. We won't do that. She needs to rest. *To heal.*"

"Jordan," Nikolai urged, looking at him pointedly. "Without her, we wouldn't have found this information… And without her, we won't be able to use it either. It was an attack on *her* life, and she should be able to share her story."

"No," Jordan said immediately, resolutely. "*No way.*"

Nikolai sat back. "It's our best shot, Jordan. If we don't use all the documents, and don't put Raven in court to talk about what Tatiana Zander has told her, Domasc has a chance to get away with this. It could all be framed as a fabricated story and fabricated documents. Without a witness, the evidence is based on hearsay. Do you want to know how many people will want to see Domasc as the liar he is? Because I can tell you that there aren't many."

Jordan shook his head. "Domasc won't get away with this."

"That's the plan," his father replied.

Nikolai sighed in frustration. "With Raven's testimony, we can ensure he doesn't."

"Raven testifying isn't an option, Nikolai. You hear me, right?"

"You can't make that decision for her, Jordan. She's a brigadier general who knows exactly what she's doing. Let her take her own responsibility."

"She's in a fucking coma!" Jordan snapped. "The moment she wakes up, *when* she wakes up—" His breath caught in his throat, and he looked away. "She needs to heal. Rest."

Kenneth took hold of the wine bottle and said to no one in particular, "I suggest we let it rest for the night and drink to Raven Renée's speedy recovery. Let me get something stronger."

Jordan met his father's eyes. Looked away again.

"Jordan," Nikolai said. "You know just as well as I do that if you try to keep this from her—a chance at retribution— she won't be happy. Far from it."

"At least she'll be safe."

"No, Jordan, *she won't*, and you know it. As long as she can stake a claim to the throne, Borzia could try another attempt on her life if we keep quiet about this."

"Natasha Zander abdicated—and now Tatiana Zander also somehow stepped down, whatever that is about. Raven could do that, too."

"And she should. But it should happen publicly. What if her son, Aleksei, grows up and feels threatened by Raven?"

His head hurt. Nikolai was right, but… He didn't want to think about it now. First, he wanted to hear her voice again, feel her fingers move on his skin—be able to kiss her again.

He wanted Raven to *wake up*.

★ ★ ★

Jordan felt restless while he waited in the restaurant. He didn't like being away from the hospital. Didn't like leaving Raven. He left part of his heart behind every time he had to leave her. Especially since she had been breathing independently for the last few days, which meant she could wake up anytime now. And he wanted to be there when she did.

Her friends had visited often. Especially Rudolfs. Kelian, her best friend, had been coming daily. Something had changed in the way he looked at her. Jordan didn't understand what, but maybe the guy finally realized she wasn't meant for him.

Ever since coming back, Jordan and Ashley hadn't talked it out. They hadn't even discussed the dinner at his parent's house or the moments that had preceded it. He was embarrassed about how he had behaved that evening. Ashley deserved better than that.

They had spoken while he had been at the mission base, and the times he had picked up Sev over the last two weeks, but the important words were still left unspoken as they both twirled around it for Sev's sake.

Jordan hastily cleared his throat as the restaurant door opened, and Ashley stepped inside. She wore a deep red dress that looked good on her. They kissed each other on the cheek.

"Hey," he said.

"Hello," she said back as they sat down. "How are you?"

Jordan shrugged. "I've been better."

She nodded. "Your father reached out, asking about the best attorneys in Barak. Is this about your last mission?"

"Yes. It'll be a large lawsuit. But I can't say much about it right now."

A quick smile. "I understand."

*Of course she did.*

It was silent for a moment, and Ashley averted her gaze. One of her hands wrapped around her throat as her gaze slowly traveled back to his. "You know… I reflected a lot on our past relationship; when we were younger, wondering what our life would've looked like right now if we had stayed together… It's sad, Jordan, that we've become these people that don't fit anymore."

Jordan inhaled. "I've thought a lot about you during those years apart. How we probably had been married, had *multiple* kids." He raised an eyebrow at her, and she smiled a little. "But I think I also knew, deep down, that it wasn't meant to be our life, Ash. However bad we wanted it to be. Sometimes I think all of this happened to get Sev into our lives. I wouldn't trade him for the world."

She blinked, a tear falling that she caught with her napkin. "I wanted this to work so bad."

"I did, too." *For some time.* Both of them felt the words hang between them.

Jordan swallowed, but held her gaze. "I'm in love, Ash. I have been for quite a while."

She sighed. "I know."

His eyes widened. "You do?"

"Yes," she said. "And I would have let you go if I hadn't been pregnant, Jordan. I would have let you go to her. But the slight chance we could make this family work, that our son would have both of us *together*. It weighed heavily on my heart."

"Ashley, I have to tell you something." Jordan swallowed. "During the mission—"

"Don't," Ashley interrupted him, hurt visible in her eyes. "Please don't. We're splitting up either way. I want to do it right. For Sev."

"I'm sorry," he said, finally apologizing.

"Me too." Ashley's smile was strained. A little sad, too. "Does Raven know?"

"What?" he asked her, lips parting.

"The moment you told me about her when we first got back together, I *knew*. You wouldn't shut up about her— your '*friend*'. Then she left abruptly, and so did that spark in your eyes. You changed. I saw you follow her to the balcony at Hunter and Nikolai's wedding—and then again at the last anniversary gala. I just—" Tears brimmed her eyes. "It was all *there*."

Shame unfurled in his chest. "I'm sorry, Ashley. I—" He didn't know what else to say.

Ashley nodded, a hand clasped over her trembling lips as a few tears escaped.

"I love you, you know?" she said.

Jordan took her hand in his. "I love you, too."

She squeezed. "We have the most amazing son."

"We do." He smiled. "And we'll do one hell of a job raising him."

Ashley nodded. "But it's not enough."

"Ashley…"

She shook her head, raising a hand. "No. I get it. It's probably the best for all of us." She let go of his hand and grabbed the engagement ring around her finger, turning it twice before shoving it off her finger. Looking at it one last time, Ashley let her eyes go to him and lay the ring on the plate in front of her. The sound of metal on ceramic resounded.

Jordan looked at it.

"I hope it's all you have dreamt of, Jordan," she said softly, and went to stand. "And I hope she'll wake up soon."

Jordan stood with her and just nodded, because he didn't know what to do with his body.

"Take care," Ashley said, as she let him kiss her cheek.

Then he let her walk out of the restaurant by herself. This time, without wanting to follow her.

# CHAPTER 26

9 MONTHS EARLIER

**(Unread) J. Locke: Sometimes I lay awake at night thinking about enlisting in the SSU, just so that I could see you again—talk to you.**

NOW

I felt like I was dying.

With difficulty, I opened my eyes and immediately closed them again when I was blinded by a bright white light.

My head was pounding like a bitch. A fit of nausea hit me, and I blinked rapidly as I tried to open my mouth—to call for help. What the hell happened to me?

A moment later, I started registering sounds.

"Raven," someone said cautiously. The name echoed through my head—it rang true. My eyes were pried open, and a bright light was forced into them again. "Raven?"

I moaned and tried to close my eyes. I wanted to tell them to leave me alone. Didn't they realize everywhere they touched me, it hurt? My mouth tried to form words, but nothing came out.

Someone smoothed my hair, and I again tried to form words.

Finally, something was pressed between my lips, and a liquid ran into my mouth.

Water.

I drank greedily as I remembered how to swallow. When I finished, I rested my head again and opened my eyes more carefully. I saw double for a moment until the image straightened and the sound was no longer distorted.

The first person I saw was Hunter, who looked down at me with a big frown. "Raven?"

"Yes," I replied.

*Thank the gods. I hadn't lost my voice.*

"Do you know who I am, Raven?"

*What a silly question.*

I rolled my eyes with difficulty. "Hunter," I croaked.

"Do you know what year it is?"

"2166?" *I hoped.*

But Hunter smiled reassuringly. "Correct."

"How are you feeling?" a nurse on my right asked.

I turned my head. What I needed was some time to organize my thoughts.

Hunter tapped something on a tablet. "A neurologist will be over in a minute to check on you, Raven."

"How long have I been here?" *What happened?*

Hunter looked at me. "Two weeks."

"Jordan?" I asked automatically. Several memories crashed into me in a confusing order. *Shadow plains. Tatiana Zander. The hospital. Borzia. My team.* "The team?" I couldn't quite figure out what belonged where and what happened when. The flood of memories made my head hurt and the world spin. Was there a pause button I could hit somewhere?

Why did my brain have to figure it all out now?

*Give me a break.*

Hunter's eyes softened. "The rest of the team is doing well—so is Jordan. He's downstairs having some coffee with your dad, but I'm sure they'll be right back."

*Jordan. Jordan. Jordan.*

"He's here?" I frowned for a moment.

She smiled. "Jordan has barely left your side since you came in. He might strangle me if he finds out I didn't page him the moment you woke up. But I think it's better to have a few moments for yourself."

I nodded. "Thank you, Hunt." I grabbed her hand with mine and squeezed it lightly.

✫ ✫ ✫

The neurologist had just finished checking my toe reflexes and cleared me, though he pressed to take it easy when the door opened, and my father came in.

Unshed tears immediately popped into my eyes. "*Papa*," I said, trying to sit up straighter as he approached and hugged me.

The memories of what had happened in the field had rushed back over the last half hour, and I needed to speak to him.

"You've been here often?"

"I have, sweetheart. Of course."

"I'm sorry I've scared you."

"Jordan got me a place close by, and he kept me company, so it wasn't all that bad," he said, squeezing my hands, as I shifted my gaze to the man still in the doorpost.

*Jordan.*

Looking at him felt like being able to breathe again.

He just stared at me as if he was looking at a ghost. His eyes were the only thing about him that looked distraught; his hair and clothes were in prime condition.

My father followed my gaze and squeezed my hand before I looked back. He winked at me and walked to the door, placing another hand on Jordan's shoulder before he and the others left the room.

"Jordan," I rasped hoarsely, tears still leaking from my eyes.

His hands opened and closed, opened and closed. He walked a little closer, and all the while, his eyes were on me.

He grabbed my outstretched hand and sat down, wrapping it in both hands—pressing it against his warm cheek. With his head tilted slightly to the side, he smiled at me. "I feel like I'm dreaming."

I grinned. "You're not the only one."

Jordan's eyes alternated between my own, and he sat back a little, but didn't let go of my hand.

Mixed emotions washed over me. My head went a hundred miles per hour, and I couldn't keep up. Like I was still in a race to the finish line. I broke eye contact and looked up at the ceiling to find some solace.

"Raven," Jordan said. "Look at me."

I did.

"I know I didn't do right by you in the past, but you have to know I will now."

"Yes," I confessed, brushing my thumb over his hand. "I know."

Jordan smiled, showing off his dimples as I did mine. "Good thing, too." He squeezed my hand. "I know we have a lot to discuss, but I want this with you, Raven—*a life.*"

My eyes filled with tears without noticing. I felt my chin

tremble. I wanted that, too—more than anything else.

"What about Ashley?" I asked.

"We broke up."

I repositioned myself. Swallowed. "She knows?"

"She does," he confessed.

"She must hate me," I squealed. *What if she wouldn't want me near Sev?*

Jordan shook his head. "She does not."

A little of the burden I felt lifted from my shoulders.

Leaning his elbows on his knees, he sat closer and planted a kiss on my knuckles. He looked at me, his eyes pleading. "What do you say?"

I nodded. *Yes.*

He pressed my hand to his forehead and let out a long breath.

"But I need some time," I said, feeling tears running down my cheeks. "Okay? Just some time. To sort it all out and—"

Jordan put a hand on my cheek, and his long fingers stroked some hair from my face. "You have all the time you need, Raven. I will wait for you."

I nodded and he brushed away some of my tears with his thumbs.

"Okay," I said.

"Okay," he replied firmly.

✯ ✯ ✯

I was released from the hospital a few days later. My father, Kelian, and Hunter had helped me through the days. Jordan also stopped by to check on me, but he had kept his distance. There were still some things I had to do before I could take this further. I knew it pained him to not be with me more often, but he never showed it.

The scratch marks on my face were getting less red with the day, save for one, which was still an angry red. It went from the bridge of my nose to my cheek. Hunter had told me it would become a silver scar if I didn't let a plastic surgeon treat it, so I decided to let it be. Part of me wished *all* of them would stay—scar my face. I would wear the marks Tatiana had left on me with pride.

The wounds on my side and back had been healing well, although they hurt with almost every movement. I had kept all functionality in my legs, although they had been fractured in several places. The only thing I could do now was take my time and heal.

When Nikolai visited, he filled me in on the situation in Borzia. What happened on the shadow plains wasn't public knowledge yet, but word *had* gone out that Tatiana Zander had officially abdicated. Instead, the new heir was her five-year-old son, Aleksei Zander.

Nikolai had told me she had been in a 'romantic' relationship with Domasc. My shock had been misplaced; he had worked together with her to deliver me to her doorstep, after all. Nikolai also told me he heard rumors she was still alive, but he would update me on any further information. I had no clue what it meant or what we would do now, but Nikolai had promised me he would handle everything.

"Jordan cares about you a lot," my father had said when we were having lunch in public for the first time. Mostly liquid foods like soup, since my stomach couldn't handle much else.

"I care for him, too," I replied, honest about it for once.

My father's laugh lines had gathered around his mouth and eyes. "Good."

"Papa," I started, and he seemed to know something was coming up as he lay down his cutlery. "We need to talk about Mama."

He nodded. "What do you want to know?"

I had to be fast if I didn't want to cry again. "I went to the hospital in Damruin—the one they brought her to—and I found out she died there."

"What?" my father faltered, mouth open. "You're serious?" Tears were filling his eyes, too.

I nodded and smiled. "She died," I whispered again.

My father let go of a laugh as he rubbed his eyes. He took hold of both my hands, squeezing tightly. "Thank you, Raven. Thank you for finding out."

"Of course." I nodded. "But the documents listed her name as Bruna, and her maiden name as Zander."

My father nodded. "I changed our last names to Renée when we came to Barak." He swallowed. "All three of us were called Bruna, but when we went to the Borzian border, I regrettably handed them your birth certificate and your mother's, including our marriage certificate, to prove you were her child."

"You knew she was a Borzian princess?"

"Yes." His eyes were glazed. "We married fast to change her last name."

I laced my fingers together. "I remember… I remember Mama telling you not to go to Borzia for help."

Shame crossed my father's face. "I know. But you have to understand, Raven… The mutation was closing in on us, and destruction followed us everywhere we went. I'm a father, and my first priority was to keep you safe. And when I didn't see another option… I was desperate."

I told him the truth, anyway. "Tatiana Zander was in the

shadow plains to kill me."

He blinked. "*She* did this to you?"

I nodded. "I think she knew because of the birth certificate, but I don't know how they figured out it was me. We'll find out soon, I hope."

"I made a mistake." He took my hands in his. "One you have had to pay for all these years later."

"You only tried to keep me safe. *They're* to blame. I get why Mama left. Tatiana Zander is fucking crazy. That whole family probably is."

Shaking his head, he said, "She never really talked about them. I think she wanted to protect me. *Us.* Or she wanted to start with a clean slate—be whoever she wanted to be. And I never pried. If she wanted to tell me, she would have."

"It doesn't matter. It doesn't change who she was to me."

"She was a special woman," my father agreed.

I swallowed the big lump that had formed in my throat again.

"So—" he began. "Jordan. I like him."

"You think Mama would have liked him?"

He shook his head ferociously. "He wouldn't have stood a chance."

My mouth dropped open. "What? Why not?"

"She would never have trusted a man that pretty."

It was the first time I laughed out loud in a long time.

# CHAPTER 27

6 MONTHS EARLIER

**(Unread) J. Locke: I'm letting you go so I can move on with my life. I have to.**

NOW

It was strange to be back in a familiar place after your life had changed.

I dumped my things in the corner of my living room at the main base and walked over to a mirror on my crutches, where I pulled up my sweater and looked at the two scars on my torso. The wounds were still an angry red and would undoubtedly leave scars. The wounds on my face, save for the one, had almost completely healed with the help of medication.

It was as if everything I had experienced on the shadow plains was a distant dream. As if I didn't have to fight for my life—that the medication did it instead.

I dropped my sweater again and sat on the couch, pulling up my braced leg. I started fidgeting with the strings of my sweatpants to loosen the fabric around the large cast my leg was trapped in.

My head started throbbing lightly.

The doctors I had spoken to told me I shouldn't exert myself again too soon, both mentally and physically. My brain needed time to recover from the coma I had been in, and my memory and concentration abandoned me now and then.

A deep sigh left my body. I was exhausted.

My eyes drifted to my desk, which had a screen on it, and I sat up straighter. It wasn't like I was doing anything illegal, but I still felt caught. My hands were itching, and after trying to distract myself for a minute, I pushed myself upright and hobbled over to the desk, pulling the chair back and pressing on the screen as I sat down.

I drummed my fingers on the wooden desk, waiting for the screen to start up.

For the first time in *years*, I opened my chat box. I had tried so hard to avoid it for so long, suppressing my curiosity—suppressing my feelings for Jordan.

He had sent me *so* many messages.

Slowly, taking my time, I read through all of them and felt ashamed of what I had done, disappearing without saying anything to him. It had been very selfish. I hurt him more than I had ever imagined. Granted, I had needed it, but still...

His last message was a message from three months ago:

**(Unread) J. Locke: I think I'm in love with you, Raven, and I don't know how much longer I can pretend I'm not. My life has been turned upside down since you walked out of it, and I have changed. But the only things that remain the same are my feelings for you, and I don't know what to do**

**about them.**

I stared at the screen and wrapped my arms around myself, tears gathering in my eyes. I realized I could finally let go of my internal struggle: the battle I was fighting against myself all these years—*over*. It was safe for me to do so. It was safe for me to feel powerless sometimes and give in to the uncertainty in life.

Wiping away a few stray droplets, I typed back a message, the only one in over two years:

**Me: I'm in love with you too.**

There was too much going on within me—too many emotions colliding at once. I logged off, got up, and pushed my desk chair back. I needed a break.

A *big* one.

✵ ✵ ✵

A knock sounded on my door, and my head shot out of the book I was reading. I looked at the clock. It was late, and I wasn't expecting anyone.

It was a way the nightmares often started. Never at the main base, but always in our old home—or me and my father's. I hadn't had a nightmare since I'd gone to the hospital and discovered my mother had died instead of becoming a mutant.

When there was another soft knock, I stumbled to the door and unlocked it.

"Nikolai?" I said, genuinely surprised to see him standing there. He was wearing a long black coat, black pants, and a turtleneck sweater.

He nodded to someone passing by. I looked at him with a frown. "What's with the incognito look?" I joked, and Nikolai's mouth pulled into a frugal smile—the one you usually got from him if you were one of the lucky people he actually *liked*. The only times I *heard* him laugh out loud had been with Hunter or soldiers he'd known for some time.

"Hunter and Jordan would be heartbroken if they found out I'm visiting you at this hour," he said dryly, mirth lacing his voice.

I laughed. "Maybe we should make a run for it while we still can."

"Too late for that now," Nikolai muttered under his breath, but something in his eyes made me pause.

I gasped.

He schooled his features into vast nothingness, but it was too late—I had already seen it. I started giggling like a schoolgirl.

Nikolai groaned inwardly. "Don't say *anything*. Hunter will kill me. Please act surprised."

I nodded, but couldn't hide my smile.

Nikolai pointed inside. "May I?"

"Of course." I held the door open.

He entered and went straight to the dining table, where he sat down.

"Want anything to drink?"

He shook his head, and I was glad he didn't suggest helping me as I poured some wine for myself—I was sick of everyone treating me like I couldn't do anything anymore. When I finished, he gestured for me to sit down, ever the general.

"What is going on?"

"Has Jordan updated you on the trial?" His face betrayed

nothing, unlike Jordan's. But I could tell by the look in Nikolai's eyes that it was serious.

I nodded, and my good leg started shaking under the table.

"It's moved to the day after tomorrow," Nikolai said.

My lips parted. "*What?*"

"And Jordan has refused to ask you for help," he continued. "I know it's extremely last minute. You're only *just* released from the hospital, and Hunter told me you had to take it slow…"

"I want to help," I interrupted him.

"That's good to hear," he responded, "because I think we need it. But Jordan has good reasons for refusing. And to be honest, I would never want to ask this of Hunter myself."

Inhale. Exhale. "That doesn't matter to me. I, like Hunter, can make that decision myself."

Nikolai inclined his head. "That's why I'm here."

"What is it?"

"We want to use the translated Borzian documents in the trial. Nobody has seen them yet, and the information in them is invaluable. It's enough to get Domasc to at least step down, probably even serve some time in jail. But your information will be out in the open if we use it all. And if we want to use it properly, we need you as a witness to declare *where* and *how* you found them—as well as what Tatiana Zander has told you."

People would know I was a Borzian princess, and many would think of me as one.

"I know."

Nikolai leaned back in his chair. "It's dangerous. There's a good chance some people won't take it lightly—won't even believe you."

I nodded. "I understand."

"It might result in you being stripped of your rank if we lose."

Tightening my jaw, I looked away from him at the uniform I'd worked so hard for. "You might lose yours too."

Nikolai nodded.

I swallowed. "The possibility had already crossed my mind. I might have an idea. One that might work around that and work toward securing Domasc's downfall."

"What is it?" he asked.

As I told him, I watched him mull it over—until he finally agreed it was worth a shot. A risky one, of course, but worth it.

Then, he asked me to go over the Borzian documents. My first instinct was to turn him down because, no, I was getting tired and didn't want to see them. But I knew it would be necessary for court, so I sighed deeply and grimaced. "All right. Let's get it over with."

When we were done, my head started hurting again, and Nikolai gathered his stuff. "I will try my best to get your plan in motion. We will do everything we can to limit the damage. I'll pick you up in the morning, and we'll visit our attorneys and teach you about cross-examination and what you should and shouldn't say. But the main objective is to take down Domasc."

I nodded. "It's long overdue."

"Indeed," Nikolai agreed.

"Give my love to Hunter," I told him.

Nikolai turned around at the door opening and smiled with his eyes only. "We'll get him, Raven."

"Yes," I promised. We *godsdamned* would.

★ ★ ★

Two days later, my clothing itched. I couldn't stop touching my suit jacket, opening and closing the top buttons of my shirt, and smoothing my pants. The white suit I was wearing fit like a glove, and I had put on my leg brace over it. My leg was healing nicely thanks to the advanced drugs, but I still needed to use crutches to move. Lisa, the female attorney, had advised me to wear a dress to appear less threatening, but that wasn't going to happen. I *hoped* Domasc felt threatened.

That was the intention.

I walked past the press into the courthouse and joined the people waiting to enter the room. Many soldiers had come to watch the high-profile trial, and many had heard about my injuries. I hadn't put on any makeup, purposefully showing off the slash across my face that was a shade lighter red thanks to our enhanced drugs.

People should be reminded I was a survivor.

Kelian had offered to walk me inside, but I told him I would see him there. I wanted to walk alone.

I finally spotted a glimpse of Hunter. My heels clicked on the smooth, reflective surface, and I was glad to have put them on—even if my leg moved like a stiff board. They made me feel braver, just as knives and guns did. Clothes were weapons, too. It depended on the setting in which they were deployed.

Closer to Hunter, I noticed Nikolai and Kenneth Locke. She walked up to me and pulled me into a tight hug. "Are you ready?"

I smiled. "I think so." I wasn't, but saying it only made it real.

Nikolai looked at me and held out a hand to Kenneth Locke, gesturing from him to me. "Kenneth, Raven. Raven,

Kenneth."

I shook his outstretched hand. "Good to meet you, Deputy Locke." He had the same eyes as his son.

"It's Kenneth." Kenneth Locke smiled warmly, his charisma shining through.

"Domasc came in through the back," a too-familiar voice said, and Jordan emerged from behind Nikolai.

He stopped the moment he caught sight of me. "Raven?"

"Hi," I replied sheepishly, and clasped my hands together. *Has he seen the message I send?* I hadn't dared to open the chat box again to check.

"When did you get released from the hospital?"

"A few days ago."

"Okay," he said, nodding resolutely, but I saw the doubt in his eyes, the concern.

Kenneth Locke looked from his son to me and started grinning, making the whole situation more awkward.

Jordan stepped closer, blocking the other men from view. "Can I talk to you?" He gestured one hand to the side and placed the other on my back.

I nodded, letting him lead me away from the group.

"Shouldn't you be resting, Raven?" Jordan asked, his eyes scanning my face.

"I'm taking it easy." The urge to put a few strands of his hair back into style took me by surprise. I was deflecting, and he knew it.

"I could have kept you up-to-date on the process," he murmured, taking my hand and running a finger over the bridge. Goosebumps erupted everywhere.

Distracted, I shook my head. "I couldn't miss this. I have to be *here*, Jordan."

"Listen, Raven." He understood—always had. "I know

you still need time, and I want you to know I won't go anywhere. But I miss you. A *lot*." His finger followed a path to my wrist, and my heartbeat quickened.

"Raven," Nikolai called, and I looked around Jordan to see him beckoning me with Micah, the head attorney.

"Sorry, Jordan. I have to go now." And I took my hand back to do just that.

Jordan blinked as if he was clearing his head. "What?"

"I have to go."

His eyes widened. "You're going to testify? No—" He grabbed my arm. "No, Raven." But I carefully pulled my arm from his grip and walked to the group. Jordan followed and rushed towards Nikolai. "You went to her behind my back," he said through clenched teeth.

Nikolai looked at him stoically. "Calm down, Jordan. Raven is her own person and doesn't need a gatekeeper. You knew we would let her make her own decision."

Micah and Lisa waited for me, and I nodded to them. We had gone over the whole trial, and I was ready. There was no time for this; we had bigger fish to fry.

I turned, lay my hand on Jordan's neck, and kissed him on the cheek, dissolving the anger and irritation on his face. "I miss you too," I whispered in his ear.

Then I walked away.

# CHAPTER 28

I waited in a small room during the opening arguments until a court officer came in to escort me into the packed hall.

All heads turned to me.

I walked past the table where the attorneys, Nikolai, and Kenneth Locke, sat: the accusing party. My legs carried me forward, but I looked at the next row behind a wooden barrier that separated the gallery from the proceedings, where my father, Hunter, and Jordan sat. My eyes locked with the latter, my smile faltering as an avalanche of emotions hit me. I averted my eyes and let them move to my friends in the following row: Kelian, Cardan, Tania... Even Keano and the rest of the team had come.

They had all shown up—every one of them here to support me—encouraging me forward with every step I took.

Even Vlad had wished me good luck that morning. He had video called because he had wanted to see me *before Lieutenant General Locke kept me away from him forever*. The conversation had calmed me—reassured me. He had made me laugh.

The court officer took my crutches and rested them

against the wall. Someone cleared their throat as I climbed a small flight of stairs, the old wood groaning before I stood in the small witness box.

People shifted in their seats, whispering to each other, and the room's buzz drowned out my nerves. The hall was enormous, but they had let in too many people, including press representatives in the back of the room, who were already writing down notes and recording audio. I tried to ignore the crowd as much as possible. *The only thing that mattered was the court case, not the public.*

*Oh, how they would eat up the information that would be revealed today.*

One judge raised a hand, silencing the room, and opened her mouth. "Taking the stand is Brigadier General Raven Renée."

I looked at the three judges in total. They were going to decide on Domasc's fate. And mine, for that matter. Nikolai and the team told me that none of the judges were outspoken in politics or affiliated with Domasc. This trial could go both ways; it was wholly dependent on the evidence.

✹ ✹ ✹

The judge closest to me looked down. "Put your hand over your heart."

She took off her glasses when I crossed my hand over my chest. "Do you swear to speak the truth and nothing but the truth, according to your *own* experiences and knowledge?"

"I swear."

She put the glasses back on her nose and nodded, reading something in front of her. "Then let's get started. Attorney of the accusing party, you may now question your witness."

I sat down, adjusting the built-in microphone on the table in front of me.

Then I straightened my back, wrapping my hands together on the dark brown table in front of me, and faced Domasc. The silver in his hair framed his dark beard and sideburns. He would have been handsome once, if he hadn't been such an asshole.

Micah walked over to me, his gaze reassuring. "We're glad you could be with us today, Brigadier General."

I leaned in slightly to the microphone. "Of course."

"Tell us, Brigadier General, how did you first hear about the assignment?" Micah wrapped his hands behind his back as he waited for my answer.

"Chief General Domasc told me about it."

He nodded. "He asked you to join the mission, didn't he?"

I swallowed. "More like demanded it."

"Objection. Argumentative," Domasc's Attorney said.

Micah gave me a reassuring look. He and Lisa had told me this often happened during court cases, and they had pressed to speak the truth no matter what. It could sway anyone's mind, even if they had to remain impartial.

"Objection sustained," the judge ruled. "Continue."

"So," Micah continued, "Chief General Domasc sent you on this mission."

"Correct."

"And what did he tell you about it?"

I sat back. "Not much. Only that it was classified, 'off-the-books'." I made quotation marks. "And that we would investigate some suspicious activity."

"Did he explain why you, in particular, had to go?"

I answered all these questions as we had practiced,

"He said it was because I had a lot of experience with the shadow plains."

"But there are more soldiers with experienced in the shadow plains, aren't there?"

"Yes."

They had made bite-sized clips of my body cam footage spanning across every part of the journey on the plains. Micah went over every little detail, which took a very long time. From solidifying facts to walking a fine line between my own opinions and interpreted activity.

When we got to the part in the hospital, some people in the room gasped as they found out who my mother was. Others were still trying to catch up to what they saw.

"When you arrived at the designated location, you quickly realized Borzians occupied it, right?"

"Correct," I replied again.

"How did you know?"

I heard the rustle of papers from Domasc's side, but remained focused on Micah. "I walked into a room and found Borzian documents. That's how I came to the natural conclusion that we were dealing with Borzians."

"And did something solidify that deduction?"

"Yes. A Borzian woman walked into the room. She told me her name was Tatiana Zander, and that she had been waiting for me."

He inclined his head. "I would like to exhibit evidence 23."

The screen in front of me, and the rest throughout the room, showed another video. This time, I was showing the Ardenian part of the documents when a woman's voice filled the room.

*"Finally, we get to meet."*

I swallowed as I relived the entire experience for the third time. We continued talking and fought until the camera broke and the footage shut off.

"Was this the moment you just described?"

I cleared my throat. "It was."

"And the other woman in the video was indeed Tatiana Zander?"

"Yes."

"Did you know who she was?"

Shaking my head, I replied, "Not immediately."

"What happened after the footage ended?"

I looked out into the crowd, meeting Jordan's eyes before looking back at the Attorney, inhaling deeply. I bowed my head ever slightly and looked at the ground. "She tried to kill me."

Murmurs arose in the crowd as people started murmuring, and journalists whispered into their recording devices.

"Please exhibit evidence 103."

"Here we can see your wounds," Micah said, as multiple photos of my wounds flashed into view, all made after they brought me back from the plains. "Tatiana Zander was the reason behind all of them?"

I tore my eyes away from the screen, my unconscious face. "Yes."

"You were in a two-week coma after this happened, right?"

"I was." My head started pounding; my throat was parched. I forced my hands to take the glass of water before me and drink from it.

"And you've only woken up… what, a few days ago?"

"Yes. Four days ago," I confirmed.

Again, the buzzing made its way through the crowd,

but I kept looking at Micah standing in front of me. His suit was a pristine dark blue, and his dark hair was styled meticulously. He was in control, his expression calm.

*Breathe.*

"And Chief General Domasc send you there, to Tatiana Zander, right?"

I forced my eyes to remain on him. "He did."

"And you found evidence that he knew she wanted you?"

"I did," I agreed again.

"What did you find out?"

"That the bird Domasc had written about was me."

"Objection! Speculation."

"Overruled," the judge immediately said, but added, "Proceed to elaborate."

Micah requested another piece of evidence of the messages Domasc had sent to Tatiana. The ones I had read in the field.

He cocked his head. "How did you know *you* were the bird?"

"I put the pieces together. My mother is Natasha Zander. Tatiana called herself my aunt. And, after a while, Tatiana confessed I was the reason she was there."

"Did she say something else?"

My aching fingers were stiff. "She told me I would never get the throne. And I told her I didn't want it."

"Objection. The question assumes facts not in evidence."

The judges sustained the objection.

"What did she want from you?" Micah asked.

I looked at the judge. "She wanted to kill me." My wounds spoke for me, did they not?

"Because you're the heir to the Borzian throne? A threat to her claim?"

I nodded. "That's what she told me."

"Let's get into exhibit…" Micah's voice ebbed away as I looked down, stashed my hands between my legs to warm them up, and focused on my breath.

This was going to be a *long* day.

★ ★ ★

During the short recess, I fled inside the toilets. I didn't feel like speaking to anyone right now—not until this trial was over. Even though my leg still hurt from time to time, it was a relief to stand after sitting for hours on end.

I washed my hands under the lukewarm water, careful while my crutches dangled on my arms. My fingers were aching and had grown stiffer with every minute that passed inside the courtroom, like the rest of my body.

The door to one stall opened, and… Ashley walked out. Surprised, I looked at her through the mirror, my hands still under the faucet.

I didn't know what to say.

"Hey," she said, which was a good start.

"Hi," I said back, turning off the tap and getting a paper towel to dry my hands.

Should I walk away? Stay? I didn't know what I would say to her if I did. I grabbed my crutches and leaned some of my weight on them and off my leg.

Before I decided my next course of action, she said, "You did well in there."

My doubt was instant. "You think so?"

"Yes," she said.

She was much better at this than I was, but I guess that's why she had become a lawyer instead of a soldier.

My smile was genuine. I slowly averted my gaze back to

the door. "Well… I have to go back." I hesitated. "Are you staying?"

Ashley started washing her hands, but she smiled at me through the mirror. "I'm staying."

★ ★ ★

"You say you didn't know what you were going to do inside the field, but that's not completely true, is it?" Domasc's attorney asked me. She walked from the accusing party's table and stalked closer to where I sat in the witness box.

I looked at her. "I don't know what you mean."

"You knew you were going to Damruin, didn't you?"

"I knew the location of the mission, correct."

They showed the fragment of me in the hospital *again*. I watched how I found my mother's file *again*, how I read it *again* and took it with me *again*.

"Can you tell us what we're looking at, Brigadier General?" The woman asked me. She barely suppressed a twitch of her lips, which was weird.

"Do I seriously have to answer that?" I looked at the judge.

Someone in the courtroom snorted.

"Silence in the courtroom," one of the judges ordered, and the one closest to me said, "Yes."

My eyes darted toward where the sound had come from, and I noticed Tania laughing silently—a fist in front of her mouth. Cardan also barely suppressed his laughter: he had a hand wrapped around the bottom of his face and tried to conjure a stern look in his eyes. Even Major Britton had folded his lips together. On the way back, my eyes trailed past Nikolai, who gestured to me to stay calm.

I looked back at Domasc's attorney. "You're looking at

me in the hospital." *Again*, I wanted to say, but suppressed the urge.

She stepped closer and continued, "Why were you in that hospital, Brigadier General?"

"To find my mother's file."

"So you could erase the evidence?"

*Evidence?* I frowned. "So I could find out what happened to her after she got sick with the mutation."

"Why did you take the files with you, then?"

"To show my father." I looked at my father, who smiled at me.

"Or," she countered, "was it because you didn't want anyone finding out Natasha Zander was your mother? So you could remain a spy for the Borzian government?"

Was this woman for real?

"I'm *no* spy." I grimaced. "I didn't even know my mother was Borzian before entering that hospital."

"But how could *we* know you didn't, Brigadier General?"

"Objection—argumentative."

"Sustained."

I clenched my fists underneath the table. *Relax, Raven. She's trying to get a rise out of you.*

"When you entered the room where you supposedly found the documents, you recognized the Borzian language on those documents, didn't you?"

"I did."

"And yet you say you don't speak or understand Borzian."

"It's not hard to recognize the language. It's very different from Ardenian."

"Did you plant the documents there to save yourself?"

I frowned. "How would I have done that?" They had seen the tapes, right?

"You tell us, Brigadier General."

My Attorney stood. "Objection—argumentative."

"Sustained."

Domasc's attorney continued like everything was going according to plan. She had woven her own narrative through mine. Disrupting it, corrupting it. Spinning it, so *I* looked like the bad guy.

"Have you met Tatiana Zander before this mission?"

I sighed. "No."

"Then how did you know the woman was Tatiana Zander?"

"I recognized her from a photo in a newspaper, and she told me who she was."

"Isn't it convenient that your camera died, and those recordings of her confessions aren't here?"

"On the contrary. It is highly *inconvenient* for me," I deadpanned.

"It's because she didn't confess a thing, isn't it, Brigadier General?"

My hands curled into fists. "No."

"It's because you were working with your aunt, isn't it?"

"Objection!" one of my attorneys stepped in. "Argumentative, *again*."

"No." My anger rose rapidly, and I had to bite my tongue to push it back down.

Domasc's attorney looked at the judge, that said, "Sustained."

The woman walked back, grabbing something else from the table. "Tatiana Zander is a respected, distinguished general."

"You're a fan?" I asked her.

"Are you?" she countered.

A humorless laugh left me. My head pounded.

"Objection—relevance."

Nikolai arched a brow at me.

*Yes. I know.*

"Sustained. Councilwoman, get to the point."

"You told the court Tatiana Zander wounded you. She scratched your face, broke your leg in multiple places, and stabbed you twice; once in the side and once in the back."

"Correct."

"And yet you still walked away from that."

"I was *carried* away, unconsciously."

"But she didn't kill you."

I looked at the judge again, wondering if they really expected me to answer that question.

"Objection. Asked and answered," Lisa said from our table.

"Sustained."

The attorney wasn't deterred. "Don't you think that if Tatiana Zander had wanted to kill you, she would have? She had way more experience than you and—"

"Objection—argumentative."

The judge sustained it again.

Was she suggesting I had hurt *myself* or that Tatiana had let me live *on purpose*? I knew she was trying to bait me, so I had to remind myself that they didn't have a case. *They didn't have a case.* They were going to lose.

"That's all," Domasc's attorney said, stepping back, proving my point.

"We have to get you out of here before the madness erupts if it hasn't already," Nikolai said, and I took his arm as I tried to walk faster. "I booked you a suite in the

Westeria, where you can stay for at least the trial duration."

"Raven!" someone shouted from behind, and I just knew it was Jordan. But as I looked around, the crowd had closed in on us with their cameras and recording devices. Other people were just plain yelling.

He couldn't get to me.

I had to get out of here. I didn't even have time to talk to my father or friends.

"*Gods*," I muttered as Nikolai led me through the crowd, out of the building, where more people had lined up.

Flashes blinded me, and I held up the hand that wasn't gripping Nikolai to shield me from the onslaught.

"Raven! Is it true you're a Borzian princess?"

"Is it true you've conspired with Tatiana Zander to take the Borzian throne?"

That didn't even make sense. What the hell was up with these people making things up out of thin air?

"Is it true you and General Zaregova are in a relationship?"

At that, Nikolai growled deeply, the crowd around us immediately backing away a step or two. "Don't tell them anything," he said in a low voice. "They will just twist it into whatever they want to hear."

A car was already waiting for us, and Nikolai opened the door, letting me step inside. "You did good today, Raven. Take some rest."

I nodded once before he closed the car and barged straight back inside, the crowd parting around him like he was a god. I tried to catch another glimpse of Jordan as the car slowly pulled away from the courthouse, but the press followed the car, obscuring my view entirely.

# CHAPTER 29

## JORDAN

Jordan was woken by a small person climbing into his bed and jumping on his chest.

"*Oof.*" The breath left his body as he opened his eyes and found Sev there. "Good morning to you, too," he said, brushing a hand through his blonde curls.

Sev squealed delightfully. "I'm hungry."

"Of course you are." His boy was growing fast. *Too fast.* "Let's get you some breakfast, then."

Sev climbed off the bed, jumping around in his little pajamas, as Jordan followed him to the kitchen.

He had sold the apartment where he and Ashley had lived together and bought this new one. The thought of bringing Raven to his previous home hadn't felt right. And Ashley, too, hadn't wanted to keep it. She had bought a house outside the city, closer to her parents, with a large garden where Sev could play outdoors.

Jordan made pancakes, per Sev's request, and he had to admit that it *was* his best dish. He'd perfected it the moment Sev had tasted a pancake at a restaurant and asked him if he could *always* get them. Ashley wasn't with them the first time Jordan tried to make it, and he'd let the pancake burn because he had not used any butter. Which, in his defense, was founded on the reasoning that the pancake mix had already been moist.

He'd done that wrong only once. And he was glad Ashley hadn't been there, or she would have surely laughed her ass off and would never not find a moment to bring it up.

Obviously, he wasn't a stellar chef, but nobody could bash him now because his pancakes were *superb*.

Sev started eating them as if his life depended on it, smearing the syrup all over his mouth in the process.

"Are they good, buddy?"

Sev nodded with his mouth full and his hands suspended in the air, fingers sticky, before he lowered them to take another bite.

Jordan walked over to his front door and opened it, finding his regular newspaper on the ground. He froze at the threshold as his eyes caught on the picture of Raven. It was a picture from yesterday. She looked beautiful from where she sat in the witness box before the court. Raven didn't smile, her mouth a stern line, but she looked into the camera with a certain glint in her eyes.

She looked beautiful. As always.

He picked it up and walked back into the large apartment, closing the door behind him with his foot.

Sitting down next to a still-eating Sev, Jordan unfolded the newspaper, revealing the headline: *Brigadier General Renée Heir to the Borzian Throne.*

He cursed under his breath, too soft for Sev to hear.

The large courtroom was once again filled with too many people. Even more than yesterday after the information about Raven had seen the light of day.

Jordan was nervous beyond anything he had ever experienced. He hated that Raven had to throw her personal life out in the open, especially the parts about her mother. He also hated that she had to sit a row in front of him and not beside him—he could count the hairs on her nape but not touch her, or hold her hand.

"Chief General Domasc, thank you for being here," his attorney began after Domasc took his place in the box where Raven had sat the day before. The asshole nodded openly, raising his eyebrows like he didn't mind sitting there *at all*. Like he was doing them a favor.

In the first hour, his attorney went over his private life, the incident at 3B, where she tried to frame Domasc as the victim, to the part where Raven found the documents.

"What did you know prior to sending Brigadier General Renée to the shadow plains?"

Domasc leaned forward. "That there had been some suspicious activity on which we had little information, but it was clear it wasn't mutant activity. In my *professional* opinion, that called for a rapid mission to investigate."

His attorney nodded. "And why did you send Brigadier General Renée?"

"Because she had just returned from the shadow plains and knew the area as one of the best."

"Did you threaten her?"

"Of course not," he scoffed. "If she had refused, I would have sent another soldier. But she had seemed keen to go."

His attorney nodded again, as if that made perfect sense. *He just failed to mention that if she refused, he would have stripped her of her title, rank, and position in the army. Convenient there was no evidence of this, either, right?*

"So you sent her because she was the most skilled?"

"Yes, I was very impressed by all she had done so far."

*I bet.* Jordan inhaled sharply and looked at Raven, who was clenching her jaw. But his eyes landed on Nikolai, who seemed completely unbothered by Domasc's entire presentation.

*We were in control.*

"What's your relationship with Tatiana Zander?"

"I have no relationship with Tatiana Zander," Domasc deflected immediately. "I met her a few times during conferences, but nothing more."

Nikolai and Jordan's father shared a look, and Jordan's body buzzed with nerves.

"How did you get in contact with her?"

"She messaged me. You see... she heard about my... *passion* for birds and wanted to see whether I could get her a specific Ardenian species."

Jordan swallowed a laugh, which instead came out as a snort. *This guy was ridiculous.*

Raven turned her head to the side and looked at him, amusement playing in her brown eyes, too, making a swarm of butterflies race through his chest.

"Did you know what she wanted to do with it?"

Domasc shook his head. "I didn't ask."

"So, what exactly did you mean by the bird you referred to in your messages to Tatiana Zander?"

He frowned, like all of this was very distant and inconsequential information. "I referred to the *king's sprout.* It's a rare bird," he clarified.

Jordan's mouth popped open at the sheer audacity.

Seeing as this was Domasc, he had expected him to save his own ass, but by doing *this*? He was reaching an all-time low. He noticed Raven in the row before him, shaking her head at the far-fetched comment.

His attorney walked back to the table and looked through her papers. She discussed some things with the rest of the team in hushed tones before walking back to the stand.

"Chief General Domasc," she began, and the man nodded like he was the king of cooperation. "Did you know Raven Renée was Tatiana Zander's niece?"

"No." His answer came fast.

His attorney nodded like she was pleased with his answer, and Jordan wondered why.

"How do you think Borzia has gotten all these documents and information on Ardenza?" she asked him.

"Objection. Calls for speculation."

"Sustained."

Slightly irritated, the attorney switched strategies. "Have you ever sent any of these documents to Tatiana Zander?" She gestured to the translated files in front of him.

"Never." He looked outraged—like it was the last thing he'd ever do, and you would have to pry that information from his dead hands.

Jordan glared at him.

The attorney continued. "Was there anyone else who had access to this information?"

"There shouldn't have been…"

"But?" his attorney asked, a little too carefully. Too curious. Too *rehearsed*.

"Well," Domasc drawled, face pinched in mock concern. "There had to have been a mole. Someone with ties to Borzia, perhaps?"

The attorney nodded.

Something ugly brewed inside Jordan's chest. *They wouldn't dare.*

"Someone like Miss Renée, you mean?" she asked inquisitively.

"Objection, your honor. Speculation."

"Overruled," the judge countered. The damage the other party wanted to inflict had been done, anyway.

As the questioning continued for another hour, they finally took a break.

Jordan tried to catch Raven's eyes, but she kept staring straight ahead as though he wasn't even there. But he noticed her clenched jaw and balled fists, which said otherwise.

★ ★ ★

At the break, Jordan walked into the hall and was immediately greeted by Raven's father, Leon, who shook his hand familiarly.

"Leon," Jordan said.

"Can he just do that?" Leon asked. "Lie like that in front of the entire court?"

The people around them looked up. Jordan recognized the storm brewing behind the man's eyes.

He shook his head. "Of course not. But you need evidence to prove he's lying."

Huffing a breath, Leon folded his lips and crossed his arms. He was so similar to Raven at that moment that Jordan smiled. "They didn't make a strong case, Leon. It was weak even."

Leon looked at him from the side, nodding once. "He can't walk away from this, *too*."

"He won't," Jordan said, and it sounded almost like a

promise. "I know Micah and Lisa. There's no doubt in my mind that they can refute this testimony. They always try to spin the story. We will have something to counter it."

"I hope so."

"You'll see." And Jordan hoped with all his might that he was right.

★ ★ ★

"Your passion for birds… how long have you had it?" Lisa asked, as some people in the audience chuckled.

Domasc acted like he was thinking. "It's somewhat new, from the last decade."

"So… if I asked you to name three of your favorite rare birds, you could tell me?"

"I could," Domasc agreed, but he had hesitated for a millisecond, which was enough.

Lisa nodded, folding her arms behind her back. "What are your three favorite rare birds?"

"Objection," his attorney stated. "Relevance?"

The judge crossed her arms. "Sustained."

But Jordan understood what she'd been doing. Domasc's attorney not letting him answer this straightforward question—especially for a bird lover—meant that something more was going on besides them not wanting to spend the time doing it.

"Let me ask an easier question," Lisa said, and Jordan had to bite back a smile. "Why did it take three years to deliver the *bird* in your messages to Tatiana Zander?"

Domasc swallowed. "We had to acquire it, of course. And as I've said, it's a very rare bird."

"Who do you mean when you say *we*?"

"I mean, *I*—I had to acquire it."

"And what did the voting have to do with it?"

Chief General Domasc blinked. "I beg your pardon?"

"The voting," Lisa repeated. "The messages said you needed time because the voting was coming up. You meant the voting for chief general?"

"Oh, yes," Domasc said. "Yes, of course. I couldn't spend as much energy on the bird as before because the time leading up to the voting is always hectic. It requires my full attention."

"So, it had nothing to do with the wish to remain unscathed before the official voting for chief general?"

"Objection, argumentative."

"Objection sustained," the judge's voice boomed.

The attorneys constantly pushed the boundaries of how far they could go to get some of the information out there. Jordan understood why Ashley loved it so much.

"Why did you have to get the bird yourself?" Lisa asked him, cocking her head.

Domasc's eyes slid to his attorney and back for a beat. "I'm sorry?"

It was the only thing of Domasc's you could read—his eyes. Jordan recognized the panic in them.

"You couldn't get someone to get the bird for you?"

"No, I'd rather do it myself."

"You were planning on catching the bird *yourself?*"

Domasc shook his head. "Of course not. I would have gotten it from a dealer."

"Very demanding undertakings to do by yourself, I'm sure."

"Objection. Relevance."

"Suspended. Please continue with the next question."

Lisa continued: "The other documents translated from

Borzian to Ardenian revealed much information about Ardenza and its army. All information *you*, specifically, had. Did you pass it on to Borzia?"

The man rocked his head, his expression turning frustrated. "*No.*"

"Objection—asked and answered."

"Sustained."

"You told the court the documents *must* have been stolen to get into the hands of Borzia... Is it that simple to get documents from your office?"

"Certainly *not*. But someone with the right connections could, I'm sure." With that, his gaze landed on Raven. Jordan followed. Raven remained seated with a neutral expression on her face—her only displeasure showed in the drooping corners of her mouth. She looked disgusted.

"Connections like Tatiana Zander?"

Domasc's eyes widened. "It isn't like that."

Lisa nodded like he was saying an interesting thing. "We would like to submit evidence to the court."

"Approach the bench."

Jordan looked as both attorneys walked over to the judges' bench, and Lisa showed something that Domasc's attorney was shaking her head about—clearly not agreeing to something. Eventually, the judge said something, and Lisa nodded to Micah as she walked back.

"Exhibit evidence 142."

Domasc looked at his attorney with questions in his eyes, but she wouldn't meet them.

*Holy shit.*

The screens turned on, showing footage of a deserted lift. When the footage started playing, the doors opened, and a couple stumbled inside—heavily kissing and clawing at each other as if it was a match to prove who was alpha. It was clear as day that the man in the footage was Domasc. But the woman…

Jordan realized she *had* to be Tatiana Zander.

The footage continued, and we watched as the woman took out a gun and fired it, targeting a person, judging by the blood we could see spreading before the doors closed again. Then they showed the accompanying messages to the videos. The audience gasped as it showed a pregnant belly with the words, *you're going to be a daddy*, underneath them.

Murmurs ran through the crowd.

*This is it,* Jordan realized. *The nail to his coffin.*

Domasc's eyes bore into the crowd where his family sat, and his wife looked away from him.

"Is the woman we're seeing in the video your wife, Chief General Domasc?"

He looked back into the crowd again before frowning at the attorney—his eyes practically spewing venom. "It is not."

"Who is in the videos with you?" Lisa asked, although we all knew the answer.

"I don't know," he rasped.

*Desperate.*

"You don't know?" she repeated.

He shook his head, his resolve crumbling like small pieces chipping away from rotting wood.

"Then why did she send you these messages?"

"I don't know."

"It said *tapes*, plural."

He remained silent.

"Objection. Vague," Domasc's attorney tried.

The judges sustained the objection.

Lisa looked at Domasc, pointing at the footage. "Is the woman in the video Tatiana Zander?"

"No," he said curtly.

"You did not sire Tatiana Zander's child?"

"Asked and answered, your honor."

"Overruled."

*Aleksei Zander*, Jordan realized. *They were talking about Aleksei Zander.*

"I did *not* sleep with that woman!" Domasc roared, slamming his fist on the table in front of him.

She merely raised her brows. "You mean the one in the tapes or Tatiana Zander? Or is she, perhaps, the same person?"

"I did *not* sleep with Tatiana Zander," he bit out.

Lisa looked at him for one more moment before stepping back. "That's all."

# CHAPTER 38

I hadn't been able to sleep. *Even* though I stayed at the most luxurious hotel in Barak, wrapped in the softest sheets imaginable.

There was no way to calm my mind.

A knock sounded on the door, and I opened it—room service. The server picked up last night's plates and glasses and unloaded the new ones for breakfast. I didn't know how much I could get down, but I was going to try my best.

Hunter had told me that the press had swarmed the main base's entrance, some even getting past the guards and sneaking inside. Most of them were still hung up about the fact that I was a *princess*. They quickly realized I wasn't at the main base, and journalists had a way of finding out where people were… So now they were here.

The hotel staff had emphasized that they respected my privacy and would warrant it.

But that wasn't what had kept me awake. It was the message Nikolai sent me last night.

**N. Zaregova: He has agreed.**

That meant we were having another revealing day in court, and I had no clue what to expect.

✯ ✯ ✯

The courtroom was packed and would have been even more so if the people had known who was coming.

The judges walked in, and we all sat down. As the two groups settled, Kenneth Locke and Nikolai on one side, and Domasc on the other, the judge read something.

"In the light of a last-minute witness statement, we're postponing the closing arguments to later today or another date." The judge paused, nodding at the court officer, and said, "Let's begin."

Micah stood. "We want to bring forward the witness King Sergei Zander to the stand."

The entire room went quiet, like they all collectively held their breath.

Not even a gasp.

Only Domasc's attorney rose. "Your honor, this is trial by ambush. We haven't had sufficient time to prepare for cross-examinations."

The judge nodded. "Of course, you will get the time if you need it."

Everyone held their breath as King Sergei walked in. It was the first time I saw him in real life. He was a statuesque man with dark hair, chiseled features, his face wrinkled, and his nose slightly crooked. But most prominent was the air of confidence he walked around with.

In a room full of enemies, he didn't look deterred in the slightest.

*My grandfather.*

He walked up the dais and sat down, moving the

microphone so it lined up with his mouth. His expression was pulled into a permanent scowl.

"King Sergei, thank you for coming so last minute."

Sergei Zander just looked at Micah, his face unreadable. He blinked—the only sign he was human at all.

The temperature in the room climbed below zero.

"Can you tell the court why you agreed to be here?"

"Sure," he said, drawing out the word, and his pronunciation dripped with Borzian. "I came because I don't want Borzia to be held accountable for my daughter's actions."

"And by your daughter, you mean Tatiana Zander, correct?"

His eyes went to mine for a split second before nodding. "Correct."

"So, you weren't aware of what Tatiana was up to? Didn't know she was going into the shadow plains?"

"No."

Micah nodded.

"You've seen Brigadier General Renée's body suit footage?"

His face betrayed nothing at the mention of my name. "I have."

"Did you know Raven Renée existed before this week?"

Sergei Zander nodded. "I did."

That didn't come as a surprise to me—I had suspected he knew. To the rest of the courtroom, it did.

"When did you first learn about Raven Renée's existence?"

"Around three years ago."

I looked up and tried to ignore the whispering.

"How did you learn about her?"

"My daughter Tatiana showed me a picture of her in an Ardenian newspaper. She told me it was Natasha's daughter." He shrugged.

*Shrugged.*

Like it was nothing.

I balled my fists as the attorney continued. "Why did she show it to you?"

"Objection—calls for speculation."

The judges sustained the objection.

Micah asked, "What did she say when she showed you the picture?"

"She told me she wanted to do something about it."

*It.*

"And with *something* you mean *kill?*"

He nodded to the judge. "Not her exact words, but it was implied."

"Objection, your honor. Speculation."

Once again, the judge sustained the objection.

"What did you say in response?"

"I told her to let the girl be. She wasn't a threat to us. I told her Natasha had left for a reason, and that her daughter probably wouldn't come back, either."

I swallowed.

"But she didn't listen?" Micah inquired.

King Zander didn't like his way of phrasing it, but agreed. Although reluctantly. "Apparently not."

They pulled up the tapes of the Domasc and the woman in the elevator.

"Do you recognize the woman in the tapes with Chief General Domasc?"

Sergei Zander looked away from the video. "I do."

Nodding, Micah asked, "Who is it?"

"My daughter, Tatiana."

I looked at Domasc to my right, who was speaking to his attorney. His family hadn't come today.

"Did you know she and Chief General Domasc were in a relationship?"

"I did not."

He didn't seem to know much about his daughter, period.

Micah walked back to the table and spoke to Lisa and the rest of the team for a moment before stepping back. He cocked his head. "Do you know who sired Tatiana Zander's son, Aleksei Zander, your grandson?"

"I do, and it isn't Domasc." Sergei's eyes nearly popped out of his skull, and I could hear his teeth crunch. The damage had already been done the day before, and he knew it. I bet that Aleksei Zander was Domasc's child, but... I guess we'd never *really* know the father of King Sergei's grandson, who was now next in line to the Borzian throne.

Sergei Zander was lying, and he had done it before— spinning the narrative so he would come out unscathed. Ardenian laws meant nothing to him, and he'd lie to us all if it would get him what he wanted.

He didn't want to smear his name—or mix it with an Ardenian. Ironic that he hated *me* so much then, wasn't it? Double standards and all.

"Let's continue," Micah said, walking a path around Sergei's mood. "Is your daughter a bird enthusiast?"

His chuckle was cold. "No, definitely not. To eat, perhaps."

Some in the courtroom chuckled at his response, though most people remained silent. King Sergei of Borzia wasn't exactly everyone's favorite person in the world.

Eventually, the questioning wrapped up.

The judge motioned toward Domasc's party. "Does the offending party want to cross-examine the witness?"

There was no way they were going to try to salvage this. There *was* no salvaging this situation. They *had* to see that, right?

"We do." But they didn't ask for more time to prepare, which meant they *knew* they would lose this case. The evidence built a strong enough case even if the witnesses hadn't been here.

*By the gods.*

"How do you know the woman in the tapes is Tatiana Zander?"

Sergei looked at the attorney, then at Domasc. If there was anyone Sergei hated more than me, it would be him. "I recognize my own daughter. I would have recognized her even if you showed me just a finger."

"Isn't it possible that she could have been interested in birds, and you wouldn't know?"

He *just* admitted that Tatiana Zander had told him she wanted to kill me. How could this be about birds again?

Sergei just looked at her, and his permanent scowl turned into a smirk for once. "No."

"You weren't afraid Miss Renée would one day steal the throne from right under your noses?"

"No."

"Not even a little?"

"Why would I? She's Ardenian. She was born here, grew up here, and will most likely stay here. She hasn't been taught Borzian morals, and doesn't know our way of living. Certainly not, if it had been up to her mother."

The only sign my father heard him was his sharp intake of breath and the arms he now crossed.

This continued for a while until Domasc's side finally relented.

While both sides made their closing arguments, I smiled at my father beside me and zoned out. I was so done with this courtroom. I never wanted to be inside one ever again.

✮ ✮ ✮

King Sergei was escorted from the hall, and I walked up to Nikolai and our attorneys. I felt Jordan following close behind like he was my shadow.

"We're going to win," was all Kenneth Locke said, and he nodded at me before departing.

"You're ready?" Nikolai asked me.

I nodded as Jordan lay a hand on my shoulder. "Ready for what?"

"I made a deal with Sergei Zander."

"You did *what*?" he asked.

I shrugged. "It was an easy deal to make, but I have to solidify it now."

"You're going to him?"

"She is," Nikolai said, gesturing for me to follow.

But Jordan couldn't let it go. "It's not safe, Raven."

I smiled up at him. "Not safe for *who*?"

He tried hard to remain frustrated with me—even bit his lip to keep from smiling. But he failed. He couldn't help himself. "You're a little monster, you know that? Over the last few weeks, I have had a million heart attacks over you."

"I'll be all right, Jordan. I *am* all right."

I followed Nikolai to a small room at the end of the hallway, and he beckoned me inside.

King Sergei was already waiting and looked at me as I walked in. I had asked Nikolai to get in contact with him.

Not because I thought he would help, but because I knew we could mutually benefit from the other.

I hadn't believed for one moment that he hadn't known his daughter had it out for me. My mother, my fierce, loving, kind-hearted mother, had walked away from her home—and it sure as hell had to have been more than just her sister that had been a thorn in her side.

No, Sergei Zander had offered up his own daughter to the chopping block. He had let her take the fall to save his precious crown.

I spoke first.

"Hello," I said, closing the door behind us.

He wrapped his arms around his back and regarded me for a second.

"I kept my promise," he stated.

I narrowed my eyes. "And I will keep mine." I stepped forward. "But I wonder... why do you even want me to sign?"

"Considering everything that has happened, I like to have some reassurance," he replied curtly.

"*Reassurances*, by eliminating yet another potential heir to the throne? It doesn't seem like you have many of them left to spare."

His eyes turned to slits. Even I could feel the change in his temperament. "Is that a threat?"

"That depends... Am I suddenly *threatening* to you?"

We stared at each other—both unmoving.

"How's Tatiana doing, by the way?" I asked, all fake concern but genuine interest. I knew she would have looked bad. Her face should have been mildly unrecognizable, swollen at the very least.

Sergei straightened a little at my taunting words. "She's

doing well."

"I wondered, though… why would she step down if she was so dead set on killing me—a *threat*—to prevent just that?"

"Tatiana hasn't been herself." He didn't elaborate further, so I decided not to push him. I bowed over the papers, scanning the text. The contract I was about to sign had me officially renounce my claim to the Borzian throne.

I read over the words I knew our attorney had already checked.

It said I had to acknowledge Aleksei Zander as heir to the throne, relinquishing any claims I had to it. It also came with a hefty sum of money. I didn't know why Sergei had seemed inclined to add that amount, but I would not pass it in favor of protecting my ego. *Hell no*. That money could do some good in the world. For Ardenza.

After some time, I picked up the pen and jotted down my signature. I paused for a moment and looked up to meet his cold eyes.

"You know, I would have signed these papers if you had asked me to." They were so desperate to keep hold of their power that they dared to put all of it on the line so that they could kill me.

Sergei said nothing.

"None of this needed to happen. I have no interest in ruling a continent—least of all Borzia." I all but accused him of making an attempt on my life.

His eyes betrayed nothing—a leader through and through. "As I said, Tatiana wasn't feeling well."

I put down my last signature and shoved the papers his way. I traded my title and any claim I had to the Borzian throne for his statement in court. And it had been the cheapest exchange I had ever made.

"Where is she now?"

"She isn't your concern. You won't see her again."

*Interesting.*

He collected the documents and put them in a briefcase.

"I'll renounce my claim today." The contract had said to renounce my claim publicly, so the people couldn't twist this story into anything both of us didn't want. I'd do it the moment I stepped outside. Every camera would be pointed my way, anyway. Might as well say it.

He nodded.

Both of us just stood there, regarding each other, neither of us wanting to be the first to break eye contact.

He was my grandfather, and he was not. He wanted nothing from me, as I wanted nothing from him. This family had hurt my mother. Enough so that she had run away. Desperate enough to find a new home all by herself. *Alone.*

"You have a Zander spirit," he remarked. "More than your mother ever had."

It did nothing to me but light a fire. I raised my chin. "That's the greatest insult anyone has ever given me."

One corner of his mouth curved up. "Spoken like a Zander." Then he picked up the briefcase and walked past me outside, where the rest of his team had been waiting for him.

He asked nothing, wanted to know nothing about me, his granddaughter, or hear about my mother's last years—his own daughter.

I stepped out of the office, flanked by Nikolai and Jordan, as I watched Sergei Zander disappear from the hallway.

# CHAPTER 31

I couldn't hear my thoughts over the noise the press made the minute my car door opened, and I stepped outside.

After meeting with Sergei Zander, there was so much to unpack and too much to process. I had made my way into the Westeria as fast as my legs would carry me, and someone from the staff was already waiting. They had stopped all the press from coming inside. I gave the older clerk a tired smile.

"Good afternoon, Miss Renée," he said.

I sighed, "I'm so sorry for all the crazy. I'll be out of your hair soon."

He waved away my comment. "This isn't the first time the press has tried to get in here, and it won't be the last."

My grateful smile blossomed for an entire second before I entered the elevator and made my way upstairs.

I stepped out of the pants and shirt and jumped into my sweats the moment I was in my room. The world had stopped watching for a couple of seconds, and I couldn't be more relieved. Taking off all my make-up, I felt liberated, and my eyes were a little less tired.

Hours later, when the sunlight lamps had dimmed, and the city was engulfed in the vibrant nightlife, a soft rap sounded, and I put down the book to stroll over to the door and open it.

A young boy with a silver tray smiled up at me. "Good evening, Miss Renée. A letter has arrived for you."

The crème envelope that lay on top of it said *Raven*. My name was written in cursive handwriting.

I took it, thanked the boy, and walked back inside. Unsure.

The letters were graceful, but demanding. My heart thudded; I knew who had written this. Opening it, I read the text. There was only an address on it—one I knew by heart.

I smiled.

My tiredness was pushed to the backburner as I jumped into some boots and threw on a thick coat; glad I had bought the woolen garment after returning from the shadow plains. It was beautiful. Expensive as hell, but totally worth it. The thick black fabric kept me warm when it was freezing outside, like tonight—like most nights.

I used the back exit of the hotel, and, after a short walk, passing almost no one, I arrived at the destination, where Jordan was already waiting for me.

He had pulled the collar of his expensive-looking grey coat up, covering his chiseled jaw. His straight nose and cheekbones seemed to cut the air, and his now shorter, blonde hair was back to its original length.

He was incredibly handsome.

I stalked closer, as fast as my braced leg would let me.

"Raven!" Ben chimed, and I grinned.

Jordan looked to the side, his attention landing on me like a blanket, taking me in from head to toe—his lips curving into a smile as if they had a life of their own.

"Hi," I said to both men.

Jordan cleared his throat. "Hey."

I arrived at the stall, and Jordan immediately pulled me closer, throwing an arm around my shoulders as a partner would.

Ben's mouth gaped open. "You're together?"

I looked at Jordan to see what he would call *us*, but he already answered, "We are." Which made the butterflies inside my chest come alive. His fingers squeezed my shoulder as he smiled down at me, eyes swirling with emotions.

"I guess we are," I mused.

"There's not a lot of guessing involved, darling," Ben said. "It *radiates* from the both of you."

Jordan chuckled. "Well, so does our mouthwatering. Can we have two hotdogs?"

"But of course!" Ben readied the little buns, being extra gleeful as he made little hearts out of the sauce.

We took the hotdogs from him, and Jordan paid. Clearly, way too much.

Ben stared at it and muttered something that sounded a lot like *gods* before he tried to give some of it back, but Jordan stopped him. "Go spend the rest of the evening with your family, Ben."

The man looked at him like he'd gone mad. "I can't take this, Jordan."

"You can. Thanks again for the hotdog." He held up the bun before taking a large bite out of it.

I waved at Ben and said, "See you later, Ben."

"You're my favorite customers; you know that, right?" Ben yelled after us, and we both laughed. I blew Ben a kiss, and he acted as if he had caught it.

I turned back around, still smiling. "Were you trying to impress me, Locke?" I joked.

He looked at me sideways and shook his head, brows furrowed. "With money? Never. He deserves to spend the evening with his family."

I bit my lip. "He does." I loved that about Jordan. He had grown up with money, but he was aware of the value of things.

We both ate our hotdogs in silence. We finished within minutes—blame it on us being soldiers—and I regarded him for a while.

"So, we're together now?" I said softly, focusing on whether his expression betrayed anything that said otherwise.

Jordan smiled both dimples into existence. "I mean... You know that if you don't want to, or things are happening too fast, you can tell me. I'll take a step back."

"But never completely?"

His expression spoke volumes. "Never again."

"I do want to be together." I bit my bottom lip.

Someone on the square we were walking on started playing music, and we both fell silent while listening to it.

"How is Sev?" I asked. I had never seen his son, and I wondered what he looked like—if he had his father's eyes, his smile.

Jordan's entire facial expression changed at the mention of his son. It was the cutest thing I had ever seen. "Sevrano is doing well. He doesn't understand why he can't live with both of his parents at the same time, but he will get used to that. He's speaking in full sentences now, too."

I smiled. The joy radiated from him in waves, and I couldn't help getting swept up in it.

We continued walking, our footsteps clacking on the pavement and the wind blowing on our backs, the only sounds we could hear. "What's it like, being a father?"

"It's…" Jordan looked to the sky—where the stars were looking down on us—and frowned, pulling a hand through his hair. "It's like my heart started beating outside my chest the moment he was born. It's the most rewarding job I have ever had."

"That sounds intense."

He smiled at me, a full teeth-baring smile. "It is."

I tore my eyes away from him and bit my lip as I looked at the ground.

"You don't mind talking about Sev?" he asked, a question I had anticipated.

"Hearing you talk about him *now* warms my heart. I can't wait to meet him one day, when everyone is ready." I smiled a little. "But when he was first born—well, even before that—it used to be hard to even *think* about him," I confessed.

"I understand," he acknowledged. "It was even hard for *me* to think about him at some point before he was born. But after… There's only a before and after he was born—splitting my life—*me*, in two pieces."

I walked closer to him, and Jordan wrapped an arm around my shoulders, his fingers playing with the side of my neck as I leaned into his touch. "I can't wait for him to meet you, too."

"I'm sorry I wasn't there for you." And I meant it. Hearing he had difficulty adjusting to all the changes in his life made me feel incredibly selfish. I had been so self-absorbed, so focused on my pain, that I hadn't once considered his.

He waved a hand my way. "You don't have to apologize, Raven. If you would've been pregnant with another man's baby, I wouldn't exactly have jumped with joy every time I was near you, either."

My brows crawled together as I inhaled deeply. "It was never about Sev. I knew he had nothing to do with everything that happened between us. It was always the thing he represented—*you*, not *with* me. *Us*, not together."

Jordan looked up at the sky. "I've lain awake more times than I can count, thinking about the scenarios in which we could have made *us* work from the beginning. I would think myself into a downward spiral in the middle of the night and wake up with the memory of you on my skin." He let a finger trail over my cheek, the path he carved sparking with passion.

I looked down at the ground. "I tried to drown my feelings for you in my work. And just when I hadn't thought about you for a day, someone would mention you, or I would dream of you—as if the universe wouldn't let me forget about you."

"I'm glad you didn't. I had long lost hope of you returning my feelings."

"Not even at Hunt and Nik's wedding?" I had been such a mess the night after that I hadn't been able to cope for a few days straight before Kelian forced me to get my shit together.

Jordan chuckled darkly, "*Especially* after Hunt and Nik's wedding."

"I read your messages, you know. A couple days ago."

"Oh, I know," he said. "I read your reply."

My cheeks tinted pink. "I wished I'd read them sooner."

We smiled at each other. It might have prevented a lot of heartbreak.

"You think this will work?" I voiced my insecurity. "Us?"

Jordan stopped walking, cupping my neck as he pulled

me to face him, my head between his hands. "Raven…" He tipped my head back. "I *know* this will work. Want to know why?"

Enraptured by him, I nodded, blinking once.

"Because we are meant to be. However much we have tried to deny it, however much we tried to stay away from each other—the idea of *us*—we are here to stay. I realized it the moment I saw you at the gala. You looked like a dream, a very specific one."

I closed the gap between us, brushing my lips over his to catch the word he wanted to speak. To savor it.

*Mine.*

My lips moved of their own accord, trying to convey all that he made me feel. Trying to tell him with words was too hard.

He made a sound in the back of his throat that weakened my knees. My lips parted, communicating my love for him. His tongue slipped past the seam of my lips, playing with my own. His hands moved over my side, pulling me closer to him as I wrapped my arms around his neck, creating a little cocoon for just the two of us. Our lips locked, our tongues clashing.

"Come home with me," he muttered against my lips, voice hoarse with longing.

I sighed, breaking the kiss reluctantly. He leaned his forehead against mine. I rubbed my lips together, closing my eyes. "I want to." But as I thought about my leg, the trial that had just wrapped up, the impending verdict…

"But it's too soon," Jordan concluded for me.

Opening my eyes, I nodded and started saying, "I'm so—"

"Don't be," he interrupted me, grabbing my hand in

a firm grip. "Like I said before, you'll get the time you need. All the time you need. I meant it. This"—he pointed between us—"*we* are here to stay, Raven."

He pulled me close again, and I nestled my face in his neck—at home in his arms.

# CHAPTER 32

Domasc was found guilty.

He was sentenced to ten years in prison for conspiring with Tatiana Zander and passing on classified information. They released him from his function as chief general, effective immediately. His wife had even publicly distanced herself from his activities, announcing an impending divorce.

We had tried to get him convicted for being complicit in attempted murder, but there hadn't been enough evidence to prove he knew about any of Tatiana's actual plans for me.

Domasc's career was officially in the gutter, and it had been long overdue. Ever since the wall had fallen at 3B, and he had sent no help our way… He had been making his own bed. And now he had to lie in it.

After the sentencing, and my injuries healing to where I was completely self-sufficient again, my father returned home. He had to pick up Benji and get back to his own life. And I was ready for mine to return to normal. Whatever *normal* was, nowadays.

I looked at myself in the mirror. With only a towel wrapped around my body and my hair semi-dried, I looked *years* younger, but felt stronger than ever.

My fingers trailed the thin silver scars on my face. They suited me.

I took a little oil from a jar and ran my hands through my curls. But before I could start styling my hair, my pager went off, and I reluctantly put it back down on the sink and walked into the living room.

"Yes?" I answered my main line.

"Raven," Jordan said, and my heart skipped a beat.

"Jordan," I replied, my voice not as affected as I was.

"I was thinking," he drawled, "since we're both invited to the Jameson-Zaregova household..."

I bit my lip. "*Yes*. Pick me up at six."

His chuckle made the butterflies in my chest fidget. "Mission base?"

"Yes, *General*."

"*Lieutenant* General," he corrected.

I rolled my eyes. "See you soon, Jordan."

"See you soon, Renée."

★ ★ ★

I could hear Jordan coming from a distance. His metallic grey sports car was allowed past the sentry at the mission base, and the soldiers standing watch whistled after him.

Jordan sat in the front, his lips curving as he spotted me. His smile and dimples had always been infectious, so naturally, my lips joined in.

He stopped in front of the curb where I was waiting.

"Looks good, Locke," someone shouted from an open window a few floors above us from the giant building. Jordan got out, put two fingers to his eyebrow and extended it to the person in a mock salute.

"Yes," I said. "Looks *good*, Locke."

Because *holy hell*, he looked fucking edible. He wore dark gray dress pants paired with a white shirt, the top buttons undone—his staple look. His ash blonde hair was unruly, and a pair of green-glassed tortoise sunglasses lounged on his perfectly straight nose.

Jordan stalked closer and grabbed my hand, which he held high in the air. He took off his sunglasses and looked me down from head to toe. "Damn it, Raven," he muttered softly. "You look stunning."

I had to admit that I had done my absolute best to look like this. I had chosen a black satin dress with a waterfall collar, which ended just above my knees—and revealed my newly brace-less legs. *All healed.*

Our dynamic had changed now, and our relationship progressed to… whatever we now were. *Together.* We were invited over for dinner at Hunter and Nikolai's, but it also felt like our first proper date.

"You too, Brigadier General Renée!" someone else called out from the same window. A girl I recognized from the infantry winked at me.

Jordan looked up, dimples still visible. "Sorry to disappoint. I don't share."

My heart fluttered at his words.

Then Jordan put his hand—*gods, his hand*—on my back and opened the car for me. I oversexualized everything about him. Is this what happened when I pined after a guy and hadn't slept with one in a while?

"Wait, I'm not driving?" I pouted.

"Another time, perhaps," he said, looking down at my legs as he put his sunglasses back on. "When you're not wearing those heels."

"Those heels can come off."

He cleared his throat and looked at me as I sat down. "Oh, I know. They will. Tonight," he said, closing the door.

Walking around the car, he hopped into the driver's seat and started the engine. The motor's loud growl sounded like a beast, and I couldn't help but feel a little euphoric as we raced through the city.

Jordan started speeding on the highway in the middle of nowhere, and I threw up my hands, whooping from the top of my lungs. Jordan laughed at the road in front of us, his face accentuated by the fabricated orange light of the sunrise.

After some time, we finally arrived at the big white house.

We walked up to the front door, which was already unlocked, and entered the house. Nobody would be crazy enough to enter the Zaregova-Jameson household without an invitation, anyway.

Jordan walked beside me into the kitchen, where our hosts were preparing dinner.

"Raven! Jordan!" Hunter exclaimed, beaming, as she walked over and hugged both of us. Nikolai had a pan in his hand, so he just welcomed us from there. He wasn't a big hugger.

Hunter guided us to the dinner table and we sat down. "Wine?"

"Yes, please," I said, and Jordan, in front of me, nodded at the same time.

She walked back into the kitchen, filling two glasses. Jordan winked at me.

The dining space was ample, open, and white. The spacious room looked out onto the land, stretching far and wide, barely visible in the fading light. It was breathtaking.

I trailed a finger over the wooden table as I felt Jordan's leg against mine.

"What did you think about Domasc's sentencing?" Hunter asked me, handing us the glasses. She sat down across from Jordan.

I tapped my nails against the wineglass and swirled it around in my hands. "I guess he had it coming."

"He did," Hunter agreed. "But you don't think he should have gotten longer?"

"Because he was an 'accomplice' in my attempted murder?" My fingers made quotation marks in the air.

Hunter nodded as Nikolai walked to the table with some bread and spreads. He sat down next to Hunter and poured a glass of wine of his own.

"I don't think he knew she wanted to kill me. But I guess it wouldn't have mattered to him if he had known."

None of my friends had talked about me being a princess or the fact that my mother had died from a mutation. I don't know whether they wanted to give me space to make sense of it on my own or if they were genuinely unsure of how to tackle the subject. I didn't even know if *I* was ready to talk about it yet.

Jordan was the exception, though. He had been with me through it all.

I caught Jordan's eyes over the table and smiled at him. They were assessing me, inquiring to see whether I was okay. I smiled to show him I was, and everywhere his eyes went, I felt a phantom caress.

His gaze turned hungry.

Just like mine, I imagined.

"Okay!" Hunter announced, breaking the spell.

Jordan cleared his throat as Hunter glanced nervously at Nikolai and then at me. "We invited you here because we wanted to tell you something."

Next to me, Jordan shifted in his seat. "You brought us here to tell us *something*?" He looked at me, brows raised, and I chuckled.

"Yes, Jordan," she answered impatiently. "Are you going to repeat everything I say, or will you shut up now?"

He raised his brows at me again. I smiled from him to Hunter and inclined my head, telling her she could continue. With a breath of impatience, she locked her hands together on the table in front of her.

"Tell them, Hunt," Nikolai said to her, all patience, and draped an arm over the back of her chair, his fingers caressing her bare shoulder.

She looked at us with a certain glint in her eye. "We're pregnant," she said, a grin blossoming on her face.

My mouth popped open. For a second, I just sat there, staring at my friend. Even Jordan was too dumbfounded to speak.

"Earth to Raven and Jordan," she said, waving a hand in front of our faces.

"For real?" I gasped.

When she nodded, I quickly stood, my eyes wide with feigned realization. "No way!"

"Yes way!" she answered, and I immediately walked over to her.

"Wait a minute," Jordan said, hands raised as if he could freeze the situation. "You're pregnant?" It was clearly not what he had been expecting.

I all but jumped her as I hugged her tightly and said into her hair, "I'm so happy for you!"

Nikolai chuckled as Jordan finally stood and opened his arms to hug him. "You're going to be a dad, Zaregova?"

"It appears so," he said proudly, accepting the hug, which meant he had to be *thrilled*.

I let go of Hunter and walked over to Nikolai. He gave me a little smile, his eyes lined with glee from more than just the news that they were expecting a baby. I winked at him before hugging him, too. "Congrats, Nik."

"Thanks."

I squeezed his arms before letting go of him.

Hunter let her hands travel over her stomach, pulling the skirt of her dress taut—revealing an already growing bump. Nikolai rested his eyes on her protectively. He looked at her like she was a goddess carrying his heart.

I imagined it wasn't far from the truth.

We all sat down again, and I couldn't help but grin at the couple. They were going to do *so* well.

Hunter glanced between Jordan and me. "And because Nik and I both have no siblings of our own, we want to ask both of you to be their uncle and aunt."

"You mean *only* uncle and aunt," Jordan commented.

"Well," Hunter said. "I haven't told Kelian yet, but he has made so many baby jokes already that I believe he will stake a claim, too."

"We will become the favorites," I said. "We will bribe him or her with toys and candy."

Jordan smiled. "I'm sure Sev will also be thrilled at having another child in the house."

We all smiled. Basking in happiness for a moment. And then—

"Nikolai was so pissed that I had gone to the Sewers with you," Hunter said.

My eyes widened in shock. "*Gods*, Hunter. You knew you were *pregnant?*"

Nikolai inhaled deeply. "We found out a few days before."

"Hunter!" I almost yelled. "Why the hell would you go to the Sewers when you knew you were pregnant? Are you out of your *godsdamned* mind?"

Hunter rolled her eyes. "You sound just like Nikolai."

My eyes met Nikolai's, and I knew I reflected his desperation in them.

"There are some really fucked up people there, Hunt," Jordan murmured.

"I can handle my own, thank you very much," Hunter chirped. "Besides, I was with all of you."

"On another note," Nikolai said, clearly not wanting to think about it for a moment longer. "I'll be running for chief general."

"Holy shit, Zaregova," Jordan replied. "Thank the gods."

He'd told me how much he hoped Nik would go for the chief general position on the way over.

Were they going to announce they would go for world domination next? That was a lot for one night. I looked from Hunter to him as I processed all the good news. "You're sure? That'll probably be a lot." It was exhausting even thinking about it.

Hunter nodded. "We've talked about it extensively, and we think we can make it work."

"We *know*," Nikolai corrected, conviction lacing the words.

"Well," I said. "That is amazing news. And if you *ever* need a babysitter, know you can always knock on my door."

"*Our* door," Jordan agreed, and the blood rushed to my

face. I bit my cheeks as he caught my eyes.

"That means a lot," Hunter said, and I had to force myself to look away from him. I smiled at her, and she winked.

★ ★ ★

The dinner they had prepared had been *delicious*. Every time Nikolai cooked, I fell more in love with his food. I had to get better excuses for coming over; my niece or nephew being a very good one once he or she was born.

As Jordan and I stepped into the car, silence filled the air. Neither of us spoke for a long time, both of us not knowing what to say and not daring to speak our minds as he started the engine and drove off.

"So, children?" I joked, breaking the silence.

Jordan chuckled. "They sure as hell make people do crazy shit."

Then he dropped a hand from the steering wheel to grab my bare knee.

The lights of the city showed up in the distance, Barak's skyline cutting through the darkness. It was a beautiful city compared to Damruin—my birthplace. Even before its fall, it hadn't been a city like this. And somehow, I just knew I would have found my way to Barak regardless of what would have happened.

I belonged here.

Jordan pulled his hand back and drove into the city, taking a couple of turns, passing familiar streets, buildings, and places, until—

"Where are we going?" I asked Jordan as he took a different turn than I had expected, driving *away* from the main base.

His hand moved over his steering wheel, knuckles flexing beneath his skin. "My place."

I swallowed, nerves clogging my throat, and my heart increased its rhythm. *His place?* As in his apartment? As in, we were going to spend the night there? Together?

His stormy blue eyes caught mine as he glanced at me sideways, and I smiled at him.

"Is that okay?" he asked me.

I bit my cheek as I nodded and whispered, "It is."

# CHAPTER 33

Jordan opened his front door and stepped aside to let me in first. The moment I entered his living room, my jaw dropped to the floor.

"What do you think?" he asked from behind.

I couldn't tear my gaze away from the views of his floor-to-ceiling windows, looking out onto Barak, bathing us in the city lights. "When you told me you bought a new apartment, you forgot to mention that it was actually a *penthouse* overlooking the whole freaking city!"

He chuckled. "*That* good, huh?" he responded.

I twirled around. "Jordan, you live in a *mansion*."

Jordan put his hands in his pockets as he said, "Come live here with me."

My breath hitched.

"Are you fucking with me?"

"No." The look in his eyes emphasized his point.

"Jordan—" There were *so* many variables to think about. He had a son, for crying out loud. What if Sev didn't like me? What if he disliked being near me? All thoughts that elicited anxiety.

Jordan waved away my words. "Think about it."

I decided not to answer. Instead, I let a few seconds pass between us. He sounded so sure. So *sure* everything would be completely fine.

I approached the window and looked outside, my heels click-clacking on his marble floor, before I halted. The world continued going around. Far below, cars were still passing down the streets—a cab driver honking to get past another car, the traffic lights switching to orange and then red, before returning the cycle all over again.

"They can't see us from outside," Jordan explained. "The windows look like mirrors from there."

I swallowed, still looking outside. "We've lost so much time," I said softly, but watched Jordan's reflection in the window until he stood behind me.

"We have so much *more* time left." He ran his fingers up my arm and pushed my hair over my other shoulder— baring the back of my neck to him. His fingertips grazed over the bare skin as I turned my head and met his gaze.

His eyes were ablaze.

Neither of us said anything, but I turned his way, and he let his hand slide around my neck as our mouths locked. The feeling of his lips on mine was like coming home. A warm bath. Soft music after dinner. A glass of wine on the couch...

He broke off contact and pressed his forehead against mine, grabbed my hand, and placed it over his pounding heart. "Feel that?"

I nodded.

"That's what you do to me, Raven."

Our gazes were still entwined as he cupped my neck with both hands, fingers splaying into my hair, caressing my jaw. He kissed me again, eliciting a moan from my lips.

His soft lips pressed to mine, hardening, as he nipped at my bottom lip. He kissed his way to my jaw, the spot below my ear, my neck.

We both let our hands explore every part of each other's body.

Slowly, I started unbuttoning the rest of his shirt, quickly peeling it off his body—revealing his muscular chest and the large silver scar to match my own.

I kissed him there, right where the scar trailed over his neck.

Before my hands could move to his belt, he took my wrists and lowered them. Then, he let his fingers trail over my arms, all the way up, to take the thin straps of my dress and push them off my shoulders. He tugged them down, taking my dress with it, and let it glide off my body in a satin waterfall.

My strapless bra and G-string were all I wore.

He took care of the promise he had made earlier and lowered one knee to the floor. Bracing on his other, he bowed to unstrap my heeled sandals and threw them to the side, where they landed on his thick rug with a muffled thud.

My dress pooled around my feet on the floor, and the city lights contrasted Jordan's muscular chest. Slowly, he stood, and all I could do was look at him—mesmerized, as Barak's lights twinkled in the dark canvas beyond.

With one hand on his neck, I guided him back to meet my lips. He grabbed my waist, squeezing the soft skin as he pulled me closer.

My hands trailed down, fumbling with his belt, but I laughed against his mouth as he pressed me harder to him, limiting the access I had. With a groan, I pushed him away without breaking contact and let my hands have free rein to zip open his pants to let them fall to the ground.

He deepened the kiss as I let my hand run over his underwear. Heat pooled between my legs, and I had no control over my behavior anymore—the attraction I felt for him, the *need* I felt for him, tempering with my brakes.

Jordan's full length sprang free as I shoved down his boxers. He was already hard for me. He unclasped my bra, letting it fall to the ground, to rest at my feet with the rest of my clothes. I wrapped my hand around his dick before he started kneading my breast—slightly pulling at my nipples.

I moaned against his lips. He heaved me up against the glass, and I wrapped my legs around him as he nipped at my throat—tongue swirling, *sucking*. Hard.

Looking at him through lowered eyes, I let my head fall back with a loud sigh—my fingers digging into his shoulders and my legs restless.

He lowered me a little, and his full length grazed my thigh, my butt, my G-string. A tremor ran through my body every time we touched, and he put pressure on my breasts at the perfect time—eliciting a moan as electricity sparked through my body.

Pushing myself down, I splayed a hand on his chest before he could try something else and pushed *him* against the glass. I tiptoed, kissing his neck, with my hand wrapped around him, moving in a steady rhythm. My kisses went lower, to his collarbone, his chest, licking over his nipple. I kissed my way down his stomach until I was lowered on both knees.

Jordan looked down at me as I looked up, neither of us smiling. I let my tongue travel down the length of him before I took him in my mouth.

He groaned. "*Fuck.*"

Before I could move, though, he had already retreated. I looked up, a question in my eyes, as he smiled down at me, shaking his head, caressing my cheek. "I won't last a minute if you do *that*."

"I know. I wouldn't have let you." He tipped my chin up when I tried to get renewed access to him. I pouted a little before straightening. "Well, if you don't want it…" I turned around to get my stuff from the floor, smiling from ear to ear, as he took my arm and pulled me back immediately.

He dragged me flush to his chest as he whispered in my ear, "You know I *want* you, Raven."

"Then *take* me," I whispered back.

That elicited a moan from him. He pushed me headfirst into the couch—the very *expensive* couch. Gods, I hope we wouldn't destroy it.

He hoisted my hips in the air, and I braced myself on the couch as one of his hands kept pushing me down, my breasts grazing the sturdy fabric, creating delicious friction. With two fingers he swept them over my entrance, passing my clit.

"I'm already wet," I panted. Never in my entire life had I been more turned on. I wanted—*needed*—to feel him inside me *now*.

He let out a hoarse laugh. "Oh, you're wet all right." He pushed two of his fingers inside—still withholding what I wanted, driving me insane.

I tried pushing myself back up, but the hand shoving me down was insistent, taking complete control over me.

Suddenly, his fingers disappeared, and I felt one long sweep of his tongue running over me—making me moan—before he lined himself up with my entrance and pushed in slowly. My hands started clawing into the couch as I heard his breathing deepen. It was the sexiest sound I had ever heard.

The pressure inside me was building, and I couldn't help but love the feeling of being completely dominated by him.

Once he was fully inside, I was breathless from his exertion on my body—pushing me to my utmost limits. He let go of my back and moved his hands to my hips, pulling me closer to feel him even deeper inside.

Then he started moving. And I. Lost. My. Mind.

He pounced, and I was utterly at his mercy.

After seconds of feeling him hit the perfect spot repeatedly, I pushed myself up, shooting away from under him before he could regain control in his arms to pull me back, and I climbed off the couch.

Jordan circled me, gauging my next move—like we were back in the ring. His eyes tracked me like a lion on the prowl.

I smirked as I let him catch me. He lowered me back on the couch roughly, but I wasn't the one to keep lying down and take it like a good girl. I grabbed his shoulders the moment he lowered and threw my entire weight into him, both of us falling back onto the rug—with me on top.

He bit his lip as he watched me lower myself onto him, taking control of the situation.

With one thrust, I sunk back down. His hands came up to my waist, moved to my hips, cupped my butt, and *squeezed hard* as he tried to set the pace.

But I wouldn't have it.

*I* was the one running the show.

As I moved up and down slowly, I took his hands and put them on my waist. I was torturing him, and I stopped moving every time his hands threatened to slide down. He laughed hoarsely as he finally gave up and let his head rest down—eyelids heavy as he looked at me.

I moved fast, slowed down again, then even more quickly until he swelled inside me, rubbing at just the right spot.

He began thrusting his hips up to meet my movements, and my body went haywire. I started trembling, my feet tingling, and I became lightheaded as my orgasm began building inside me.

One of his hands moved to my breast, pinching my sensitive nipples, and I shattered.

Jordan moved his hand to my neck to keep me from falling and took control.

He hammered into me from the floor as I clamped around him, still finding release. I moaned deeply as he watched me come undone, his hand still secured around my neck—keeping me upright.

With one last thrust and my name on his tongue, he came.

Jordan lowered his hand, and I let myself lean forward, collapsing on top of him. One of his hands moved through my hair, massaging my scalp.

I purred like a cat.

His hand wrapped into my hair, grabbing it, and he pulled, forcing me to look up. He kissed me roughly, claiming my mouth like he had claimed the rest of my body, and made me look at him. "I love you, Raven. I love you so fucking much."

"You love fucking me so much?" I joked, but he only pulled one corner of his mouth.

"Must've gotten the words wrong," Jordan murmured, winding one of my curls around his fingers.

"You know I love you, too," I told him. "*Have been* in love with you for years."

He braced his hand on the floor, his muscles shifting as he pushed us upright. I wrapped my legs around his waist as he climbed off the ground, with me still in his arms. "I know." It was barely a whisper, but the depths of his dark blue eyes spoke volumes.

Jordan walked me through the apartment, and I burrowed my face in his neck, kissing him there. He took me with him under the shower and dried me off, too, before guiding me into his bedroom and laying down beside me underneath the dark grey satin sheets—his warm chest a blanket to my back.

Home.

This is what *home* felt like.

# CHAPTER 34

### JORDAN
### 6 MONTHS LATER

Despite everything that had happened, Ardenza had the mutation situation under control. More territory was taken back every week, and plans for rehabitation were in the works. They were going to put Ardenza back to how it used to be—including the rest of the world. Of course, Borzia hadn't made a sound, but they received word of protests within the continent. Other continents, like Kolon, had made inquiries about possible future partnerships.

Jordan talked with Raven about their future and the world's—and what it would look like. How would they, as a human species, survive all that nature was going to throw at them? How could they harbor the safety of generations to come? What other potential problems could arise—and what would be their solutions?

Raven had mused about a solution many times. They had talked often while she practically lived at his place, sleeping over on the days Sev wasn't there.

After Domasc had been sentenced and she had publicly

renounced the Borzian throne, Raven had also opened up about her past. She had spoken to him about her fears and her mother. About what had happened when she and her father fled to Barak. Her nightmares had stopped, too.

The last few months of Jordan's life were the best he'd ever had. For once, everything in his life made sense and went how he hoped it would. He had tried to get Raven to move in as soon as possible, not wanting to spend another day away from her, but Raven had wanted to take it slow. See how they did first, before meeting his son.

There hadn't been a doubt in his mind that this wouldn't work. He loved her as he'd never loved another woman, and knew she was his forever. His happily ever after.

Raven knew, too, but she didn't want to hamper Ashley and do anything she wouldn't be okay with, or rush Sevrano into anything.

What she didn't know was that Ashley had already accepted Raven. She'd been asking Jordan when Sev would finally meet her, but he hadn't told her. He didn't want to pressure *her* into anything she wasn't ready for, either.

Raven was in the bathroom, fidgeting, although she had been ready for a while. She looked beautiful. But as Jordan had told her Ashley and Sev were on their way, she'd gone back in there saying she needed to have a moment to herself.

Jordan walked over to the floor-to-ceiling windows, looking out into the city. One building portrayed an enormous banner with Nikolai's face on it. He chuckled. Nikolai hated it—he had explicitly asked for his face not to be projected anywhere, on *any* building. But that's just how Barak celebrated its new *chief general*. Or at least how Jordan and his father liked to celebrate it.

Jordan smiled every time he saw it from his apartment.

One of the bathroom doors opened in the hallway and Raven walked back in. She was wearing simple black boots, black jeans, and a white, slightly oversized t-shirt. She sat down at the bar and let her head rest in her hands.

Jordan walked over to her, rubbing his hand over her back. "It'll be fine, Raven."

"What if he doesn't like me?" she groaned, sighing deeply.

He suppressed a chuckle. "He'll like you."

Another groan. "But what if he doesn't?"

"Relax, Raven."

She straightened her neck and shot him a look that could freeze over hell.

"Well, probably not if you look at him like *that*."

Her expression cracked, and she laughed. "You're not nervous he won't like me?"

Jordan put his hands in his pockets. "No."

"Why not?"

"I don't know. It's a feeling. Call it fatherly instinct." He shrugged.

The doorbell rang and Raven had a minor meltdown. "Oh, gods." She stood, rubbing her palms on her pants.

Jordan walked over to the hallway, where he opened the door and was greeted by Ashley and Sev.

"Dad!" Sev said happily and jumped up to him, hugging his legs.

Jordan hoisted him into his arms as he kissed Ashley on her cheek and let her in.

"How's she doing?" Ashley asked. Jordan had been texting her with updates.

He smiled. "She's okay. Still a little nervous."

When they entered the living room, Raven stood at the

kitchen island, a little awkward, unlike herself.

"Raven," Ashley said as she walked up to the other woman and kissed her on the cheeks.

Raven smiled a little, saying something to Ashley, which Ashley brushed off. "Don't worry about it," he heard her say, and was suddenly overcome with a feeling of gratefulness for his ex. She and Raven had already met a couple of times, even going to lunch, before Raven wanted to meet Sev.

"Who is that?" Sev whispered in his ear, cupping his little hand as if to shield his voice.

Jordan looked at him. "I told you about her. She's a very good friend of mine."

"Like mommy?"

"Sort of," Jordan agreed. Explaining the differences between their relationships would be a little much for now.

He put his son back on his own two feet as he waved Raven over. Sev looked up but scurried behind Jordan's legs as she walked closer, as if he was hiding. Raven's eyes turned a little panicky when she looked at Jordan, communicating something in silence, but Jordan shook his head to say that it was okay.

"Hi, Sev," Raven said as she lowered into a crouch, leveling the playing field. "Is it okay that I call you Sev?"

Ashley looked at them with her bottom lip between her teeth, like she was trying to hold back a smile.

Sev nodded and let go of his father's leg.

"I'm Raven," she offered, holding out her hand.

"I want to do a fist bump," he said matter-of-factly.

Jordan nodded seriously. "He's in his fist bump phase."

She folded her fingers into a fist. "Sure."

Sev's fist collided with Raven's, and she grinned at him.

Then, back at Jordan, who was still standing behind him.

"What is that?" Sev asked, pointing to the silver scar on Raven's face.

Raven smiled. "That's my battle scar."

Sev nodded. "Want to play a game with me?" he asked, pulling his hands through his short blonde curls.

"Of course," Raven said. "I *love* games."

Sev said, "Hide and seek."

Ashley took that as her cue to leave. "I'll see you guys for dinner in a couple of hours." She waved to them and planted a kiss on Sev's cheek. He was also in his hide-and-seek phase, and it took him forever to find everyone.

Sev looked at her. "You won't play?"

"You will see me tonight, okay? Why don't you start counting, sweetie?"

"Yes!" Sev was immediately occupied otherwise, and Ashley left the apartment with another wave to them. Later that night, they would meet each other again for dinner reservations in one of the best kid-friendly restaurants in Barak.

"How long do we have?" Raven asked as the door closed, but Sev had already started, hands covering his eyes as he put his head to the wall. "One…"

Her eyes widened as she looked around. She asked Jordan, "How far will he be counting?"

He shrugged. "We never know."

Sprinting, Raven took off toward the master. Jordan followed her. Jordan thought she was being so cute, going above and beyond to leave a good impression on Sev.

He saw the door close to their—well, *his*, for now—walk-in closet. He opened it immediately after her and burst out laughing as he saw her trying to disappear behind a clothes rack. She jumped when she heard his laughter and tried to shoo him away.

"*Shh.* He's counting!" she hissed.

Jordan stepped up to her, locking her up behind all the clothes. "Yeah, but he only knows the numbers one, two, and three and repeats those. He has absolutely no sense of time. And unlike other kids his age, he likes to stretch it instead of jumping it."

Raven chuckled. "*So?*"

"So, it will take him forever to start searching."

"Hmm." She pouted her lips. "You think I passed the test?"

He let his thumb caress the corner of her mouth. "There was no test, Raven. And if there was, you already had."

"You think so?"

"Sev likes everyone I like."

"Careful now, you just admitted to liking me," she said playfully, grabbing the collar of his shirt and pulling him closer, brushing her lips over his.

Jordan made a sound that was a mix of laughing and a groan. "You're *it* for me, Raven," he murmured against her lips.

Raven kissed him once more, then pushed him away. "Now go find a place to hide!"

"Can't I stay with you?"

She shook her head. "You'll make me lose."

He crossed his hands over his heart. "That hurts." But he walked out of the closet, closed the door behind him, and went back into the living room, where Sev still stood against the wall. "Three... One... Two..."

Jordan took a blanket from the sofa and pull it over himself, looking like a bunch of blankets. Totally obvious, but not for his kid.

He had been right. It took Sev another full minute before he decided the time was up and started searching.

Jordan was the last to be found.

# EPILOGUE

The musty, sweat-filled air greeted me the moment I set foot in the Sewers.

It wasn't my first time back at the fighting pit since my mission to the shadow plains, but I still hadn't fought. Something inside me was brewing, *restless*. It was bubbling to the surface—a new idea, a new direction. And although I didn't know what it was yet, I knew it would be big.

I shouldered through the raging crowd, their sticky bodies gliding past mine. The familiar thrill of being in this place ignited a tingle in my hands.

I wanted to fight.

*But not tonight.*

Walking over to the side of the room where many people sat on the wooden steps that ran halfway up the brick wall, I inclined my head to one of them. The boy was young and had a large scar running through one of his eyes—blinding him to that side. He couldn't be much older than eighteen, but somehow, acted like he was forty—had the mouth for it, too.

He had a reputation, and called himself *Bravo*, although I had no clue why. Nobody seemed to know his real name—

I'd asked around.

"Hey man," I said, shaking his hand as he approached—his minions looking away from us as they recognized me.

We had an understanding, him and I. And although he was over a decade my junior, I felt pretty smug about it.

Bravo took off his hood, showing his buzz-cut and the tattoo that ran over the side of his neck. "I got somethin' for you," he said, nudging me along to a quieter part of the room. Bravo took a paper from his inside pockets and handed it over.

I already knew what it was—a fake order for some bullshit supplies I didn't need.

He spoke in a tone only I could hear. "There's been no sign of life from Auntie Zander."

"*At all?*"

"None."

It had been *months*. It made no sense.

"Got more?"

Bravo smiled, his teeth all perfectly white and straight. The guy was an enigma. "What'd you think?"

I'd started asking around about someone who could provide me with information on Borzia. I wanted to keep an eye on the Borzian royal family. When it came to them, trust was non-existent.

To get information like that, I'd gone to the Sewers. All kinds of people walked these floors, especially the illegal ones. And what I needed was, well, illegal.

That's how I met Bravo.

The boy folded his lips. "They're setting up a program to go to space."

"What?" I frowned. "*Space?*"

"Apparently, they want to go to the stars."

*To the stars?* My heart thudded in my chest at this news, more so than any other news I had received so far. Why would they be going to the stars? Knowing Borzia, it couldn't be anything good. *Personal gain* was a corner stone of their monarchy.

"Do you know why?" I asked him.

Bravo shrugged. "No, but I'll ask around."

"Okay, keep me posted," I said, handing him this month's money. I paid him well.

The crowd roared, and we both looked to where a fight was in full swing.

Bravo turned an eye to me—literally, because he had just the one. "When are you steppin' back in that ring?

I smiled. "Soon." Looking at my watch, I sighed. "But not tonight."

"Aight. See you around, *sparrow*."

"Sure," I snorted, shaking my head at his grinning figure.

★ ★ ★

I arrived at the entrance to the opera hall just in time. My make-up, hair, and dress were immaculate. Nevertheless, Jordan had been left waiting.

"Where were you?" he said, after pulling me close and kissing my red lips, so his words got muffled as I had to rub the smudges off his lips while he spoke.

I smiled mischievously. "I *might* have visited the cleanest place in Barak, although the name would suggest otherwise."

"You were at the Sewers?" Jordan groaned, like he couldn't believe me.

"Being an individual with an independent spirit, I fear I must tell you I have a life outside of this relationship."

Jordan's hand traveled over my back and into the nape

of my neck, where he squeezed a little. "*Oh*, all the things I would do for you."

My heart lifted in my chest at his sudden declaration. He did that often—throw me off-guard.

Jordan took hold of my wrist, wrapping his long fingers entirely around it, tugging me closer until he engulfed my hand in his. He led me through the empty hall toward the balcony and sat us down just before the lights dimmed and the music started.

Goosebumps erupted over my skin.

I would love to bring Sev here one day. Let him experience the beauty of music. Even after the short time I had been in his life, he had won me over. I would catch a bullet for that boy—and it had nothing to do with him being Jordan's child. My dad, too, was a big fan, and had taken Sev in as if it was his own grandchild.

Jordan's hand traveled up my leg, and my mind blanched. As the music continued, a man and woman walked onto the stage—singing their hearts out—his fingers curved a path upward between my legs.

I trembled as his fingers grazed my slip. I suppressed the urge to turn to him—kiss him—fuck him right then and there. But my restraint was wavering.

When Jordan's hand traveled further, my pager suddenly buzzed.

"Fuck," I hissed, taking the thing from my bag while Jordan retracted his hand from my skirt.

Multiple eyes were on us, and I did my best to hide my burning gaze, but luckily, the room was dark, and the sound hadn't been loud enough for all to hear.

Jordan chuckled. I glared at him.

I looked at my pager, which read: *Baby has arrived! Room*

*102.*

*Oh my god.* I stood, attracting even more eyes to us as I showed Jordan the pager. His face broke into a grin, and he grabbed my hand to tear me away from the box.

I knew they were having a girl because Hunter had misspoken once, but I had promised not to tell anyone.

"I can't wait," I squealed, and Jordan squeezed my hand in agreement.

As we walked through the hallway, my pager beeped again, and I reopened my bag to read what it said: *1st to arrive = fave.* This one came from Kelian. We all carried the pagers around so we would be the first to know and could come see the tiny human *immediately.*

But there was *no way* Kelian was going to get there before me. Absolutely no way. I was going to be the favorite, *for sure.*

"Kelian is already on his way from the base," I told Jordan as a valet brought out his car.

He walked closer to me and planted a kiss on my forehead. "The opera is closer to the hospital. We'll be faster."

"Yeah," I said, taking the keys from the valet before Jordan could. "Because I'm driving."

## JORDAN

Jordan looked at Raven behind the wheel and smiled to himself.

The tiny velvet box in the pockets of his suit seared a hole through it.

It would have to wait.

# ACKNOWLEDGMENTS

I want to do something different for acknowledgments. Instead of thanking all the (primarily the same) people for standing by me, supporting me, and possibly forgetting to mention others, I'm going to briefly reflect on the journey of how this book came to be.

As I said before, Battle Heat was a passion project. A standalone book. I wanted to experience self-publishing for the first time with something other than the large-scope, daunting project that felt like my life's work.

While writing Battle Heat, I fell in love with Jordan and Raven as characters. Not together, at first, but separately. They stole my heart, and I sensed another story to tell, but I was not quite sure what it was yet. So, by the time Battle Heat got sent off into the world, I decided on my next project. Liking the idea of a sequel to explore more of the world, I started brainstorming the next logical steps for the characters and story.

This is where the first "problem" emerged. I hadn't planned for a sequel other than hinting at the thing going on between Raven and Jordan, and even that was vague. I didn't have many threads to work with; it was more like a

BRITT VAN DEN ELZEN

blank canvas.

Earlier this year, I almost threw this book out of the window (along with my laptop) before deciding I needed a break. The plot didn't work. I wrote the book twice and bumped my head against the wall both times. The desperation was real, but I stuck with it instead of quitting—which would have been the easy road in this case. I didn't turn my back on this book and didn't give up when things got hard. I faced the flaws and worked with them to reach the finish line.

In my opinion, this book is better than the first, and the process of writing it made me grow as an author. And I guess that's the point; doing the hard thing makes us grow—overcoming makes us stronger. Choosing the easy way out keeps us stagnant and in the same spot.

I want to thank all the readers who loved this story (or are going to) despite all its flaws. It means the world to me that people read my work and enjoy it—experience some of the escape I know all too well. And, of course, I want to thank everyone in my corner who keeps cheering me on. I appreciate you.

All of you.

BRITT VAN DEN ELZEN ALWAYS WANTED
TO EXPLORE OUR SOLAR SYSTEM BUT
INSTEAD DECIDED TO CREATE HER OWN
UNIVERSES. WHEN SHE'S NOT TRAVELING,
SHE RESIDES IN THE NETHERLANDS,
WHERE SHE LIVES WITH HER FAMILY.

WWW.BRITTVANDENELZEN.COM
**INSTAGRAM** @BRITTVANDENELZEN
**FACEBOOK, TWITTER & TIKTOK**
@BRITTVDELZEN

Lightning Source UK Ltd.
Milton Keynes UK
UKHW010246170223
417160UK00018B/868/J